NICHOLAS

Beth Williamson *writing as*

EMMA LANG

Published by Beth Williamson
Copyright 2014 Beth Williamson
Cover design by Kim Killion

For more information on the author and her works, please see www.bethwilliamson.com.

ISBN: 978-0-9885666-4-4

Circle Eight: Caleb

"In Lang's first full-length self-pubbed novel, readers must hold onto the reins tightly as she takes them on an unforgettable ride..."
— 4 1/2 stars, TOP PICK!, RT Book Reviews

"Caleb is an absolutely delightful read."
— 5 cups, Coffee Time Romance and More

"Emma Lang has given us another great family to enjoy in her Circle Eight series..."
— 4 1/2 stars, Guilty Pleasures Book Reviews

"I love how lost Caleb is, but also how determined in life and even willing to fall in love with the unconventional Rory."
— Romancing the Book

"Emma Lang's newest release Circle Eight: Caleb is a fast-paced and action filled historical romance...Another wonderful installment of the Circle Eight series that fans are sure to enjoy."
— Book Reviews & More by Kathy

"With Emma Lang's strong and colorful characters, the Graham legacy promises to continue on, and excitedly so."
— 5 Stars, Book Obsessed Chicks

"Caleb and Aurora are not instant combustion, they are a slow burn."
— 4 Feathers, Under the Covers

"Caleb is a great western romance with a sultry cowboy and a fierce heroine that take you on one wild adventure...."
— 5 Stars, The Romance Reviews

Circle Eight: Brody

"A hot, raw western romance. If you like 'em gritty, this one's for you."
— New York Times bestselling author Kat Martin

"Lang has grabbed reader attention with her Circle of Eight series and continues to hold it with Brody, as a bold Texas Ranger meets his match in a determined rancher's daughter. Not only is Lang's latest a powerfully realistic western/adventure, but a sizzling hot love story as well…"
— 4 Stars, Romantic Times Book Reviews

"Hotter than a habanero, and a thrill-a-minute action adventure to boot, "Brody" is a very intense romance read."
— Red Room, Virginia Campbell

"Brody is a wonderfully well-written, good old-fashioned western love story. And when you get done, you'll definitely be anticipating which of the next Graham siblings will fall in love!"
— 5 Stars, Affaire de Coeur Book Reviews

Circle Eight: Matthew

"Book one in Lang's new Circle Eight series is a delicious tale of passion and betrayal. Opposites attract in this fiery tale, with memorable characters, fast-paced action and emotional rewards."
— 4 Stars, Romantic Times Book Reviews

"Wonderful love story, featuring the well thought out theme, filled with mystery and heroic women and strong western men."
— 5 Hearts, Romance Book Scene

"Go back to the days when Texas was a Republic in Emma Lang's first book of her Circle Eight series, Matthew. From its opening page, I became engrossed with the Graham family"
— 4 1/2 Kisses, Two Lips Reviews

"MATTHEW is one of the rare novels a reader picks up and never wants to end. Luckily for all of us, this is only the beginning of The Circle Eight series."
— The Romance Reviews, Top Pick

CHAPTER ONE

July 1844

Nicholas Graham wanted to vanish. Simply disappear from here, from life, until he existed in a place where no one knew him. He didn't remember how he got to this point, or why, just that he was there. Needing, *aching*, to be anyone but himself.

A hole had opened in his chest, one so vast and wide he doubted it would ever be filled.

"Why are you standing here?" His sister Rebecca had hiked up the hill to speak with him. Flowers hung from various points of her light brown hair and a wreath sat atop her seventeen-year-old head. "You're supposed to be helping with the barbeque pit. The wedding guests will be here in an hour."

Nicholas scowled. "The pit is dug. Stop being so damn bossy."

She scowled back. "Eva won't like you cussing."

"Too bad she isn't here to scold then." He turned his back and waited for his sister to leave. He'd found a quiet place amongst all the hullabaloo of their sister Elizabeth's wedding and Rebecca had ruined it. His family usually ruined things. With seven brothers and sisters, and now spouses for three of them plus young'uns, it was near to impossible to be alone. Ever.

"You mad or something?" Elizabeth was usually the quiet peacemaker of the family, finding ways to soothe even the most fractious situations.

He sighed. How could he explain what he didn't understand? Nick wished for the millionth time he could disappear. Being a Graham was a lodestone.

"No. I'm not mad. Just…tired." He was. So very tired. The ranch sapped him of everything.

She placed her hand on his shoulder. "Then you rest here a while. I wouldn't be late for the wedding, though. Ellie is counting on all of us to be there."

Nick waved her away. "Don't fuss. I'll be there on time. I haven't let the family down and I don't intend on starting."

That was part of it. Always doing what was expected, no matter how much he wanted to say no. Or how miserable he was.

"All right." She patted him. "I won't tell anyone where you are." With that, Rebecca walked away, her boots scuffing through the dirt around the big oak tree. She'd found his favorite thinking spot, just beyond the rise before the valley opened up to the Circle Eight ranch. He could see for miles from the tree, even more when he climbed up, although it had been some time since he'd scampered up the bark. Even climbing trees had lost its allure years ago. Although he was twenty-three, he felt eighty-three, an old man trapped in a young man's body.

Something had to change. And soon.

His thoughts drifted to Houston. To a certain blonde woman who had haunted his dreams since he'd seen her a few months earlier. He shook his head to dispel her image. Winifred Watson was not for him. Not only did she make that clear, but a boardinghouse owner in a big city was not the right match for a rancher from the middle of nowhere.

If only he hadn't met her, held her while she fought for her life. Their experience had been intense and ill-fated. Now they were tied together by a memory he could never forget. She made him realize that the numbness he'd been feeling was much more than boredom. It was misery.

He blamed her. She had awakened the sleeping beast within him. Now he would do anything to shut it up.

Nicholas's gaze strayed north. To Houston. To her. He shut his eyes and breathed in through his teeth.

Fuck.

He pushed off the side of the tree and started back toward the ranch. Being the middle Graham brother always meant he was expected to do what everyone wanted. He wanted to hide but he didn't want Elizabeth to suffer for his twisted soul. It was her wedding day, even if she was two months gone with a babe. Her husband-to-be was a shyster who had gotten her in the family way. Nick didn't like it but he would be there for her. The Grahams were nothing if not always there for family. Happy or unhappy.

Wagons were scattered around the yard and folks milled around, no doubt chatting about the latest Graham wedding. Their three older siblings had married and now suffered from wedded bliss. Now it was Ellie's turn, although Nick was not convinced Vaughn Montgomery was the right man for her. Done was done.

Nick took his time walking down to the house. Perhaps if he timed it right, the ceremony would begin right as he arrived. Their eldest brother, Matt, was set to walk Ellie down the aisle. The rest of them only had to be present.

The twins, Meredith and Margaret, ran in circles around the dog. The seven-year-olds sported shocks of red hair unlike their parents, Matt and Hannah. Behavior-wise, they took after their Aunt Catherine, the youngest of the Graham siblings at fifteen, and the hellion of the lot. Matt and Hannah's young son, Michael, danced around behind his sisters with his cousin Stuart, Nick's sister Olivia's boy, squealing like only four-year-olds could.

It was a happy scene. Too bad Nick felt nothing. He was hollow inside. Something was wrong with him, that was for certain. And he didn't know what to do about it.

He pasted on a happy face for Elizabeth. It wasn't her fault he couldn't actually be happy. The day wasn't his—it was hers. Nick could ignore Vaughn. After all, his future brother-in-law was held in doubt by all the Graham men. The man had spent his life as a confidence man, bilking people out of their money and goods. The last job he'd had, to swindle a family named the Gibsons, ended in the Circle Eight burning to the ground. Then, after the Gibsons kidnapped Elizabeth and Vaughn, she somehow fell in love with him.

Nick didn't understand it and he doubted he ever would. The Gibsons had helped rebuild the ranch but that was a crime against the Grahams Nick would have trouble forgetting. There was too much lost in the fire, not the least of which was Martha Dolan, grandmother to Hannah, Matt's wife. That particular wound was still fresh. Damned if Elizabeth hadn't asked them to the wedding but Tobias Gibson was smart enough to not appear on the ranch.

Nick wouldn't be responsible for his actions if he saw the eldest Gibson again. Good riddance to the entire family. The Grahams would rebuild their lives without their help.

"You look like you swallowed a thunderhead." Caleb's voice interrupted Nick's internal rant.

Nick forced himself to take a breath before he turned. All the Graham brothers were similar in build, not only because they were kin, but because ranching was hard word and tended to put slabs of muscle on them. With the exception of the youngest, Catherine, they all had blue-green eyes, something that set them apart from most.

Caleb and his blacksmith wife, Aurora, lived in a cabin nearby, which had not been damaged by the fire. Although he was only a few years older, Caleb had worked as a Texas Ranger for four years before he returned to the Circle Eight. Now he worked the beeves every day, side by side with his brothers and Javier and Alonzo, the two ranch hands who had grown up with them.

Of all his siblings, Caleb was the hardest to fool. Texas Rangers could smell a lie from a hundred paces. Nick had no choice but to be honest.

"Some days I think I did. It tastes damn bitter too."

4

"You should try to hide it today." Caleb looked concerned, but thankfully didn't offer any more wisdom. That was the last thing Nick needed.

"Yep. Planned on it." He didn't know how he would accomplish it, but he would.

"You should start now because here comes our future brother-in-law." Caleb didn't trust Vaughn Montgomery yet either. Perhaps it was because he had already gotten their sister pregnant, or perhaps because he was a former swindler. No matter the cause, the Graham brothers were polite to him but nothing more yet.

Montgomery was tall with black hair and light blue eyes. He wasn't as big as the Graham brothers...but he was big. The man obviously had done some hard labor in his life, and recently. In the last month he'd been helping out and demonstrating he could sweat alongside everyone else. It didn't mean Nick trusted him. That would take some time, if ever.

"Less than an hour left." Montgomery rubbed his hands together.

Caleb and Nick remained silent.

"She's still going to marry me, isn't she?" Now Montgomery looked worried.

Caleb smiled and walked away. Nick crossed his arms and spread his feet. "Is there a reason she shouldn't?"

"No, of course not." Vaughn straightened his shoulders, looking affronted. "I've been nothing but a gentleman. And I did everything your family asked."

Nick shrugged. "I'm not judging. Ellie is the one who has to marry you, not me."

"You don't plan on giving me a chance." Vaughn didn't whine or accuse. He simply stated a fact.

"Since I met you in Houston, I haven't seen anything to make me change my mind." Nick had helped Vaughn get back the deed he'd stolen from the Gibsons, although the shyster had spent a two months in jail after his boss's murder. No matter that Vaughn hadn't been the one to do the killing.

"Fair enough. I haven't lived life as a saint but I am not the same person I was when I landed at your sister's feet." Vaughn nodded and walked away, his charcoal gray suit shining in the sun.

Nick probably should have been nicer. Ah, well, spilled milk now. If he thought too long about Vaughn, Nick's mind would slide to her. Vaughn's friend and confidante. To the blonde who rode within him every day.

Winnie Watson stared ahead at the seemingly endless plains and sighed. Beside her on the carriage seat, Bartholomew Johnson turned to look at her. The older man had been her father's servant and soon after he died, or rather when Winnie shot him dead, Bartholomew showed up at her doorstep. He hadn't left and seemed to have appointed himself as her guardian. The sixty-year-old man had nowhere else to go and, truthfully, she was glad of his company.

The white-haired former butler was barely five feet tall and had a balding pate currently protected by a ridiculously floppy hat. He was a city dweller and out there in ranching territory, they were both out of place. Yet there they were, plodding along in a rented carriage on their way to the Circle Eight.

Her two friends, Elizabeth and Vaughn, were getting married. It was a happy day, and she was excited for them, yet she was melancholy. If she were honest with herself, it was more to do with the other person she would see at the ranch and not the wedding.

Nicholas Graham.

The man had saved her life when she'd been shot. The still-healing wound picked that moment to twinge. He had been the first man she'd allowed close in a very long time. Theirs had been an intense few days, ones that had shaken her, scared her, and left her heartbroken.

People didn't fall in love at first sight or in only a few days. That was a ridiculous notion. She had stopped believing in love ten years ago when the darkness came. Then she saw Vaughn and Elizabeth, two people who would die for each other, and knew that love existed.

Nick had woken her heart, swiping off the cobwebs with his sweet care of her. His gentle touch had made her feel cherished, special. A foreign concept and one that sent her sideways. She'd had to send him on his way, albeit in the guise of bringing his sister home. Now she was riding toward him and didn't know what would happen.

Discomfort and confusion warred with excitement and joy for Elizabeth and Vaughn. Winnie was a mess and she knew it.

"What's got your tail in a twist, Miss Winnie?"

She shook her head. "I am tired, Bartholomew. It's been a long, dusty drive."

The older man harrumphed. "Don't be thinking that fib fooled me."

A smile threatened her lips at Bartholomew's words. "It's not a fib. I truly am tired. I didn't sleep well last night."

"There's more to it than that and you know it." He had the reins held loosely in his gnarled hands but he took the time to point a finger. "You ain't been the same girl I knew since I come to work for you. I think it's 'cause you got shot."

Bartholomew knew part of what happened but they had never discussed it. He didn't know what she'd done or what it had done to her. Some days Winnie wondered if she was anything more than a series of scars, some old, some new, all on top of each other to form her into what she was.

No one truly knew the depth of how far she'd fallen or how much it took to pull herself out of that hole.

Now that her father was dead, she should be free. However she didn't feel free. She felt trapped by those scars, drowning in dark memories that hung on her. Nick had shown her a glimpse of a normal relationship and she knew then it was not for her. However, she was excited for Vaughn and Elizabeth, believed in the love they shared. That was why she'd left Houston and headed to the middle of nowhere for the wedding.

The wide open plains were beautiful but confusing. She couldn't judge distance as she could in a city. It wasn't as though she could estimate ten blocks to a building. No, out here, it was miles, or even hours, until they found what they sought. In fact, they had started out before dawn yesterday for the Circle Eight. She hoped they'd been going the right direction or they would be hopelessly lost.

The heat shimmered on the horizon. A trickle of sweat meandered its way down between her bosoms. She resisted the urge to scratch and focused on squinting into the distance. Between the lazy ribbons of summer, something brown wavered. She leaned forward as though an extra foot of room would make the object clearer.

"What is that ahead?"

Bartholomew shook his head. "I can't rightly tell, Miss Winnie. Might be a barn of sorts. Maybe."

Winnie hung on to the hope it was a building and the Circle Eight. She was tired of sitting in the carriage and the endless rolling green hills of Texas. Her bottom was numb and her nerves frayed.

As they drew closer, the brown smudge took on a distinct shape. A large house with a barn behind it. Her excitement over arriving for the wedding was tempered by the reality of seeing Nicholas Graham again. After flipping once, her stomach flipped again and she tasted the coffee she'd consumed that morning. Perhaps even yesterday's coffee.

"There's lots of folks around and plenty of wagons. I think we found what we're seeking." Bartholomew sounded tired, more so than she. He was an old man, not used to driving for two days in a carriage, even one with a top to keep the sun off their heads. Guilt lanced her.

"We can stay for several days nearby. I, for one, look forward to not being in this vehicle for some time." Her fervent hope was there was someplace to stay, such as a boardinghouse like her own. She straightened her shoulders and swiped at the dust on her skirt. Arriving just before the wedding was not what she intended, neither was being so filthy, but it couldn't be helped. After some trouble at the boardinghouse, she hadn't left Houston until two days after they were scheduled to depart.

Now they were riding in, caked with dirt, less than an hour before the wedding. She made a face. Vaughn and Elizabeth would not mind but Winnie did. They were her friends and she owed them much. The quilt she'd had made, carefully wrapped in brown paper in the back of the rig, was only a token.

As they rode up to the sprawling house, she noted the shiny windows and the scent of new wood. The Grahams had rebuilt their house into a solid home for a big family. A very big family. She'd never seen the like in Houston. In a city, everyone built up, not out. This house was nearly as wide as a city block.

A variety of wagons, curricles and carriages were parked all around behind the house. People stood in groups dressed in fine clothes.

"Winnie!" Vaughn stood at the corner of the house, waving and smiling. She could almost feel the happiness in the air, emanating from her closest friend. He looked very handsome, as usual, but the joy on his face made him almost glow.

"There's Mr. Montgomery." Bartholomew pulled the carriage to a stop. "I'm powerful glad we found him." She could almost see the relief in his posture.

"Please relax and find a quiet place to rest." She squeezed his gnarled hands. "You are a good friend, Bartholomew."

The older man shrugged off her touch. "Now don't be getting all female on me, Miss Winnie. I'm too old for that kind of nonsense."

She smiled and turned to greet Vaughn. His face held a grin brighter than the sun. She accepted his help in descending from the carriage. He bussed her cheek and took her hands.

"I cannot tell you how glad I am to see a friendly face." Beneath the obvious happiness, she sensed stress.

"Elizabeth has four brothers." She raised one brow, waiting for confirmation the Grahams didn't welcome him with open arms.

"And each one of them has interesting ways to torture me." Vaughn shook his head. "I always wondered what it was like to have a big family. I wonder no more."

This time Winnie laughed. "How is Ellie?"

His expression softened. "Beautiful. Bossy."

"Healthy too? She wrote me about the baby. I am so very happy for you." And indeed, she was. Regardless of the dark moments in her own past, she was genuinely pleased for her friends.

"Thank you and yes, she is healthy. With Eva, the housekeeper, and Hannah, her sister-in-law, clucking over her, she is well taken care of." He glanced at a group of women to his right. "No doubt they are comparing notes on how often I bring her tea or a pillow for her feet."

Winnie patted his arm. "They are simply making sure she is well taken care of. You do not have the shiniest history, Vaughn."

"You need not remind me."

"I only meant to reassure you if they didn't want you to be with her, you would not be standing here today waiting to marry your love." She waited while he considered her words.

"I believe you are correct. Ellie's brothers are fierce as hell. Even the fourteen-year-old, Benjy. Remember him?"

"I do." She took his arm, eager to be part of his day. "Why don't you introduce me to the rest of the new family you are about to join?"

"It would be my pleasure." Vaughn was always such a gentleman, no matter the situation. Elizabeth was the perfect match for him. Winnie couldn't imagine how it felt to be so connected to another human being, and for that, she envied them.

As she and Vaughn walked toward the barn where the men had gathered, Winnie belatedly realized she hadn't washed the dust from her face, hands or clothing. She no doubt looked like a vagabond.

Just like that, Nicholas was there in front of her. All the breath whooshed from her body and her face heated. She felt like a twelve-year-old girl and not a twenty-five-year-old woman.

He was incredibly handsome with thick, dark, wavy hair and those blue-green eyes like Elizabeth. His jaw was set, seemingly carved of granite. He stood with his legs apart, arms crossed and hat down toward his eyes. Dangerous. Unfriendly. A shiver ran up her spine despite the warm summer day.

Beside him were three other men; two were obviously kin, with the same eyes and build. The other had hair as dark as pitch and the coldest blue eyes she'd ever seen. The four of them were a wall of muscle and guns.

"Montgomery. Who's your friend?" One of the other men spoke to Vaughn.

Vaughn squeezed her arm. "This is Miss Winifred Watson. She is a friend of mine and Ellie's. Benjy and Nicholas also know her."

The men's gazes cut to Nicholas, who hadn't moved so much as an eyelash.

"That true, Nick? You know her?" The same man spoke, and she came to the conclusion he must be the eldest, Matthew.

After a few moments of excruciating silence, during which Winnie's cheeks heated, he finally nodded. It wasn't as if she came armed and threatened the family. She was a wedding guest. This type of greeting was unacceptable even in impolite society.

"I am also able to speak for myself. Elizabeth and Vaughn invited me to the wedding. I was unaware there was an inquisition involved to attend." Her sharp words made three of the men smile.

"She reminds me of Aurora." The second brother spoke. "And Hannah when she gets a bee in her bonnet."

"Damn sure is tart like Liv too." This from the dark one.

"We're pleased you could come, Miss Watson. I'm Matt Graham and this is my brother Caleb and brother-in-law Brody Armstrong." Matt tipped his hat. "I'm sure Ellie will be happy to see you. The Graham ladies are in the house. Why don't you take her there, Montgomery?"

"I'd be happy—"

"No." Nicholas finally spoke.

"Pardon me?" Vaughn's tone told her he was near his breaking point with his new family. They were tough men— she didn't blame him. If she hadn't been dealing with men her entire life who were harder, darker and more evil, she might have been intimidated.

"You go near that house, and the women are gonna shoot you." Nick unfolded his arms. "I'll take her."

Winnie blinked in surprise. He treated her as though he didn't want her there, yet he offered to escort her to Ellie? Where was the Nick she'd met in Houston, who held her so tenderly and kept her alive? He'd been replaced by the cold stranger made of icy stone.

"I know you don't spend much time around polite society, but it's customary to ask a woman if you may escort her." Winnie's words made at least two of the other men snicker.

Nick's lips tightened and something flashed in his eyes, but was gone before she could identify it. "Miss Watson, can I walk you to my sister?" The words were polite but the tone was contained annoyance. Good. She didn't like this man, didn't recognize him. They had shared one of the most intense experiences of her life. He shouldn't trivialize it by treating her like a stranger.

"Thank you, Mr. Graham. I would be pleased to accompany you." She patted Vaughn's hand as she pulled away from him. "I shall see you shortly."

Vaughn smiled. "Please tell her I love her."

Nicholas made a harrumph of disbelief. Winnie tipped up her chin and waited for him to take her arm. Who was this man? His behavior had already tainted her fond memory of being with him.

With obvious reluctance, he took her arm and they turned toward the house. Immediate warmth flooded her, along with a sharp awareness of the man beside her. She'd felt nothing but pleasure at seeing a friend when she'd touched Vaughn. With Nicholas, the experience was completely different. Her body was aware of his, painfully aware.

Each breath he took, the warmth of his hand, the hardness of his arm, the length of his stride—all of it assaulted her senses. She could hardly think with him beside her. His height was another issue. She was not particularly tall and he was. In fact, she only came to his shoulder.

It occurred to her that he had shortened his steps to meet hers. It was a small concession but she noted it. Beneath the stiff exterior, perhaps Nicholas was still there. The man she'd met in Houston, who'd carried her bloodied body in his arms, may still be there.

The revelation gave her hope. She had missed him, the long conversations they'd had, and the warmth of his company. If she were honest with herself, she had been looking forward to seeing him. Secretly hoping he'd smile and she would have an excuse to see him again. And perhaps again.

Instead he treated her as someone he'd never met, worse, someone he didn't like. Until the moment she recognized his shortened stride. They would reach the house in moments. She had to say something or lose the opportunity to do so.

"Although I don't believe the feeling is mutual, I am glad to see you again, Nicholas."

His arm tightened even further, nearly steel beneath her hand. He did not respond.

"I thought we had become friends in Houston. At the very least, more than casual acquaintances."

"I was there for my sister." His gruff reply made her heart thump.

"That doesn't mean nothing happened." Anger crept into her voice. "You saved my life, Nicholas."

He was silent for a few moments. "The doctor saved you."

She came to a halt, yanking back on his arm. "I refuse to allow you to cheapen what you did for me. I won't forget it and you will accept my gratitude and my friendship."

He dropped his gaze and blew out a breath. "I wasn't saying nothing happened and I don't meant to cheapen anything. I don't know how to be your friend. Truth is, nobody wants to be my friend."

Relief flooded her. He hadn't forgotten and neither had she. "There is no secret formula to being a friend. Vaughn and I don't see each other often but when we do there is no artifice required. We simply accept each other for who we are."

"You might change your mind if you have to accept me."

Beneath the cool words, she heard something else, dark and thorny. She knew that place well, had fought with it many times in her life. He might also be damaged emotionally, and pushed everyone away to avoid feelings. There were months

13

that passed when she spent her days alone, avoiding everyone except for the strangers who rented rooms from her. A boardinghouse gave her the opportunity to insulate herself. It was not only a business decision to survive but to protect herself from her emotions.

Oh yes, she knew Nicholas, probably more than he knew himself. Winnie knew what she had to do.

CHAPTER TWO

Nicholas wanted to drop her arm and run. His heart thumped almost painfully at her nearness. She was as beautiful as she was smart. It would take her no time at all to discover his dark secret. Her directness bothered him more than he wanted it to. Hell, he didn't know what he wanted.

As they approached the house, he told himself to keep walking, making sure each foot moved forward. Being so close to her reminded him of how beautiful she was, even if she had an inch of dust on her from the trip. Hell she could be wearing a turnip sack and cow shit and still be stunning.

All he had to do was get through the wedding. One day. He could do it and then go back to his life. Not that it was a lure for him. The yawning hole inside of him was proof positive of the misery he lived with every day. Winnie made things darker because she was all lightness and good.

"Oh dear, I need to wash up. Is there someplace I can splash some water on my face?"

He sighed inwardly and turned toward the back of the house. The well pump was always available, including a bar of soap and a towel. It might not be the fancy basin she was used to but it would get her clean. He wasn't sure what he expected her reaction to be, but it wasn't gratitude.

"Thank goodness. I think I've swallowed a bushel of dirt since yesterday morning." She took hold of the pump handle as though she'd done it a thousand times.

Nick stood there like a fool while she used soap and water

like a normal person. Nick watched her small hands, ivory white and delicate. Her fingers were thin and elegant. He remembered holding them in his callused, darker hands and wondering at the differences between them.

Nothing had changed.

They were still different. Night and day. Darkness and light.

She dried her hands and face on the towel and then used it to pat at her clothing. He couldn't help but gaze at her lushly curved form as she pressed the damp cloth to the dust she'd collected. His body tightened with longing, an ache at his core, a hunger he would never be able to satisfy.

But oh how he wanted to.

Nick was no stranger to bedding a woman, but his experience was limited to two, and both of them were professionals. Good thing Eva didn't know about it or he would never hear the end of it. The housekeeper had been a mother to the entire clan since the Grahams had lost their own.

Yet this thing—whatever it was—that drove him to crave Winnie was different. It was intense and consuming. He thought he had conquered it by leaving her behind in Houston, but seeing her again only served to remind him of what he was shunning. His mouth actually watered to taste her skin. And her scent.

Yes, he'd spent many nights remembering the scent that was uniquely Winnie. He'd breathed in deep, inhaling her into his body, into his soul, until he could not rid himself of her. He wanted to kiss her, to taste her, to lose himself in her softness.

No. No. No.

It couldn't, *wouldn't*, happen. His body was tight and hard, eager, regardless of how much his brain told him no.

"Thank you for allowing me to freshen up." She smiled at him and he froze. Something must have shown in his face. "Nicholas?" She reached toward him and he flinched. Her hand dropped.

"What did I do?" Her whispered question held a wealth of pain. Pain he'd inflicted.

"Nothing. You did nothing." He struggled to find the right thing to say. "It's me. I'm not a good person, Winnie."

She shook her head. "You are wrong, Nicholas. You saved me in more than one way." Her blue eyes held genuine emotion. He turned his head, unable to look at her. His heart shifted, but he resisted the urge to allow it to actually beat. "Nothing will change what happened between us. Only you can determine what happens now."

"Not a thing gonna happen." The words were pulled from his gut, rusty and rough.

"Then you've made a choice." She kissed his cheek before he could react. Her scent filled his nostrils, and the urge to pull her to him, lose himself in her essence, roared through him.

This could not be. Could not. With an effort that bordered on pain, he stepped away from her. His muscles tightened to oak as he restrained himself from moving close to her again. It would take years, if ever, before he forgot the feel of her soft lips on his skin.

"I won't give up." Winnie stared at him a moment longer before she turned toward the house, chin in the air. "Stubborn man." Leaving him behind, she walked away.

Nick shook with the need to follow her, beg her to forgive him. Tell her...what? That he was an idiot, a black hole of misery, or that he could never be who she needed?

She looked back at him. "Do I have to escort myself or will you be a gentleman?"

He forced himself to move. She was right, of course. He had said he would bring her to Elizabeth and the rest of the women. Eva would have him hogtied if he let her walk in while he stood outside like a fool.

Nick held the back door open and gestured for her to step inside. She nodded regally and swept into the house. Feminine voices and giggles permeated the air. His sisters were like a gaggle of geese, honking and flapping their wings. They all stopped in the cacophony of female silliness and stared at him.

Elizabeth wore a light blue dress with her brown hair in a wreath of intricate braids on her head. She radiated joy, bright enough to make his eyes sting. "Winnie!" She pulled the petite blonde into a hug. "I am so happy you're here."

"So am I." Winnie slid a telling glance at Nick. "Although it

17

was a long journey, I wouldn't miss this wedding."

"*Hija*, is this Miss Watson?" Eva watched the embrace with her all-knowing dark eyes. She wore a lacy dress that accentuated her olive skin.

"Yes, this is Winnie." Elizabeth turned to smile at everyone. "Winnie these are my sisters Olivia, Catherine and Rebecca. My sisters-in-law Aurora and Hannah. And of course, Eva, she who keeps us all in check."

The girls descended on Winnie and Nick took the opportunity to sneak out the back door. Eva followed him, her brow furrowed.

"Nicholas, you run."

His shoulders clenched. "Let it be, Eva."

"One day you cannot run. I think perhaps that day will be soon."

Nick left as fast as his legs could carry him. Seeing Winnie had been even more difficult than he imagined. He resisted the urge to retreat to his favorite thinking spot. All he had to do was get through the next few hours. It couldn't be any harder than the last ten minutes.

Winnie had a clear view of the bride and groom as they were joined in matrimony by a preacher. Her eyes stung as the love surrounded them, permeating the air with all that would come from such a marriage. On this day, everyone should have been smiling.

Yet she knew without checking that Nicholas was not.

Darkness surrounded him, she saw it, felt it, knew it. Perhaps that was the reason she had a strong, instant connection to him. The reason she had almost fallen in love with him. The reason she had turned into a quivering mess inside when she saw him. They were connected at an elemental level. Two kindred souls searching the dim caverns for some sign of light, then refusing to go toward one when found.

Amidst the congratulations after the bride and groom were married, she and Nick stood apart from the others. Winnie was strong enough to hide the darkness around her, but he wasn't. His family noticed it, scowling in his direction as the happy backslaps and hugs abounded in the Circle Eight yard.

The wedding celebration took off in full swing with mounds of food appearing from people's wagons and inside the house. Winnie had never seen so much food at one time. The makeshift tables with wood planks and sawhorses groaned beneath the weight of the bounty. She watched as the Graham men retrieved barbequed steer from the pit near the barn; the delicious smell made her stomach rumble.

The brothers were all teasing each other, except Nicholas. He carried his end of the grate with the meat on it, his expression void. There were no smiles or happiness to be found in that man. It made her heart hurt. Although she fought against her own demons, she felt something for Vaughn and Elizabeth. It wasn't quite joy but it was happiness they had overcome all the obstacles to their marriage.

Her gaze kept straying to Nicholas. She found herself moving toward him, a still fish in a pond of activity. While the wedding guests milled around chatting and filling their plates with food, he stood by, alone and frozen.

She wanted to touch him, comfort him and show him that someone cared for him. The urge became an ache. Her feet moved of their own volition until she stood beside him. Before she thought about what she was doing, her hand crept into his. The callused paw was much larger than hers, but it was a perfect fit.

His fingers tightened and he turned to look at her. "Winnie?"

"Nicholas."

He glanced down where their hands joined. "I don't understand."

"There's nothing to understand." She couldn't explain it if she tried. Being there with him, alone in a crowd, was where she was supposed to be.

He walked toward the barn with Winnie in tow. The rest of the crowd disappeared. She focused on Nicholas and the spell woven around them. Her heart thumped steadily while a tingling spread from the contact with his skin. His lovely, warm skin.

19

He pushed the barn door open and stepped inside, pulling her along. After he closed the door, the dimness of the barn surrounded them. Dust motes danced in the sun's rays that broke through the slats. The smell of new wood hung in the air along with the sounds of soft nickers from the horses.

Neither of them spoke. Winnie followed him into the last stall where the hay appeared to be stored. She trembled with anticipation for whatever was about to occur. Nicholas pushed the stall door closed and looked at her.

Desolation and sadness were etched on his face. A sob rose in her throat but she swallowed it back down. Now wasn't the time to weep for him. Now was the time to show him she cared. Winnie didn't fool herself into thinking she would heal him, but she could give him a few stolen moments of intimacy.

She unbuttoned his shirt with deliberate care, waiting for him to protest.

He didn't.

Sounds from the wedding revelry were muffled in here, where only the two of them existed. She kissed the exposed skin as she worked, until she pulled the shirt free of his trousers. His belly contracted as she drew closer to his cock, which strained against the buttons and fabric constraining it.

Winnie knew much about copulation, more than she wanted to, but at this moment, she wanted to make love for the first time in her life. There was no artifice, no pretending to be something she wasn't.

When she reached for his buttons, he made a sound of protest, but she ignored him. His staff sprang free, the velvet steel hot and heavy in her hands. He groaned as she squeezed and caressed him.

"It's gonna be over before it starts." His voice, low pitched and gritty, reached through the haze of arousal.

She gentled her movements and then finally stepped away to rid herself of her own clothing. His gaze followed her movements as she shed everything until she stood in nothing but her skin.

"Sweet angel on earth." This time his tone was softer.

Winnie smiled and finished removing the rest of his

clothing. She laid them on the hay to make a bed of sorts and then crawled on them. When she held her arms up, he started as if she poked him.

"Please, Nicholas."

He lowered himself with agonizing slowness until they were fused from top to bottom. It was incredible, like nothing she'd ever experienced. Perhaps it was because she had feelings for him, or perhaps because her experiences were more like a chore.

Pleasure ricocheted through her as he cupped her breasts and rolled the nipples between his fingers. His cock pressed against her thigh, eager and hot. She opened her thighs, inviting him to join them together.

She pulled at his back until he slid into her welcoming heat. Inch by inch, he entered her and was finally seated deep within her core. Tears stung her eyes as the perfection of the moment washed over her.

This was what making love felt like.

Then he started to move and her wonder increased, as did her passion. She pulled at his hips, urging him faster and faster. Soft moans escaped her throat but she made no other sound. They hid from the world, creating a cocoon of ecstasy only they knew of. When she crested, stars danced behind her closed lids and her breathing ceased. Pure joy exploded throughout her body as she clutched him, pulling him even further into her trembling body.

His back tightened and his breath gusted past her ear as he pushed into her one last time, finding his own release. She thought he said, "Angel," but her own ears rang with the aftermath of their joining.

Their labored breathing echoed in the stall and Winnie heard the murmurs of the crowd outside the barn enjoying themselves. Anyone could have walked in on them at any moment. She wouldn't, and couldn't, regret what they'd done.

He lifted his head and stared in her eyes. This beautiful, haunted man already owned a part of her heart, and now he'd taken even more.

"Are you all right?"

She smiled. "I don't think I have ever felt more right in my life."

He frowned and then rose, stealing his heat from her and tearing a bit of her happiness with him. She accepted his offer of a handkerchief, cleaned herself up and they both dressed silently. He stood behind her and plucked a few pieces of hay from her hair. The entire time they worked, he would not look in the eye.

Dread began to push aside the contentment she'd been experiencing. Something was wrong.

"Nicholas?"

He shook his head and looked at a spot somewhere over her left shoulder. "This was a mistake."

Her stomach dropped to her knees. "You don't believe that."

"Yes, I do." He turned to leave and she fisted her hands to keep from slapping him.

"You cannot hide forever. I see you for who you are, Nicholas Graham." She damned the tremble in her voice. "Now you need to do the same."

He left the stall without a word, leaving her to quake and swallow the bile that had risen at the way he ran from her. Wasn't he affected by what they'd done? How could he be so cold after what they'd shared?

Coming to the Circle Eight had been a mistake. Now Winnie had experienced something else for the first time—heartbreak.

CHAPTER THREE

Things couldn't possibly get any worse. Nick stared at Matt as though he could force his older brother to change his mind. As if that ever worked in all his life.

"You want me to escort her back to Houston?" Nick hated the way his voice broke, like he was a thirteen-year-old boy.

"None of us know her like you do. We can't force the old man to do it. Hell, he can't even hold a fork." Matt glanced at Bartholomew, who sported a sling and a pained expression while Eva hovered over him. "Damn fool drank too much of McRae's homemade whiskey and fell down drunk. I think his arm is busted."

Nick had missed it all since he'd been in the barn. With Winnie. Where he'd had the most incredible experience of his life. Hell, his goddamn knees still shook.

He wanted to forget it happened because it would color everything for the rest of his life. Yet he also knew he would never, ever forget.

"I can't help what the old man did. It's not my fault."

"I didn't say it was, but it don't change the fact she has a business in Houston and needs an escort back." Matt scowled in his typical older brother way.

"I'm not gonna do it." Nick crossed his arms.

"You will do it." Matt leaned his close, his gaze brimming with anger. "I don't know what made you so angry at the world, but Miss Watson is a friend of this family. You saved her life in Houston. She trusts you. I don't care what excuse you have. You *will* do this."

Nick wanted to argue. He wanted to shout and yell until his throat was raw. Yet he didn't. Matt was right and Nick had no excuse. Not one his brother would accept. Winnie was sweet, polite and deserved better than an idiot cowboy. Even if he had fallen in love with her the first time he saw her.

"I don't *want* to do this."

Matt ran his hand down his face. "I think that's clear. To everyone. Including her. If you don't escort her, the women will kill both of us."

"What about the old man?"

"Eva is enjoying fussing over him. He can stay here until he's healed up." Matt met Nick's gaze. "I don't know what's wrong, but you gotta find a way around it."

Nick swallowed the lump in his throat. "I'll take her." He turned and walked away before he said something stupid.

The guests had gone and the Grahams were busy cleaning up the remnants of the wedding feast. Vaughn and Elizabeth sat beneath Mama's tree speaking quietly to Winnie. The young'uns were tuckered out, likely inside napping. The sun hung low in the sky. It was a peaceful scene, one he watched but couldn't become part of.

He passed all of them and went to the barn. Probably not the wisest decision but he wanted to ready the wagon and the horses. The sooner they left for Houston the better. He knew they wouldn't leave tonight but they would leave before the sun rose. Nick had done some dumb things in his life but being intimate with Winnie during the wedding feast topped them all. And now he walked into the very place they'd found incredible bliss. His gut tightened to the point he tasted bile in this throat.

"What are you doing?" Benjy appeared from the shadows. The lanky fourteen-year-old was silent as a cat and rarely spoke. They had become closer during the trip to find Elizabeth after the Gibsons had taken her. The brothers weren't exactly best friends but they understood each other more than the others did. Benjy had suffered unspoken horrors during the five years he'd been gone as a child. Nick hadn't, but he still carried the darkness in him.

"Matt is making me take Miss Watson back to Houston in the morning." Nick sounded petulant even to his own ears.

Benjy shrugged, his too-wise gaze uncomfortably sharp. "She's a nice lady."

Nick couldn't disagree. She was a nice lady, and so much more. "I've got things to do here. Taking four days to drive to Houston and back isn't gonna get things done."

Benjy didn't reply. What could he say? The excuse was ridiculous, bordering on stupid.

"You want to come with us?" A final effort to save himself from being alone with Winnie again.

With a shake of his head, Benjy squashed that idea. "Both of us can't be gone at the same time."

He was right of course. Nick was being a ridiculous fool, but as was his way, he couldn't seem to stop himself. "Then help me grease up this rig's wheels. It's ancient and I don't know if it will make it without a bit of work."

The work helped to take his mind off the impending trip. They checked the rig over, greased up the axles and checked the traces. The leather was worn but not ready to fall apart yet. Whoever they'd rented it from should have been horse-whipped for letting an old man and a woman drive it all the way to the Circle Eight. At best, this was a ride-around-town rig.

Darkness had fallen when he finally decided it was good enough to make it back to Houston. Benjy sat on an upended bucket watching him. The boy had probably decided Nick had lost a bit of his mind, which wasn't too far from the truth.

"Supper time." Benjy pointed toward the door. "Eva rang the bell a few minutes ago."

"Get yourself cleaned up then, or she'll tear my hide off if you're late." Nick wiped his forehead with an already dirty rag and blew out a breath. He was tired. Beyond that, though, exhausted. It had been so long since he'd slept well, if at all. Physical labor helped him forget all of it, for a short time.

Benjy stared at Nick a moment longer before he stood up. "You gotta let the light in sometimes. Darkness will eat you alive." With that bit of sage wisdom, the young man left the barn.

Sometimes Nick forgot everything his brother had endured. Benjy had lived under the thumb of a kidnapper, sold as a commodity to a man who'd done unspoken things to him. Nick's problems paled in comparison. He felt petty and ridiculous, but it was what it was. Perhaps driving Winnie to Houston was a good idea. It could be the knock to the head he needed to climb out of his hole.

Rebecca watched from the corner of the house. Her heart did a pittypat as Vaughn picked up Elizabeth's hand and kissed her palm before they climbed in the wagon and drove away for their honeymoon. Her sister had found a hero—a man who'd changed his life and swept in to marry her. It was terribly romantic.

One day Rebecca might find a man who would do such a thing for her. She had no illusions about actually finding that man, not out in the middle of nowhere Texas. Nope, she would have to travel to locate such a hero, or settle for a man who would provide her security, a home, children and a future.

It wasn't a very fair choice, to be certain. She dreamed of more, though. Now seeing Ellie with Vaughn, it made Rebecca ache for her own slice of heaven. Being seventeen was prime marrying age. Many of the girls she knew had already decided on their choice of husbands. It was slim pickings.

She hadn't told anyone, but Rebecca had a man in mind. It was no one her family would approve of and she wasn't sure he would be a hero. She couldn't love a man if he couldn't be a hero.

The sunrise brushed the sky with a swath of pink when Nick led the horses to the rig and hooked up the traces. An early morning mist hung in the air, the humidity of the day making itself known. Summer had its grip on Texas and it wasn't letting go anytime soon.

The horses were not the cow ponies he was used to but they were solid animals, a matched set of bays. Both geldings were well taken care of, unlike the carriage. He double-checked the gear and then led the rig out of the barn.

Winnie stood there, bag in hand, wearing a light blue dress. Her beauty stunned him, knocking the words out of his mouth. He nodded at her, avoiding her gaze lest he make an ass of himself. Again.

"Eva packed some food for the journey." Winnie held up a burlap sack.

Nick grunted. He stepped toward her and reached for her traveling bag. She pulled back, surprising him.

"Perhaps you can actually look at me again one day without flinching." Her words were harsh but her voice was the opposite. Hurt.

"I never meant to hurt you, Winnie." His soft apology wasn't enough.

"I do not give myself lightly, Mr. Graham. Your behavior since yesterday has been insulting and belittles what we shared." She swept past him and her clean scent washed over him.

Nick had wrestled with his conscience since they had been together. Now it stabbed him. And he deserved it.

"Would it help if I said I'm sorry?" The words were out of his mouth before he realized it.

"No, but it's a start." She placed her bags beneath the seat and pulled herself into the carriage. "We'd best be on our way."

No response was needed. He tucked his saddlebags beneath the carriage, tied his horse to the back and hoisted himself into the driver's seat. The next two days would be difficult, to say the least. He hoped he didn't make too much of an ass of himself.

Winnie kept her head turned, looking out at the landscape. The awkward silence made the first hour pass slower than a molasses drip. Each minute crawled past. She sat beside him, stiff as a board, her entire body screaming, "Never again," in his direction.

"You're gritting your teeth so loudly you scared a flock of birds." The first words she spoke startled him. He tugged on the reins, in turn making the horses toss their heads and pick up speed.

"Whoa, boys, whoa." Embarrassed and annoyed, he slowed the horses back down to an appropriate speed for the carriage.

"You have no reason to be angry with me, Mr. Graham." He knew this Winnie. She was the one he'd met in Houston. She was hard as an oak tree and tougher than its bark.

"No, I don't." He loosened his grip on the leather and flexed his fingers. He'd been gripping them so hard he'd given himself cramps.

"Then stop acting as though you've been wronged. I will not accept your anger for an unsubstantiated reason." Her hands were folded neatly on her lap but her grip appeared to be as tight as his had been.

Guilt assailed him. Winnie damn well didn't deserve to be treated the way he'd been treating her. Their experience had been mutual and he damn sure was a willing participant. If he could stop acting like a horse's ass, things would be better for both of them. Too bad he couldn't stop.

"I know why you do it."

"Do what?" He wanted to be done talking.

"Why you push people, me, away. Why you're angry all the time. Why you spend so much time alone."

Every word slammed into him. She couldn't possibly know all that.

"I don't know what you're talking about."

Her sigh was so soft he nearly missed it. "I know because I've been through it myself. For years."

"What are you yammering about, woman?" He told himself not to be angry with her, to let it pass. That worked out badly.

"I'm talking about being so sad some days you can barely drag yourself out of bed." She had turned toward him, her face flushed with anger. "Or so angry that even the smallest incident incites fury. Or not caring if you take another breath."

Nick stared at her, his heart hammering hard enough to make his ears hurt. "What are you talking about?" His words were barely a whisper.

She grabbed his hand. "I know, Nick. *I know.* I lived it for a long time. The only reason I survived was because I met Vaughn, the very first person who cared about me. He helped me realize what I was doing, how I was destroying myself. As you are doing."

Horrified, he could only stare. Nick was not destroying himself. He was going through a bad patch.

"Let me help you, Nick."

"I don't need help." He shook off her hand. "There ain't nothing wrong with me."

If he'd thought the silence before was awkward, he'd been wrong. The air between them was thick enough to cut with a knife. It fairly crackled with tension and the lies he'd just spouted to her.

"You don't have to be honest with me now. I wanted to be sure you knew I understood." Her tone had lost the bite it had a few minutes earlier. Instead it held the promise of revisiting the conversation. Something he did not want to do. Ever.

The best response, in his opinion, was no response. He simply stared straight ahead and ignored her huffing beside him. She was likely thinking of ways to punish him for being stubborn and obnoxious.

His throat was drier than the ground beneath the wheels. Hell, he could hardly swallow. Just thinking about how thirsty he was made it worse. He licked his lips and tried to get past it.

It didn't work.

"Do you, uh, have water?" He, undoubtedly, sounded pitiful.

"Yes, of course I do. Would you like some?"

He counted to five before he answered. "That would be why I asked if you had water."

"I know. I just wanted to hear you ask for a drink rather than peering around the corner silently." She handed him the canteen, much to his confusion.

"You confound me, Winnie."

"Good." She turned her head away.

He was annoyed, upset and completely off-kilter. She deliberately stirred the pot and then threw it at him. He refused to acknowledge she'd spoken the truth. Straight like an arrow to his heart.

Nick knew driving her to Houston would be a disaster. Now he expected it would be worse than that.

Winnie had pushed him too far. She hadn't meant to but once she started, the words fell out of her mouth. Then it was too late to snatch them out of the air. Her heart hammered with the raw emotions surging through her.

No one but Nick had ever pulled such deep feelings—ones she had buried so far deep inside her they should have never resurfaced. Something about Nicholas Graham coaxed them out and she had to face their ugliness.

The trip back to Houston should have been she and Bartholomew, not the man who haunted her dreams and whose hands still ghosted their mark on her skin. He made it clear he had sampled the cow's milk but didn't want to have another sip. She knew what rejection was, plainly, but it didn't mean she wasn't hurt by it. If only Bartholomew hadn't fallen and hurt his arm. They could have had pleasant conversations all the way back, or at least civil ones.

She wondered sometimes if the universe had a twisted sense of humor. It threw all manner of badness at her, then goodness, then more badness. She could hardly catch her breath some days. Nick was too much like her. Digging into his darkness had brought hers back to hang over her like a thundercloud.

There was no help for it. She would have to tell him everything. The poison had already started to bubble up in her gut. She had to expunge it or choke on its acid. It took an hour to find the courage to speak again. He could not listen to her, or worse yet, think her a liar.

"When I was five years old, I came to realize that my father used me to entice men to give their money to him. I was such a pretty child with impeccable manners. It wasn't until I was nine that I realized some of the men were interested in more than my father's schemes."

She took a shuddering breath, the warm air coating her throat, forcing her to swallow twice before she could speak again. "When I was eleven, he sold me to one of them."

"Jesus. I knew that man was a sick bastard. Can say I'm glad he's dead." His voice was raw, angry. His words gave her the courage to continue.

"When I was fifteen, I became pregnant by another of my father's business associates. My daughter was born on May first in eighteen thirty-five. I never held her, never looked at her... because I couldn't." She gripped her hands hard enough to make her knuckles pop. "Now she is nine years old and I don't know where she is or who has her."

The silence was only broken by the twittering of birds that could not know how painful her confession was. How broken her heart still was after nine years. How much she wished she could turn back the hands of time and fight for her.

"What is her name?"

Of all the questions he could have asked, this was the one that made her cry. Big, fat crocodile tears rolled down her face as she choked on the sobs that threatened to burst forth. It took several minutes of noisy snuffles and a neckerchief offered up by her unwilling companion, before she was able to answer him.

"Grace. I named her Grace."

The name was precious to her, as was the memory of a daughter she'd given away.

"That's a right pretty name." For the first time since she'd met him, he wasn't angry, annoyed or impatient. He was simply there, beside her.

"Thank you. On her birthday I imagine what she looks like and hope someone is celebrating with her." She was alone on that day, never leaving the boardinghouse or seeing anyone. It was too painful, too private, to share with anyone.

Until now. Until Nicholas.

"I've never told anyone. Even Vaughn doesn't know and he's my closest friend." She'd kept her secret, festering deep inside her, never to heal.

He was silent for a few moments. "Why tell me?"

She shook her head. "I don't know. The words jumped out of my mouth."

To her surprise, the air between them had eased, no longer

thick or heavy. She was able to take a deep breath, even as she continued to wipe the tears from her face. Her heart ached; the pain from having her daughter taken from her was as sharp as if it had been yesterday.

"It was a secret."

"Yes."

"And you shared it with me."

"I've told you, Nicholas, we are very much alike. I know you'll keep my confidence." And she did know, somehow, how trustworthy he would be with her deepest secret.

He sighed. "That's quite a burden to heap on me." There was no rancor in his words, only sadness.

Before she could respond, he spoke again.

"But I have my own burden. I know how heavy they are. I don't mind sharing yours."

Her hands tightened on the now damp neckerchief. She had to admit he surprised her again. "Thank you, Nicholas."

He shrugged. "Sometimes I think my mother might be proud of me."

His words sliced through the air, full of self-loathing and ancient pain. She wanted to touch him, tell him again she would listen if he wanted to speak. Their truce was fragile and she dared not risk falling into the acerbic words they'd shared earlier.

"I have no doubt she is proud of you. Your family is tough, smart and amazing. I wish I had a thimbleful of what you share." She had no one, except Grace, and she was lost to her. Vaughn was her closest friend, but now with Elizabeth by his side, his life would continue in another direction. Yes, Winnie was well and truly alone.

"They're annoying."

Winnie snorted. "So are you."

A hint of a smile twitched the side of his mouth. "You surely have a way of speaking your mind."

"I suppose that's correct." She sighed. "It's gotten me in trouble more than once."

"Truer words were likely never spoken."

She tapped his knee with the neckerchief and the tension

within her began to loosen. The confession exhausted her, but she wouldn't regret it. She had held it inside for a very long time; it was past time to be honest with someone. Nicholas had been the right person. Her heart agreed with her. After the intense couple days with him in Houston when she'd been shot, she was more sure than ever they were connected. Perhaps for the rest of their lives.

Winnie did not give her affection or trust lightly. He might not realize it, but he was part of a very small group of people. She might hope someday to have him as a partner like Vaughn and Elizabeth, but she wouldn't allow herself to wish for it. Wishing got her nothing but heartache and scars.

The movement of the carriage soothed her and her eyes began to close. It hadn't helped that she'd not slept the night before. That was, of course, Nicholas's fault.

Rebecca smiled as the children played in the yard. Childish squeals and laughter rang in the bright summer morning. As the de facto watchful aunt, she was generally in charge of the five scamps while their mothers took care of activities that were too dangerous for young'uns to be present.

Her sister-in-law Aurora was working on some new tools for the ranch while Hannah and Eva were canning the first vegetables from the garden. With a family as large as theirs, canning was a necessity to get them through the winter with vegetables and fruits.

The twins, Margaret and Meredith, were directing their brother and cousins in a rousing game of tag. Rebecca made notes in her book of remedies. She had been writing and building her knowledge of herbs and medicines for more than five years. Eva had helped her get started but now Rebecca was the keeper of healing arts.

It gave her a thrill to find something that would staunch bleeding or sooth a skinned knee. The children went to their mother when they were injured but looked to Aunt Rebecca to make the pain go away.

"Hey, girl, where is your brother?" The question, nearly shouted across the yard, startled Rebecca and she smeared ink on the page.

"Good Lord, mister, are you trying to scare the life out of me?" She set the book down along with the pen and inkwell on the rock beside her.

"I'm looking for your brother." It was a man on horseback. The sun was behind him and she couldn't make out who it was.

Rebecca got to her feet and shaded her eyes. Her breath caught when she recognized him.

Tobias Gibson.

He wore a blue shirt that had seen better days. Various stains decorated the fabric. Eva would have had a fit to see one of the Grahams wear such a garment. His horse was a familiar one and she petted the side of his neck as she looked up at his rider.

This was the man she had decided was the man she would marry. If Matt, Caleb and Nick knew, they would shout at her until her ears bled. None of them wanted Gibson on the Circle Eight, not after he'd burned it to the ground earlier that year. Even though he spent months—every day—helping rebuild it, including providing the wood, his crime against the Grahams had become a grudge her brothers couldn't forgive.

She could and had. In him, she saw the man who could be her hero.

"Mr. Gibson, you'll need to give me a bit more information than that. I have four brothers."

His mouth tightened. "Matt. I need to find Matt."

"He's out working with the cattle. I don't expect him back before sundown." It was barely mid-morning. Since the Gibsons lived a half-a-day's ride away, he must have left in the middle of the night to arrive.

"Damn." His curse was soft enough the children didn't hear him. He might have acted the gruff stranger but beneath it all, there was a good man. She saw it, she wished for it.

"Is there something I can help you with?" Her heart sped up at the thought of spending time with him without the family around. She had watched him work for days, and grown more sure he was the right man for her with each day that passed.

"I was wanting to borrow your Eva to help Pops. He's in a

bad way and there ain't no doctor that will come out to our cabin." Beneath the words, she heard the concern over his grandfather.

"Eva can't leave but I can."

He looked startled. "You? You're a child."

She bit back the angry retort she would have thrown at her brothers. "I am seventeen years old, Mr. Gibson. I'll be eighteen in just a few months. I am not a child."

"Seventeen? I've got ten years on you, girl. You are a child for certain."

She tilted her chin up and straightened her shoulders. "I am the healer of the family." She pointed at the book on the rock. "I have more knowledge of the healing arts than anyone you'll find."

He didn't look convinced.

"Let me speak to Eva and gather my things. Watch the children for a minute." Without waiting for an answer, she dashed into the house. From what she knew of him, he was good with children and had five younger boys that lived with him. He knew how to take care of young'uns.

She ran into the house, slamming open the door. Eva and Hannah started and stared at her open-mouthed. The older man, Mr. Bartholomew, sat at the table shelling peas. His reaction was to raise his brows.

"What is it, *hija*?" Eva wiped the sweat from her brow with her apron. Canning was hot work, hotter still in the summer. The air in the house was near oppressive even with the windows wide open.

"Mr. Gibson's grandfather is ill. I'm going to go see if I can help." She didn't wait for anyone to respond. She ran to her room and retrieved her precious bag of herbs she had carefully collected over the last several months. What she'd had before had burned in the fire, so everything was fresh.

She almost made it out of the kitchen before Hannah's voice stopped her. Her brown gaze was full of concern. "I don't think you should be riding off with Mr. Gibson without talking with Matt first."

"There isn't time. I know they rode north but with six

35

hundred acres, there's no way of knowing exactly where they are. The elder Mr. Gibson might be in dire circumstances."

Hannah's frown deepened, joined by Eva's.

"I will be back as soon as I can. You know where I'll be and who I will be with." She edged closer to the back door.

"That's my biggest concern. You know how Matt feels about the Gibsons." Hannah had a point.

"He was here for two months helping us rebuild. I think he's proved he can be trusted." Rebecca opened the door. "I'm a grown woman, nearly eighteen. I can make this choice without my brother's approval."

"What about the children?"

"I can keep an eye on them." Mr. Bartholomew, bless him, saved Rebecca from further obstacles.

"Thank you!"

She dashed out the door and found the children gathered around in a half-circle around Mr. Gibson and his horse.

"I'm leaving now. Mr. Bartholomew will come out and play with you."

Meredith raised one brow, imitating her father so much Rebecca had to hold back a laugh. "I'll be back as soon as I can." She nodded at Mr. Gibson although her palms were sweating and her heart racing. "I'll go saddle my horse."

Rebecca was smiling as she ran toward the barn. Her adventure was just beginning.

Nick was being slowly tortured. Blissfully unaware, Winnie's head lolled back on the seat before she slumped sideways. Damned if she didn't end up with her warm, soft body pressed against him from stem to stern. It was a sweet weight, one that made him forget who he was, if only for a few moments.

Her clean scent drifted up toward him, along with the unmistakable fragrance of grief. She had grieved for the daughter she'd never been allowed to keep and the girl Winnie had never been allowed to be.

He understood grief all too well. Her words, her raw

emotions, had scraped at him until he almost made a confession of his own. She was unique, unlike anyone he'd ever met. He might not ever admit it, but he agreed with her—they were very much alike. More so than he wanted to accept.

He had dark secrets and his own grief. It was buried deep inside him and there was no way it would ever see the light of day, no matter how much she might weep and tell her own stories. Nick wasn't about to blow his own cork and let the evil genie out of its bottle.

She shifted closer and sighed. Her warm breath tickled the skin on his neck. He wanted to move away from her, to break the contact with her incredible softness. At the same time, he didn't. He could imagine having that weight close to him every day, every night, every morning.

Enticing.

Dangerous.

His muscles had tightened until his legs started to cramp. He forced himself to relax, breathe slow and easy until his body eased. Even asleep she did things to him. There was always a reaction, good or bad.

Nick had spent so much time keeping people at a distance, but Winnie had snaked through his defenses before he realized she was there. Before he realized she was much more than a woman he'd met.

She was brave, outspoken and smart, not to mention tough. Not many young, beautiful women ran boardinghouses on their own. Hell, none of them had the balls to kill their own father, regardless of how evil and twisted he was.

Winnie had almost died because of her courage and her rage. Yet here she was a few months later, hale and hearty, and full of passion. She amazed him, humbled him and made him recognize just how pitiful his life was.

He was yanked in all directions when around her and he still was drawn to her. Irresistibly moving like a moth heading toward certain death in the flames of a lantern. He couldn't stop himself. It wasn't only because of their experience in Houston when she'd been shot by her father, or even when they'd found bliss in each other's arms in the barn yesterday.

37

No, it was her story, her loss and victory over that tragedy. Winnie was who he wanted to be, who he could be. She was everything he wasn't.

Her hands lay on her lap, small and open, the fingers slightly curled. For being so delicate and dainty, she commanded a great deal of power. How had she survived what she'd been through? What's more, how had she remained whole and full of life?

Nick's gaze kept driving back to her hands, how she had touched him, brought him pleasure and peace. He craved more. His body ached to experience it again. To feel something besides despair and anger.

He shifted his shoulder until she slumped completely against him. It felt right, perfect perhaps. He hadn't experienced much in his life he could call perfect. Except Winnie.

She made him want to be a better person. How could he do that when he couldn't fight his own demons? He could do something for her. He needed to do something for her. The question was, what could he do? She was independent, had her own money and would doubtless not appreciate his help if he poked his nose in her business.

Yet he felt compelled. It was the first time in a long time that he'd felt anything but dark emotions. It was the same feeling that had overcome him in Houston. He had watched himself transform into another person, someone who forgot his own darkness and worried about another's happiness.

He had forgotten how that felt, perhaps deliberately. When he was caught within the despair that was his constant companion, he closed his eyes against everything else. Nick didn't want to feel that way, but he couldn't seem to stop himself.

Now with Winnie so close, he allowed himself to remember that feeling. It was addictive, and he hadn't wanted to remember it when there was no chance of experiencing it again. Here he was, back with her for another two days, lost in Winnie Watson.

She'd had tragedies in her life, as had he. She had

triumphed; he had not. Maybe, just maybe, if he stayed near her long enough, he might find a way to be as triumphant as she. And if he helped her, he might even find peace, not happiness, but contentment. Enough to allow him to live and beat back the ghosts that rode his back.

She made a sound, a small hiccup of distress, and her hands fisted. His protective instincts flared to life. She needed him; she just didn't know it yet.

Inspiration rushed through him so fast and hard, he sucked in a surprised breath. He knew the one thing that would make a change in her life.

Nicholas was going to help her find her daughter, Grace.

He didn't know how but he was damn well going to find that child. Impatience licked at him as he waited for her to wake. He was amazed to recognize what he felt was excitement. He was *excited*. It was as foreign as happiness. Nick didn't know how to react or act.

Nothing was more important than family and Winnie had none. Vaughn and Elizabeth were friends, extended family, but not blood. The Grahams had accepted Winnie as though she were a cousin, but again, she had no one of her own. Or rather, she did, but that daughter was lost. Nick would right that wrong. He would damn well give her back her only kin.

Decision made, he found himself relaxing. Now he had to tell Winnie what he wanted to do. Or rather, convince her it was right thing to do. He would be fiddling with her life and her future. This was not a small thing. He had little time to figure out how to do what he had to do.

"Nicholas?"

Less than that. He had no time.

"I'm here."

She sighed and sat up. "I was more tired than I thought. My apologies. I didn't mean to fall asleep on you."

"It's all right. I didn't mind." That was an understatement, of course. He might have begun this trip full of resentment, but now he was bubbling with something very different.

She yawned and rubbed her eyes with the heels of her hands. "I didn't sleep well last night."

"I haven't slept well in years."

She was quiet for a few moments. "Neither have I."

A comfortable silence ensued. Somehow their conversation had cleared the air between them. Nicholas had time to consider how to convince Winnie to let him find her daughter. Although he had hours to concoct a plan, the best he could think of was starting with whoever delivered the child and dig until they found her. It wasn't much of a plan but it was what he had.

The summer heat settled over them as they rode onward. Sweat rolled down his back, pooling at the waistband of his trousers. Winnie looked fresh as a daisy.

"I think we should stop and have some dinner. Eva packed plenty of vittles." He wanted to talk to her face to face about his plan.

"I am parched. That sounds lovely." She adjusted her bonnet. "I would also love to put a cold cloth on my neck."

Nick wanted to be the one who put that cloth on her neck, or anywhere else she wanted one. The memory of her skin, the scent, the incredible softness, raced through him. It took great effort to push it aside and look for a likely place to stop.

Then he would change her life, and his, forever.

CHAPTER FOUR

"I want to find your daughter. I want to find Grace."

Winnie stared at him, shock keeping her immobile. His expression was serious, completely, utterly serious. She had to swallow twice before she could speak. Her voice had deserted her.

"Why?" Her heart ached as she tried to understand what he wanted. "She is nothing to you. A nine-year-old memory of a dark time in my life."

"It's not who she is to me, it's who she is to you." He set down the biscuit he'd been toying with as he spoke. He brushed off the crumbs stuck to the tips of his fingers. His gaze found hers. "I'm not doing this right."

"Doing what right? I don't understand, Nicholas." She hated the trembling in her voice and the way her heart thumped with pain.

He took her hands, his were surprisingly cool and damp. "I haven't done much right in my life. My brothers can tell you how many times I do the wrong thing. This is something I want to do right. For you."

She looked into his blue-green eyes and saw earnestness. Whatever he intended, he was being honest with her.

"For me?"

He blew out a breath. "You were right about me. I'm a mess, not worthy of much except working with cattle. You showed me I could do something else, be something else. Please let me find her for you. Let me find your family."

Family.

The word had meant nothing to her most of her life. She hadn't known her mother and wished she hadn't known her father. Now that she understood how family was supposed to treat each other, and how much she envied the Grahams, Nicholas dangled her own family in front of her.

He had no idea what his request was doing to her. Even allowing a small speck of hope to dance across her heart was dangerous. She managed to suck in some air but she still felt lightheaded.

Family.

"I didn't tell you the story of how I lost her to prompt you to find her." Her voice was rough. She didn't sound like herself.

"I know that. I appreciate you telling me about Grace. More than I can tell you." He squeezed her fingers. "You've given me something I'd lost. I want to do the same for you."

She might embarrass herself by vomiting. Winnie got to her knees and extracted her hands from his. She turned away and leaned forward until her forehead touched the cool grass. Winnie attempted to suck in a much-needed breath, but instead a sob escaped. A broken sob. Her throat closed.

A warm hand landed on her back. "I'm sorry, Winnie. I didn't mean to make you cry. Hell, I never use the right words."

She wrapped her arms around her waist and squeezed. He rubbed her shoulder with awkward movements.

"Forget I said anything. We'll get to Houston and you can shoot me dead. That ought to make you feel better."

She managed to swallow. "I don't want to shoot you." To her own ears, her voice was rusty as an old nail.

"You should. I'm a complete jackass."

This time, her mouth twitched at his miserable humor. "I won't disagree with you."

"Hell, I'm worse than a jackass. Olivia would kick me in the balls."

His idea was not unknown to her. She had toyed with the notion of finding Grace but it never went beyond a few wispy dreams. She never let it go beyond that. Now Nicholas threw it over her, dousing her like an icy bucket of water.

"Winnie, I'm sorry. Please say something." His voice broke and she heard much more than an apology in his voice. She heard desperation and a darker emotion.

She pulled herself upright and relaxed her hands, ignoring the crescent shape dents and perhaps blood on her palms. He thrust a handkerchief at her, his expression one of pure misery. When she took the cloth from him, she squeezed his hand.

"I know you meant well."

His normal scowl slipped back over his face. "I meant to pay you back for the kindness you've shown my sister and her husband."

That made her angry. Almost furious. Her face heated with every pulse of ire.

"Don't you dare turn this around into something it's not. Your gesture has absolutely nothing to do with Vaughn or Elizabeth." She poked her finger into his broad chest, remembering the slabs of muscle beneath the shirt. He was perfectly made outside if not inside.

Guilt flashed in his beautiful eyes before he looked away. "I don't know what you mean."

"Don't you start lying, Nicholas." She poked him twice for good measure. "You're doing this for yourself."

His gaze snapped back to hers. "For myself?"

"Yes, you are selfishly hoping I'll say yes, fall at your feet and you can be a hero. I don't even want your help, damn it." She wanted to curse long and hard at him. Her childhood was anything but traditional, including an extensive array of curses and other inappropriate terms. "You will not use me like that."

He opened as mouth as though to refute her again.

"Don't you dare deny it."

He shook his head. "Winnie, I'm gonna try my best to explain this to you, but sometimes what I feel in my heart or my head is mixed up. My words don't come out right."

She didn't want to believe him. He had already laid her heart open, filleted like a fish under his knife of helpfulness. What could he possibly say that would make up for poking his nose in her business and causing her such distress?

He sat back and pulled his knees up, wrapping his arms

around his legs. "As a Graham, I spend most of my days trying to keep my distance from my family. They are noisy, pushy, and I don't get many moments to myself. I pick chores that let me spend as much time as possible away from home." He shook his head. "I couldn't see anything beyond breathing in and out. Then I met you."

She stared at him, pleased to hear him finally talking but still angry he had chosen to use her secrets to do so. Winnie might not ever forgive him for that.

"Nothing in my life shines the way you do. Even the color of your hair glows in any light. You are so damn brave and strong. I felt less than worthy to help you when you were shot. When I saw what you did, killed your father for his crimes against all and sundry, I was humbled." His voice had grown thick with emotion and she resisted the urge to pat his arm or take his hand. He needed, not to mention deserved, to experience his feelings. "It almost hurt to look at you. There was nothing I could offer you that you couldn't do on your own."

"Not true." She couldn't help it. The fact this big, strong man was intimidated by her independence was foolish.

"Then you shared your story about Grace and how you lost her. I can't be the man for you to share your life with, but perhaps I could give you a gift you would remember me for during that life."

Share her life? He wanted to share his life with her? Winnie digested that piece of information, or at least attempted to, and couldn't stop her heart from thumping. She'd never met anyone who understood the struggles she endured, sometimes on a daily basis, until she met Nicholas Graham. His struggles were equal to if not greater than hers.

"If I can find her, then maybe I can chase away some of my own darkness." He flexed his hands and then fisted them. "God knows I haven't been able to do it."

"Is that all? That is the only reason? To chase away your own shadows?" She punched his arm. "You are selfish." Winnie's disappointment washed over her. He was a good person who had helped her to survive the gunshot that nearly took her life. Now he was showing her he only thought of himself.

"I want to find your family," he whispered. "Everyone needs family."

Her breath caught. "What did you say?"

"Family."

She stared at him, heart in her throat. "I don't understand."

"For all the complaining I do about my family, I know I wouldn't be here without them." His gaze met hers. Honesty. Truth. Desperation. "Please. Let me find her."

Winnie's stomach turned in a circle once, then again. She tasted food from the previous day's wedding feast. He knew what he offered her, what it meant to her and how much it hurt to even imagine such a thing. Yet he asked her to allow him to rip the scab off the biggest, deepest wound on her soul.

She got to her feet and walked a few feet away, her arms around her middle. Nausea continued to assault her. And along with it was something she never expected...hope.

Hope was such a dangerous thing. She had it bled out of her at the age of ten. Now the notion she could find Grace raced through her, followed quickly by the one thing she knew she might not survive.

Hope.

Before, Winnie endured pain and anger. Now, she shook from the possibility of what his request meant. She hadn't allowed herself to open that door before. Now he was pushing it open, albeit in the guise of asking her permission.

She should say no. She should climb back in the wagon and go home. To her safe boardinghouse and safe life. To never think about what might have been if she said yes to Nicholas Graham's crazy plan. She opened her mouth to tell him no.

Then she found she had lost her mind along with him.

"Promise me you won't break my heart. Promise me you will find her."

Nicholas's expression spoke of surprise and determination. "I promise you I won't stop until we find her."

"We?"

"Yes, we. You're smart and you know people in Houston. I

have a gun and a bad attitude. Together we can do anything."

She couldn't stop the snort that escaped. "You can be formidable."

"And you are smarter than any woman I know."

"I doubt that is true. I've met your sisters and sisters-in-law. They all appear to be quite smart women."

He waved his hand. "I don't consider them when I think of females."

This time Winnie smiled. "You have a certain charm, Mr. Graham."

He frowned, the wrinkles between his eyes a familiar dent. "I don't reckon anyone would call me charming."

Before she could think about changing her mind, she kissed him. "Let's find my daughter."

"Goddamn right we will."

Winnie couldn't stop the well of excitement that raced through her, leaving goose bumps across her skin.

They were going to find Grace.

Matt Graham rode home with his brothers Caleb and Benjy ahead. It had been a good day and the summer had proven to be the right combination of sun and rain. The grass grew, the cattle ate and got fat. In the not too distant future, they would bring the beeves to market and fill their coffers for the winter. If things kept going well, it would be a nice profit for the Circle Eight.

It was about time things evened out for the Grahams. After some rough years and tragedies, they were due for some good things to happen. What with Granny Dolan passing, Hannah had carried a touch of sadness about her. The children grew and she was happy, but he knew she missed her grandmother. An uneventful summer and fall would go a long way to making things normal for everyone.

The three reached the barn and dismounted. As he led his horse into the darkened interior of the building, he rolled his shoulders. He could use a bath and possibly a rubdown by his wife. The thought was very appealing and he wondered how he got so lucky. Life was damn good.

As he passed a few stalls, he stopped and cocked his head at the empty spot where Rebecca's horse should be. He frowned. It was too late in the day for her to be riding. Hell, it was nearly suppertime.

"Do you know if Rebecca had to go to town today?" Matt asked the question to no one in particular.

"Damned if I know." Caleb poked his head up from the stall. No doubt he was rubbing his horse down and preparing to get him settled for the night.

"Dunno," was Benjy's murmur from farther down the barn.

"Shit." Matt made quick work of his own horse's care and then strode toward the house with a bit more speed than he would have had before discovering his sister's absence.

He opened the door and the smell of supper washed over him. Eva had made something spicy and it smelled incredible. First he had to find Rebecca and the food would wait. The women were in the kitchen with Mr. Bartholomew at the table playing some kind of game of sticks with the children.

Catherine leaned against the table munching on something she'd pilfered from the stove no doubt. The teenager was a hellion and never listened to a thing anyone told her.

"Where's Rebecca?"

Eva glanced at Hannah.

"I ain't seen her since this morning." Catherine was not particularly helpful.

"She went to go help that man who came to the house." This from the older man with the sling.

"What man?" Matt's words were clipped.

Eva and Hannah looked at each other again.

"Hannah? Eva?" He looked at his sister-in-law, Aurora. "Rory? Somebody tell me where the hell Rebecca is."

"She has it in her mind that her role is as a healer and she won't hear anything else." Eva spoke to the pot she was currently stirring.

"What man?" Matt stood in front his wife until she met his gaze. Her brown eyes were full of guilt.

"Tobias Gibson."

Matt cursed under his breath, mindful of the passel of

children currently staring at him, their eyes wide as saucers.

"Why did you let her leave with him? The man is not to be trusted, no matter how much he helped rebuild this place. He burned it to the ground first." Matt tried his damnedest to control his temper but it was already near to boiling.

"His grandfather was very ill and Rebecca thought she could help." Hannah wiped her hands on her apron. "She took her medicine box and that book she writes in every day."

"You let her leave her with a man you know I wouldn't lct step foot on this ranch?" His voice had risen.

"She *is* a woman grown. She'll be eighteen in September. You can't stop her from doing what she wants."

"I sure as hell can. I am the head of his household, no matter how many of you want to fight me about that." He glared at Eva and Hannah. "I'm going after her."

"No, you won't." Hannah put her hands on her hips, a sign she was about to get mighty stubborn. "She is a good healer, the best I've seen. Elizabeth told me about Pops Gibson and while he was an old curmudgeon, he kept that family together. They might not be us, but they are a family who needed help. Tobias was here for months building this house. His penance is finished."

He wanted to argue with her, to tell her it was wrong. Rebecca was his responsibility. Hell, she couldn't possibly be almost eighteen. She was a girl in braids and dirty knees, not a female who would go off with a man without telling Matt.

Apparently she would.

"When is she coming back?" His hands itched to go saddle up and go after his errant little sister.

"When she is no longer needed." This from Eva.

"Traitor."

The older woman shrugged. "You are all my children, *hijo*. Fighting with any of you does no good. Sometimes you have to make your own mistakes to learn from them."

"I can't believe none of you stopped her." Matt ran his hands through his hair.

"Do you want to ride after her?" Caleb had come in at some point and stood behind him.

"No. Much as I don't like it, she is a Graham and she knows how to protect herself. Besides, if the old man was bad enough off to make Gibson come to us for help, he might be dead within a day."

Eva gasped and Hannah looked ready to punch him.

"If she's not back in a couple days, I'm going after her." With that he turned and walked out of the back door. He would use the cold pump water to cool his temper. At this rate, he'd need fucking snow to make a difference.

Rebecca slid off the horse with a plop. The hard ground jarred her bones after the exceptionally long ride from the Circle Eight. She'd thought it was farther away, at least half-a-day's ride, but it was only eight very hard hours. No doubt Tobias had fooled Vaughn and Elizabeth into believing his property was further away to confuse them.

Not so with Rebecca.

No, he drove them both until she couldn't feel her behind and her thighs screamed with a thousand pricks of pain. Tobias didn't seem to care he drove her to such discomfort, not that she could begrudge him the sense of urgency. He was obviously very worried about his grandfather.

Three little boys stood beside the modest cabin. They were of varying ages and thankfully somewhat clean and quiet.

"Where's Will?" Tobias barked at them as he secured the horses to a post beside the door.

"He's with Jeb hunting up some supper. We ain't, I mean, we didn't eat yet." The tallest one, skinny with buckteeth and thick blond hair, spoke. He glanced at her as though it was for her he'd corrected his grammar. She resisted the urge to smile. The situation was far too serious to be distracted by the boys.

"How's Pops?" Tobias put his hands on his hips, although standing over the boys, he was not threatening. She couldn't say the same for how he treated everyone else. Rebecca wanted to see the soft side of the man. She was still annoyed with him though, the grumpy sourpuss that he was.

"Sleeping." The tall boy spoke again. "He's been coughing

something fierce, Tobias."

"I know." Tobias blew out a breath. "That's why I brought Miss Graham." He gestured to her. "She's a healer."

Rebecca didn't know if she was a healer, but she had the knowledge to do her best to try to heal someone. Tobias's opinion, albeit a little cockeyed, warmed her.

The boys stared at her. "Miss Elizabeth?" This from the smallest of them, with a lisp and adorable cheeks.

"Next best thing, her sister."

Oh, now that wasn't nice. Rebecca might be seventeen but she was just as good as Elizabeth, not a substitute.

If possible, the boys' eyes widened even further. "Now get yourselves gone so she can take a look at Pops. Gather some kindling and help Jeb and Will clean the kill when they get back."

The small Gibsons scampered off to do as they were bade. Tobias looked at her from beneath the brim of his hat. The sun had set a short time earlier, leaving the air cloaked in gray shadows. The air was pleasant, a surprise for Texas summer evenings. Nevertheless, a chill ran up her spine at the dark visage Tobias presented.

"Let's get to work. Pops ain't getting better while we stand out here."

Rebecca held up her hand. "I am more than happy to help your grandfather. First, I need a moment to perform some personal, ah, business."

His mouth tightened. "Fine then. Privy is out back. Well pump is on the side of the cabin. I'll meet you inside when you're done."

She didn't get a chance to respond before he left her, quite abruptly, and entered the house. Rebecca glanced up at the evening sky. "Too late to change my mind now, I suppose." With a sigh, she made her aching legs move. She had much to do and whining about her personal discomfort wasn't going to get anything done.

Rebecca was a Graham through and though. Pops needed her and she would help the older man. She would not give up without a fight.

Houston had a bustling atmosphere that never seemed to stop. Nicholas steered the wagon through a bevy of obstacles including horses, pedestrians, runaway barrels, a screaming mother and a ladder that had fallen into the street. It was a wonder anyone got anything done in this city.

He'd had the same reaction the first time he had come to the city. Growing up where he did, there was plenty of open sky and room to stretch your legs. Here he couldn't fart without someone catching wind of it. Literally.

He remembered the way to Winnie's house and steered the wagon around to the back. Tomorrow he would see about getting the rig returned, beat the snot out of whoever rented it to Winnie, and then secure her a horse to ride. Thank God he'd brought his gelding.

They would need to be able to move quickly and a horse-drawn conveyance would be cumbersome. Hell if he knew where they'd go but they had to start somewhere. Transportation seemed a good place to him.

Winnie had been very quiet for the rest of the trip after she agreed to his crazy plan. They'd spoken but it was inane topics like the weather and when to stop to eat. She'd retreated into herself and he didn't know how to draw her out of it. For most his life, he had pushed people away. What the hell did he do now?

If Ellie were there, he could ask her. Hannah would help too. But none of his family was around. He'd left them behind, gladly at the time, and decided he didn't need them. Ha! Well, wasn't he a complete idiot. Helping Winnie was something he needed to do. Failing her was not an option.

He stopped the wagon in front of the small barn and set the brake. Before she could get down, he hurried around the back of the wagon and held up his hands to her. When the hell had he become so solicitous? Had someone knocked him the head?

"I, uh, thank you, Mr. Graham." She leaned into his hands and he plucked her from the perch.

She weighed no more than a bag of feathers—a curvaceous bag of feathers, he remembered all too well. His body tightened with the memory of the perfection he'd touched, tasted and caressed. Perhaps staying at the boardinghouse was not such a good idea. It would be near to impossible to keep his hands to himself if she was so inclined to offer her bed.

Shit.

"I think you can call me Nicholas. Or Nick. I reckon we're past the mister part, seeing as how I've seen you naked."

He wouldn't be mistaken for a charmer.

"Well then, I certainly hadn't forgotten what a plain speaker you are, *Nicholas*." She reached up and took her traveling bag from beneath the seat. "Please take care of the animals and then come inside. I'll get a late supper ready."

He wanted to kick his own ass, which wasn't uncommon. Damned if the wrong words fell out of his mouth again. He cursed as he unhitched the team and brought the horses into the small barn. The rig would sit outside until the morning and they could return it. Winnie kept a clean stable although she had no animals of her own except for a barn cat, which meowed at him with fervor when he opened the door. Nick lit the lantern hanging by the door and then led the horses in.

"I'll end up out here with you fellas." He settled the first horse into a stall and then the second. There were oats and fresh water readily available. She must have someone keep the stable stocked at all times. He supposed that was part and parcel of owning a boardinghouse. Folks who stayed with her would have mounts. She was probably popular just for the equine accommodations, not to mention the beautiful house, good food and the exquisite hostess.

He brushed the horses down, made sure they were comfortable with food and water. Nick knew he was avoiding going into the house. He didn't want to admit why.

Nick was afraid.

Now that he'd admitted so much to Winnie and turned her life upside down by concocting a scheme to find her daughter, he didn't know what to do. What if she wanted to talk more? Or, God forbid, share what he felt? The very thought of more talking made his stomach flip.

Then again, she'd been quiet for more than a day since the last time they had truly held a conversation. There was nothing to be afraid of, yet he still dragged his feet. The cat, a yellow tabby with half an ear on the left side, stared at him from the open door.

"I suppose I should get on up there. She likely has supper on the table."

Meow.

"She had good vittles if I remember right."

Meow.

"She even takes in ugly strays like you."

Meow.

"And me."

Nick turned out the lantern and closed the barn door. The cat loped along beside him as he walked to the back door. A warm glow emanated from the small window he knew was above the sink. It looked like a home. A welcoming one.

His heart clenched. Pure need pulsed out from within. Need to come home to her, and feel her warm body against his each night. A fairytale.

Did he have the courage to find out if the fairytale could be a reality? He sure as hell didn't know. Maybe he never would. Or perhaps this adventure would prove him wrong about what happiness meant. His steps faltered at the thought.

Nick thought courage was something men had to face down danger. Now he knew differently. Courage was having the balls to be scared shitless and still be foolish enough to move forward. He dug deep to find it. After a fortifying breath he walked up the steps and knocked on the back door.

"Come in." Her voice came from within, light and lilting.

Meow.

The cat darted inside as soon as he opened the door. It headed straight for Winnie's legs, winding around beneath her skirt and meowing for all he was worth.

"Cheddar, what are you doing in here?" She glanced down at the cat, a lock of her golden hair swaying across her cheek.

"I'm afraid he latched on to me." Nick took off his hat and

held it in his hands, turning it this way and that. He wasn't sure what to do. Staying in her house when she was shot was a different situation than this one. Now she was hale and hearty. And alone. It hadn't occurred to him they would be in the house together without a chaperone.

Heat raced through him at the possibilities. And the memories of the barn on the Circle Eight. He resisted the urge to adjust his growing erection in his trousers, even as his circulation suffered.

"He's a pest when he wants to be, which is more often than not." Winnie shooed the cat away with her foot but the feline didn't go far. It sat a foot away and meowed, growing louder each time. Soon it was louder than any infant that ever wailed.

Nick, feeling guilty since he'd let the cat in, squatted down and scooped it up. "I prefer my eardrums in one piece." As he walked back toward the door, the cat wriggled, attempting to escape. "Oh no you don't. Out you go."

It took him three tries before he was able to get the critter on the other side of the door. It yowled in protest. Loud enough to wake every bird within two miles. Shaking his head, he turned and found Winnie laughing silently.

"Wrangling cats is different from wrangling cattle, hm?" She appeared to be highly amused by his battle with her crazy cat.

"Not so much. Cattle are just as annoying." He folded his arms and scowled. Her smile disappeared and he cursed silently for being the cause of it. Nick forced himself to relax and attempted to calm his unruly brows.

She shook her head. "You cannot stop yourself, can you?"

"Stop myself from doing what?"

Winnie stepped up to him and lifted her small hand toward his face. She smoothed her finger above his eyes. "You're barely twenty-four and already have dents in your forehead."

His cheeks heated and he damn well hoped he wasn't blushing. "I'm in the sun a lot."

"You wear a hat in the sun."

He wanted to move away from her but at the same time, he wanted to stand there and let her touch him all night. "I am who I am."

She cupped his cheek. "As am I." She stood on her tiptoes and brushed her lips across his.

Nick closed his eyes and hoped for the strength to resist her. He couldn't be distracted by their physical pull. If he wanted to help her find her daughter, he needed all his wits about him. That wouldn't happen if he spent his time thinking about her beautiful breasts or how soft her thighs were.

She moved away and he swayed toward her. Foolish man. Fortunately she didn't see the lovesick idiocy.

"I have plenty of food left from what Eva packed. She must have thought there were six of us." Winnie, unaware he was fighting the urge to do more than stand there, set out food on plates. "I have water to drink. I hope that will do. I normally have milk delivered from a farm nearby but since I haven't been here—" She stopped and turned to look at him. "Nicholas?"

He shook his head. "I'll sleep in the barn."

Her expression fell and he refused to acknowledge the pain in her eyes.

"You don't have to."

Nicholas wanted nothing more than to stay with her in the boardinghouse. To stay with her. But he couldn't, not yet. If ever. Before he could even consider living his life, he had to stay the course and find Winnie's daughter. It had become his banner, one he would fly high as he traversed the unknown battle ahead.

"I do."

She sighed. "I don't agree with you but I won't argue with you. Please at least eat some food before you hide yourself from me."

"I'm not hiding." He slapped his hat against his leg.

"Yes you are." She stuck her nose in the air and returned to the food on the counter. Her back was straight as an arrow, her shoulders stiff. Nick had hurt her, of course. He seemed to be good at that, no matter how much he didn't want to be. "Eat up and go where you need to go."

They sat down at her large table, the room echoed with

emptiness with just the two of them. The damn cat still yowled outside, while inside, a very awkward meal progressed. Nick swallowed the slightly tough biscuits and ham but he didn't taste a bite of it. Winnie picked at her food, which was his fault. The cool well water washed down the food although he was afraid he might see the supper again later.

Sometimes when Nick was twisted up in knots, so was his stomach. He never told anyone about it, preferring to do his business privately. No one knew any of his secrets.

Except Winnie.

She was the only person he ever confessed anything to. There were other things she didn't know. Those shadows would stay hidden.

It would be a very long night with only the horses and a meowing cat for company. In the morning, he had to be at his best. For her. For him.

He was afraid if he wasn't, there was no future. Ever.

Winnie slammed the coffee pot down onto the stove with a definitive *clang!* It felt so satisfying she did it again.

Clang!

She was annoyed and frustrated. Nicholas had refused to sleep in the same house with her. What did he think she was going to do, seduce him while he slept? While not a bad idea, it was something she wouldn't appreciate herself, therefore would never consider it. The man was stubborn as the day was long. He made her angry and, at the same time, sad for the tight box he kept himself locked in.

She should be more patient but her emotions were wound up tighter than the cogs of a clock. Ticking away inside her second by second.

Her anger wasn't solely targeted at Nicholas. Her anxiety more about searching for Grace, of starting down a path she had been afraid to follow for ten years. The sad fact was she had no earthly reason not to look for Grace except her own fear. She'd given away her own child. No matter that she was sixteen years old and recovering from childbirth. She should have fought her own helplessness.

Regrets were useless. They left a bad taste in her mouth. She ought to kick them out of her mind for good. Easier said than done. Her world had been inundated with regrets for so long, she didn't know how to purge them.

Nicholas had pushed her, and for that she would be grateful for the rest of her life. She didn't want to hope too hard they would find her daughter. If they didn't, or found out something Winnie couldn't bear to hear, it would break her heart all over again.

The coffee burbled merrily in the pot and she poured cool water from a pitcher to settle the grounds. As she reached for a cup, a masculine voice sounded from behind her.

"Ah, can I help with breakfast?" He surprised her at every turn. She'd heard from Elizabeth that her family had grown up with everyone knowing how to do all household chores. An unusual arrangement but one Winnie respected.

She poured a cup of coffee and turned to hand it to him. His brown hair curled in damp waves at the edges while his freshly shaven jaw gleamed in the sunlight coming through the window over the sink. Heat rushed through her at the sight. The man was handsome as sin.

"I don't have much here. I usually have a local farmer who delivers eggs and milk. Plus Consuela cooks when I have boarders. She also makes the bread twice a week for me." She winced at the meager offering in the larder.

"I don't think I could eat anyway." Nicholas's expression was tight with tension, mirrored on her own face, she was sure.

"Coffee?" She held up a cup.

"Fine. Then I've got to get that rig back to whatever idiot rented it to you."

"Old man Sylvester is quite nice. I'm sure he didn't realize the conveyance needed repair." Winnie had always rented from him. The elderly livery owner had lost much of his clientele. She felt sorry for him and wanted to be sure he ate and had enough money to survive.

Nicholas snorted. "Like hell he didn't know."

She scowled at him. "You make judgments too quickly."

"And you trust too easily."

It was her turn to snort. "Me? I very rarely trust anyone. My circle of trust extends to three people right now." She couldn't trust people. Not after all she'd been through in her life. Too many disappointments and pain.

"I'm not one of them." His glanced out the window, the sun's rays highlighting the beautiful blue-green eyes and the pain within them.

Winnie wanted to lie to him but couldn't. It wouldn't be right or fair to him. She had feelings for him but their relationship was too new, too fresh, to consider trusting him. "Not yet."

"Yet." He shook his head. "You trust me with your body."

She inwardly winced at his bald speaking. The Grahams definitely didn't believe in dissembling.

"I suppose that's true. Nicholas, Nick, we don't know what will happen between us. Until we know, I, well, I can't." Her hands itched to take his, touch him.

"Uh-huh. I'll take that coffee now." His jaw was tight enough she thought she heard his teeth crack.

She refused to feel guilty. If he stayed at her side and showed her that he could be trusted, then she would trust him. For now, however. The tension between them had to break. They wouldn't be successful at their journey to find Grace if they couldn't have a civil conversation.

"No."

"No?" His brows rose. "Pardon me?"

Winnie gritted her own teeth. "No. I'm done with this anger and your foolish inclination to always be unpleasant."

If possible, his brows went up farther. "Unpleasant?"

"And repeating what I said is annoying." She banged the coffee pot down once more and then strode toward him. He watched with surprise until she grabbed his collar and yanked him toward her.

The moment her lips touched his, fire licked at her skin and her clothes were entirely too constrictive. He reared back and stared at her, this time with an intensity that made her shiver.

"You kissed me."

"Do you have an issue with my actions?" She trembled with the need to touch him again. Even her voice shook. It was madness. Sheer madness.

He didn't answer and her heart dropped to her feet. Instead, he pulled her back against him, breast to chest, hard to soft. She wrapped her arms around his neck and sank into his kiss. Sweet, wet heat swept across her skin.

The man was like a strong drink, bracing and enough to make her mind malfunction. Winnie held onto him, anchored by the strength of his muscles honed by years of ranching. It was like embracing a living, breathing, hot oak tree.

Her nipples hardened to aching points, needing more than to feel her underclothes. She yanked at his shirt until it popped free of his trousers. He grunted when she reached down to find the soft skin of his back. She slid her fingers lower and grasped the top of his buttocks, then squeezed.

"Do you think this is a good idea?" he murmured against her mouth.

"No, but we're going to do it anyway."

"Damn right we are." He released her long enough to finish removing his shirt, then made quick work of his trousers. He stood before her, deliciously naked. A few scars puckered his skin, but otherwise he was perfect. Soft whorls of brown hair decorated his chest, leading down a flat stomach and lower still, to the hard cock that stood in a nest of curls framed by an impressive pair of testicles. Winnie had never considered a man could be beautiful.

Nicholas changed all that. He changed everything.

"You've far too many clothes on."

Winnie smiled and unbuttoned her dress, dropping it to her feet. His gaze raked her up and down, once, then again. His finger traced the scar from the bullet on her shoulder.

"You forgot to put your frilly underthings on."

This time she smiled, knowing by the second just how hard her nipples were becoming. "No, I didn't forget."

His nostrils flared at the same time his cock jumped, slapping against his stomach. "Holy hell, woman."

"Indeed." She stepped back until the table was behind her.

"What are you—"

Before he could finish the sentence, she slid up onto the table and spread her legs. He was there in an instant, nestled between her thighs. Her body nearly sighed with relief. He belonged there.

"You're so wet." He slid his hardened staff in her ready folds. She closed her eyes and pulled him closer still.

"In an instant. Only for you." So very true. There was no one in her life, before or after Nicholas, who would evoke such a reaction.

"I can't wait."

"Don't." She took hold of his rod and it pulsed beneath her hand. Her heart thundered as she guided him to her core.

He pushed in slowly at first, inch by inch, until she scratched at his shoulders, urging him to do something other than tease her. When he thrust into her to the hilt, she gasped. They were made to fit together, perfect as a custom key in a lock. She spread her legs wider, pulling him deeper. Until she didn't know where he ended and she started.

Her forehead pressed against his. Their breaths mingled and she breathed in his essence. Their combined heat spiraled up between them. It was instantaneous combustion.

Winnie wrapped her legs around his hips and grabbed the edge of the table. He thrust in a slow rhythm, sending tingles through her from her pussy to her breasts, radiating out. Every small hair on her body stood on end.

"You're so damn tight." His voice had dropped to a husky whisper that skittered across her ear.

Pleasure was something she hadn't expected to feel with a man but with Nicholas, her past disappeared. Anything she shied away from previously, she now embraced. He had found the person inside her who had been buried away for nearly all her life.

The more she touched him, the more she needed. She was addicted and out of control. And for the first time, she welcomed the feeling.

The morning sun bathed them as they made love. She

pressed kisses against his collarbone, the salty tang of his skin lingered on her lips. He cupped her buttocks and pulled her closer, his cock sliding impossibly deep within her.

He filled her, in more ways than one. She kissed him hard and leaned back, spreading her legs further.

"More."

His eyes widened and a smile played around his full lips. "Yes, ma'am."

His hands moved up her thighs, whispery soft. Shivers raked her, making her pussy walls clench around him. He grunted and dug his fingers into her skin. Her breasts bounced with each thrust and his gaze locked on them.

As though he read her mind, he leaned forward and captured one nipple in his mouth. He sucked while his tongue swirled around on the hardened peak. She groaned and pushed her flesh further into his hot mouth. When he bit her tender bud, she started and grew even wetter.

"More."

To her delight, he bit her again while he continued to pound into her core. Pleasure streaked through her, stealing her thoughts and reason. Winnie should feel guilty, but she couldn't. Finding bliss with Nicholas was natural as breathing. Unbelievably natural.

His pace quickened and she barely held onto all rational thought. Pleasure soared through her, crashing over her. Stars danced behind her lids and for one perfect moment, the world fell away and there was nothing but this. The two of them, the bliss found in each other's arms. Nicholas whispered her name as he found his own release, shuddering in her arms.

Harsh breathing and the scent of sex filled the kitchen. Winnie managed to lean back and smile. His gaze, for once, was unguarded and relaxed.

"Breakfast?"

To her delight, he smiled. A genuine smile from the unhappiest person she ever met. "I reckon I worked up an appetite."

To this, Winnie laughed and kissed him hard. The tension in the room was gone. They would eat and then start on the journey to find Grace. She was determined now. This quest was the right thing to do.

Rebecca stretched the kinks out of her back and yawned. After two days of nursing Pops nearly day and night, she was exhausted and sore. He was a bit of a codger but it was evident he loved his family. The second pot of coffee was already on the stove and breakfast consumed.

The Gibson men all had hearty appetites, except for Pops. Will, Jeb and Tobias were the oldest of the bunch and devoured food as though they hadn't eaten in weeks. The three little ones barely spoke but they knew how to stuff food in their mouths. She had taken to calling them sweetie, honey and sugar. None of them spoke while she was around. Elizabeth mentioned they liked to be read to but Rebecca had to spend her time nursing Pops.

He was dying and he knew it. She knew it. Tobias knew it but refused to accept it. Pops had obviously been sick for a while but had kept it to himself. He had a wasting sickness, one that was stealing him breath by breath. Rebecca used her knowledge of herbs to locate those that would help him, but it was a temporary fix. The man had less than a month to live if she were to hazard a guess.

"Why aren't you in there helping him?" Tobias was always angry at her, at Pops, at the world. Rebecca, however, refused to rise to his anger.

"He's sleeping. Would you like me to wake him so I can wipe his brow?" She shook her head. "He managed to a bit of bread and some eggs this morning. It's more than he's eaten since I got here."

Tobias looked terrible. A few days' worth of whiskers darkened his cheeks and his eyes were red as beets.

"When was the last time you slept?" She reached for a cup to pour him coffee.

"I'll sleep when Pops is better." He sounded as though he'd swallowed rocks.

With four brothers, not to mention brothers-in-law, she knew not to argue with a stubborn fool. With a shrug, she handed him the coffee.

"You must realize he is very ill." She chose her words carefully.

His eyes narrowed. "I reckon you'd better make him better than."

Rebecca frowned. "Mr. Gibson—"

"You'd best call me Tobias. We've been under the same roof for two days. There ain't going back now."

She blinked as the knowledge sank in. Matt was going to be furious with her but she had to come. The old man needed someone to make him comfortable, to ease his pain. She wouldn't regret whatever came next.

"Tobias, your grandfather is more than ill. He's dying."

Mixed with the rage that nearly exploded from his expression, Rebecca saw grief and despair. Tobias Gibson was more than an angry man. He was a grandson who hurt for his grandfather.

"That ain't true."

"Whether you believe it or not, it's still true."

He threw the coffee cup against the wall, splattering hot coffee everywhere. Pops stirred in his sleep across the open cabin. Rebecca held onto her own temper, by a thread, but she held on. Someone had to be the adult.

"Fix him!"

"I can't." Her throat grew thick with the certainty that Pops would die with the love of his family around her. Tobias was rough but he cared. A great deal.

"Fix him!" He took hold of her arms and lifted her from the ground. His grip was tight but not painful. She stared into his eyes, this complicated man who she found herself drawn to.

"I can't." Her voice was barely a whisper.

To her utter shock, Tobias kissed her, hard enough to make her teeth cut into her lips. Her first kiss. Not what she'd expected. And she definitely was not enjoying it.

He wrenched his mouth away and let her drop to her feet. Rebecca swayed, grabbing the table to steady her. His breath was loud in the small cabin.

"Shit. That shouldn't have happened."

She couldn't agree more.

CHAPTER FIVE

Nicholas hitched up the team with practiced ease to the rattletrap conveyance. The horses both possessed a good temperament and were placid as he secured the traces. They were good animals although they were old. He savored the opportunity to return the rig to the idiot who rented it to Winnie and the old man.

She was getting herself ready to travel. After their early morning interlude in the kitchen, he'd needed the time to himself. To recover. To think. To stop his knees from shaking.

Each time he touched her, he lost control of his senses. She was softer than the petal of a rose and just as beautiful. The sad fact was, Nick had never experienced such an intense reaction to anything. Ever. Until he met Winifred Watson.

She was dangerous to his equilibrium but he couldn't help himself. No matter how much he pushed away, she drew closer. And he let her.

Now they were about to embark on a quest for which there might not be a happy ending. It had been his idea but they both knew there was only a slim chance they would find the girl. Slim was better than none.

He could not fail her. Would not. This was too important. For both of them. Redemption. Absolution. Forgiveness.

Nick had penned a letter for his brother, Matt, to let him know he would be away from the ranch longer than planned. He knew his oldest brother would not mind. In fact, Matt might breathe a sigh of relief to have Nick gone for a week.

Winnie stepped out of the house with her usual grace. Petite and curvy, she cut an amazingly appealing figure. One that made his body tighten although it had been scarcely an hour since he'd been inside her.

"We have to get another mount for you." He again hooked his horse to the back of the rig. "Can you ride?"

She frowned and her lips twisted. "I can but it's been some time." She glanced down at her dress. "I have a riding skirt inside. Let me change. It won't take but a few minutes to brush it out."

"I can go return the rig without you." He didn't want to think about her changing her clothes.

"No, you won't. I need to be the one to speak to Mr. Sylvester." She speared him with a "don't argue with me" look and marched back into the house. "I won't be a few minutes."

Nick told himself to be patient. They didn't have an appointment, only a stop on a rather unusual journey. He checked his horse's gear, noting he needed to polish the leather. Everything was in tip-top shape, unlike the rented rig. The carriage had groaned and creaked, barely making the journey across the rough Texas terrain.

He wasn't about to be nice with Mr. Sylvester. Anticipation about tearing into the livery man had been the high spot of getting everything ready this morning. She was not about to take that from him. No matter how sweetly she batted her blue eyes or, more than likely, told him what to do. Winnie was a strong-willed woman, one who had been through much in her short life. He respected her for a great many things, but in this, he would not bow to her will.

Twenty minutes later, she stepped back out wearing a light brown split riding skirt that hugged her delicious curves. She wore a matching vest and a dark green shirt. On her head was a flat-brimmed, practical, brown hat.

She smiled as she walked toward him and his heart thumped so hard his bones vibrated.

"I'm glad the sun decided to shine on us today. It will make our traveling easier." She carried a basket on her arm. "I packed what food I had."

He could only nod and take the basket from her, then hold

her hand as she climbed into the rickety rig. It rocked from her weight and she was half his size. No matter what he was going to speak his mind to the livery owner.

Mr. Sylvester was a wisp of a man, ninety years old if he was a day. Nicholas's anger fled in the face of such an ancient man.

Winnie smiled broadly at the old man. "Mr. Sylvester, how lovely to see you. As promised, I'm returning your carriage and horses."

Nick bit his tongue and forced himself to remember to respect his elders. Granny Dolan, who had left them earlier that year, would have stripped off a layer of his skin if he'd yelled at her the way he planned to yell at Mr. Sylvester. She had been a feisty old woman and spoke her mind as often as she wanted. He missed her, which was a difficult thing to admit. He didn't want to need anyone, or express his feelings.

"Good morning, Miz Watson." Sylvester had barely a fluff of white hair ringing his head but a full white beard on his bony chin. Scrawny and frail looking, the livery owner tottered over to them. "Where is Mr. Bartholomew?" He shot Nick a distrustful glare.

"He was injured during our trip and is staying with friends." Winnie patted the old man's shoulder. "My friend, Mr. Graham, escorted me back."

Sylvester's bushy white eyebrows lowered. "Graham? Is that the same family I heard about?" He pronounced "heard" as "heer-ed".

"Mr. Graham's family is the highest quality, good people." She gestured to the carriage. "They even did some maintenance for you."

"Hmph. I'll have to check it to make—"

Nick couldn't keep the words in any longer. They burst forth on a single gust of air. "Listen, old man, this rig barely made it to my family's ranch. I'm surprised the axle didn't snap for lack of grease. The traces were cracked and in desperate need of some damn work. You're lucky Miss Watson wasn't injured."

"It ain't that bad." The old man looked to Winnie. "Were it?"

She met Nick's gaze with reproach in her gaze. "I'm afraid it was." She sighed. "However, no one was injured."

"I ain't got nobody to help me so I do all the fixing 'round here." His slight shoulders slumped.

Guilt sliced into him. He didn't know there was no one to assist him. However, Nick should have recognized that by the tiredness of the building. Certainly there were a number of liveries in Houston in better shape, with better equipment and horses that weren't born two decades ago.

"After Miss Watson and I finish our, er, quest, I can come back and help you. My sister-in-law is a blacksmith. She can fashion some new gear for you." Nick had no idea why he was offering to help the old man. When Winnie turned that brilliant smile on him, he understood.

"Thank you, Mr. Graham. That's very kind of you."

"If you tell me he's good folk, then I'll believe it. I ain't no charity case, though." Old man Sylvester had his pride, which Nick could relate to. What man didn't?

"Then you can rent us a mare for Miss Watson to use for a few days, maybe even a week." Nick gazed down the stalls in the barn. "I'll pick her out."

"That sounds fair enough." Sylvester led them into the bowels of his establishment. Each moment they walked further in, the worse the smell of horseshit became. Likely the elderly man couldn't lift the shit to shovel it. Things were worse than they seemed. Truly, he ought to sell the place and make arrangements to live there until he died. This was too much for one man, much less one who had passed the far side of sixty long ago.

The animals weren't neglected. They were well fed and groomed. That was something the old man did well. Nick glanced at all of them before deciding on a healthy roan mare. She wasn't the prettiest of the lot but she was sturdy and took to touch without shying away.

"This one here. What's her name?" Nick blew into her nostrils to give her his scent. The mare tossed her head, nudging his shoulder.

"Her name's Juliet."

Winnie stepped up beside him. "A Shakespeare fan?"

"I don't know nobody named Shakespeare. She already come with a name." Old man Sylvester scratched his balding pate.

"It's a lovely name and a lovely horse." Winnie ran her hand down the horse's neck.

"I think she's stick ugly but if you want her, she's yours as long as you need her." The old man shrugged his shoulders. "I gotta saddle that should be good for ya, Miss Watson."

"Thank you, Mr. Sylvester. I'll ask Consuela to send her boys over to help you with the clean up." She smiled at him. "I'm sure they would appreciate some extra coin and I've got some lying around doing nothing."

After a few more grumbly words about not being a charity, Winnie paid him for the use of the mare and Mr. Sylvester stopped complaining. Just like that, they were headed away from the sad livery on horseback. Nick watched Winnie as she settled herself on top of the horse. Her wary expression told him she wasn't comfortable on the animal.

"You need a few minutes to practice?"

Her lips tightened and she flicked him a dismissive glance. "I do not need practice, nor do I appreciate your implication I do."

If she could have, she might have stuck her nose way up in the air and stomped away. However, she leaned over and whispered in the horse's ear. He wished he could hear what she told the mare. After a short conversation with the equine, she sat up and patted the horse gently.

"All set then?" He wanted to smile at her but she probably would not appreciate it.

"Of course." She straightened her shoulders and nodded regally at him.

"You said we were going someplace near Houston." He was a little frustrated with her. She refused to name where they were going to return only that it was where she gave birth.

"Espejo."

Nick concealed his surprise with a nod of his head. He kneed his horse into motion and kept the animal at a slow gait knowing she was still getting used to riding.

Espejo? That was a surprise. He knew where it was from his previous trip to Houston. The small town was nestled between the hills and could be missed if you blinked. There were less than twenty buildings, and only a few hundred residents. What set the town apart was the reputation of just one building.

The brothel.

His younger brother, Benjy, had been goggle-eyed when they'd ridden passed the infamous building. The brothel had been the nicest structure in Espejo, with gleaming windows downstairs that allowed potential customers to see the goods.

His gut bubbled with questions. "Why Espejo?"

She was silent for long enough he nearly repeated the question. "The midwife who delivered Grace lives there. At least I hope she still lives there. The last time I saw her was three years ago."

"Is she a friend?"

Another lengthy silence before she spoke. "Of a sort. Sometimes women help each other because there's no one else to do it. In a world where men make the rules, women have to survive any way they can."

He didn't quite understand it all but he knew from her tone of voice that she believed every word of it. He knew how hard it was to survive for a man. A woman had other problems to contend with he didn't. No doubt his sisters would give him an earful if he dared to ask them.

"Will she tell you what we need to know?"

Winnie sighed. "Yes, I think so. It has been some time since I saw her but she owes my father no loyalty. And since he's dead, he can't threaten her."

Nick was startled. "He would have threatened her if he was alive?" He knew her father was a ruthless bastard, the kind who would stop at nothing to get what he wanted. That apparently included threatening a woman who was kind to his daughter.

"Of course." Her tone was off-hand, as though it should have been obvious.

He chose his words carefully. "Does she have a house in town?"

Winnie snorted. "You are being far too circumspect, Nicholas. No, she doesn't have a house in town. She lives at the Slipper and takes care of the girls. "She's always lived there. Josie was born there and she hasn't left. She is a fixture there as much as the Ruby Slipper."

Nick's mind whirled with the notion the midwife lived at a brothel. She had told him her father used her to entertain the men he wanted to steal from. He hadn't imagined that it involved an actual brothel, though.

"I didn't want to presume anything."

"She is a good person, no matter where she lives or what she does. Good people are who they are. There are too many rich people with more money than God and they have the blackest souls on earth." Her jaw tightened as she spoke. "You may not pass judgment on her or anyone else at the Slipper."

Nicholas deserved some of her accusations but not all of them. "I ain't gonna pass judgment. Hell, Winnie, I was trying to figure out where we're going and who we're going to see. I'm not doing this for me."

She let out a breath through her mouth, nearly whistling through her teeth. "I'm sorry. I don't know why I'm acting like such a ninny. You've been wonderful."

"Let's not exaggerate now."

She laughed, a tinkling sound he soaked up like a dry sponge. "You have been wonderful. Not sweet or accommodating, but without you, I wouldn't have looked for her." She glanced at him with suspiciously shining eyes. "For that, you are wonderful."

His heart thumped at the emotions, the genuineness of her words. "Remind me to have you repeat that to Matt and Caleb."

Another laugh and he almost smiled at her. The woman was turning him into a blithering idiot.

"No matter what, Nicholas, I wanted to say thank you."

"There ain't no—"

"Yes, there is. We may be on a fool's errand but for the first

71

time in a long time, I'm doing something for me and me alone." Her smile was blinding in its beauty and joy. "Thank you."

Nick hadn't experienced humbleness in his life very often. Rarely, if ever. Winnie had given him a gift, although she probably didn't know it. He took her thanks and its implications and tucked it away in his cobwebby heart. He managed to swallow the big lump in his throat.

"You're, ah, welcome." Nicholas didn't know what being in love was supposed to feel like, but he sure as hell had never experienced such things before. Winnie made him want to be a good person, to make her happy if only to see her smile and hear her laugh once more. The sad truth was he hadn't wanted to leave the Circle Eight, but now that he had, he wanted to punch himself. His life had changed, literally, during this trip with Winnie and he doubted things would be the same. For that, he couldn't be sorry. Perhaps the deep pit he had existed in was growing shallower.

He might even escape it.

Buoyed by the general air of good feelings and the beautiful summer day, they rode in companionable silence. Espejo was only an hour outside of Houston and in no time the tops of the town's buildings came into view.

They passed several wagons and a few men on horseback as they drew closer. None of them were friendly or welcoming but no one was hostile. People minded their business around this kind of town. Without the brothel, there wouldn't be a town. Yet the people who lived in town couldn't approve of the brothel as good Christians. They also would starve without it.

It was a conundrum that no one spoke of but everyone thought about. They rode straight to the Ruby Slipper. Winnie had no qualms about it, so neither did he. No matter what anyone thought, he had more respect for her than anyone. He quelled a few overly curious stares with a scowl, once even having to touch the butt of the pistol riding his hip.

The brothel was in a two-story building, nearly unheard of in a town of this size. The house gleamed with a fresh coat of white paint and, of course, a painting of a Ruby Slipper on the top left corner of the building. The crimson shoe stated proudly to all that the inhabitants didn't care what anyone thought.

The second floor sported a balcony the full length of the building. The rails were as gleaming white as the rest of the house. No one was visible upstairs or down. It was if the building, and its inhabitants, slumbered. Perhaps they did. It was only ten o'clock in the morning.

They stopped the horses in front of the brothel and Nick dismounted. He held up his hands to Winnie and with a frown, allowed him to help her dismount. She grimaced. Damned if he didn't want to rub her ass to whisk away the pain from riding.

"Can you walk?"

She jerked her head back and speared him with a narrow eyed glare. "I am perfectly capable of walking, Mr. Graham. Don't worry your pretty head about my abilities."

A smile crept up on him. "Pretty head? My brothers would disagree with you about that."

She shook her head. "You always surprise me. That smile is quite a weapon. If I ask you to use it, don't question my motives."

His smile was a weapon? Nick had no response to that. Not one. Instead he tucked her arm under his elbow and led her to the front door of the notorious Ruby Slipper.

"Should we knock?" He didn't know the protocol for such a situation.

"No, we are welcome here anytime."

He surely didn't want to respond to that statement. A man was usually welcome at a brothel, of course. Women were another situation altogether.

The door was as red as the slipper painted on the outside. The knocker was a shiny brass lion's head. Something he might expect on a fancy mansion such as he'd seen in Houston. Whoever owned the building took meticulous care of its upkeep. The brass knob also sparkled in the sunshine. No doubt many men had used this very door to enter a world of pleasure.

She grasped the knob and the door swung open easily. Expecting the usual smells that accompany such a location, he was surprised the gentle scent of lemons wafted out on a cool breeze. She stepped in and he followed, curious.

The interior wasn't dark but a single lantern burned in the gloom of the large room. The curtains were shut on the large windows. At least a dozen tables with chairs nearly stored beneath them sat waiting for the night's customers to arrive. A tall counter sat on the right side. He assumed they served liquor from that spot.

In the center of the building, an elaborate staircase led up to the second floor. A master carpenter must have carved the winding bannister as it ended in a swirl of polished dark wood. A red and black carpet decorated the center of the steps, also no doubt of the highest quality.

The Ruby Slipper must have clientele with pockets to let. Someone had spared no expense to make this house of ill repute into a palace. The smell of lemons was stronger, likely whatever was used to clean and polish everything.

Winnie walked toward the stairs, bringing him along with her.

"Shouldn't we wait until someone greets us?" He didn't want to be shot for trespassing.

"No need. I told you I am always welcome here."

Nick was bursting with questions, but the hushed silence of the building quelled his need to voice them aloud. With more than a bit of trepidation, he followed her up the stairs.

"Ruby?" she called out as she neared the top.

"Winnie?" A door opened somewhere. "Is that you?" The woman's voice was husky, like a fine whiskey and just as rough.

"Yes, it's me and I have a friend with me."

"Does she need a room?"

Winnie turned and grinned at Nick. "No, he doesn't."

A brief silence from the woman named Ruby. "Well, then, come on up and bring *him* with you."

They turned right at the top of the stairs toward the only open door. A warm glow emanated from within. Nick had no idea what to expect and, to his surprise, his gut was tight with apprehension. He was afraid of Ruby? Of course not.

Winnie squeezed his arm as they approached the door. Her

expression was open and excited. Nick didn't know much about her life other than what she'd told him, but it was clear this woman was her friend.

She knocked lightly on the door as they walked in. Nick should have been prepared for shocks, after all they were hunting down a baby who had been born and given away ten years earlier. Anything could happen. However, he experienced a jolt when he walked into Ruby's room.

The room itself was swathed in cream and light purple. A canopied bed dominated the left side of the room with fluffy bedding fit for a princess. Matching curtains hung on the windows, giving the room a hushed atmosphere. The right side of the room held a fancy desk with gold leaf detail, claw feet and a neat stack of papers beside a rather girlish lantern. Behind the desk in a fat leather chair sat a woman, presumably Ruby.

The madam of a brothel had to be a tough old bird. Or at least that was what he thought until he saw Ruby. She was tall enough to dwarf the large chair, with square shoulders and a strong jaw. Her hair was the color of burnished copper, deep and full of a thousand shades of the sunset. Her face was exquisite, beautiful as one of the angel paintings he had seen in a church once. Her eyes were blue like a robin's egg. She wore a dark brown dress, quite conservative in nature, buttoned to her neck and down her arms. Her hair was in a fat braid, resting on her shoulder.

When she spotted Winnie, she smiled with obvious delight. "I can't believe you're here."

"Neither can I. I should have visited sooner." Winnie let Nick's arm go and crossed the room to embrace her friend.

He looked away, unable to watch the tears in the women's eyes as they reconnected. Whatever they were to each other, their love for each other was patently obvious. Nick had never had that type of friendship with anyone. He had love for his family, but for nothing like what Winnie had with Ruby. Envy speared him, for what the women shared, and for what he wanted with Winnie.

They finally separated, grinning broadly. Ruby spoke first.

"And who, may I ask, is *him*?"

They both turned to look at him. The petite, curvy blonde and the tall brunette, a mismatched pair but both feminine in their own way.

"Nicholas Graham, may I present Ruby Fleming. Ruby, this is my, ah, friend, Nicholas." Winnie stumbled over her words and he couldn't help but wonder what she was going to introduce him as. Lover perhaps?

"Friend, hm?" Ruby's left brow raised and she regarded him with unabashed curiosity. "It's lovely to meet you, Mr. Graham."

She was well spoken and had impeccable manners. Then there was the opulence in which she lived. Ruby was not at all a typical madam, if there was such a thing. He wanted to know how Winnie was acquainted with her but didn't want to show her friend just how rude he could be if he let his mouth take over his brain.

"How do you do, Miss Fleming?" He had manners, if he forgot to use them sometimes.

"I do very well, Mr. Graham." An amused twinkle gleamed from her brown eyes. She turned to Winnie. "To what do I owe the pleasure of this visit? I haven't seen you in a dog's age."

Winnie gestured to Ruby's oversized leather chair. "Please sit and I'll explain."

Nick watched as the ladies sat and then lowered himself gently into the delicate looking guest chair identical to the one Winnie had taken. She smoothed her hand over the riding skirt and kept her gaze down for a few moments before she spoke.

"I need to find her."

Ruby apparently needed no explanation as to who "her" was. "I wondered if you might get around to that one day."

Winnie's cheeks grew pink. "I might not have if it weren't for Nicholas. He made me realize what I had been missing for nine years."

"A life with your daughter."

At this Winnie started as though she'd been poked. "Yes, a life with Grace."

Ruby smiled. "I'm happy for you, Winnie. Very much so.

How can I help?"

"I need to speak with Josie."

Ruby's good humor faded. "She's in a bad way, Winnie."

"What happened?"

Nick was alarmed the one person who knew what happened to the baby would be unable to help them. Perhaps there was someone else.

"She has a wasting sickness. Doctor doesn't give her but a couple months left to live." Ruby shook her head, a choking sadness in her voice. "I hired a woman to take care of her but she coughs up more blood every day."

"I'm so sorry, Ruby. She doesn't deserve such a fate." Winnie reached across the desk and laid her hand on her friend's.

"No, she doesn't, but God doesn't seem to favor those who fall off the path of the righteous." Now he saw a hint of Ruby's anger. "She helped more than her share of people. An angel on earth if there ever was one."

Nick wondered who Josie was to the imposing madam. She was definitely angry about the fate of the woman who had helped so many. A wasting sickness was a horrible way to die. He'd seen one of the men from town turn into a skeleton over the course of a year until he finally died.

Winnie sat back and wiped her eyes. "Where is she?"

"Down the hall in the corner room. The one with the two windows facing east. She loves the morning sun." This time Ruby's smile was a mixture of sadness and regret.

"Can I speak to her? I need to find out where she took my daughter. Without a place to start, I'm afraid my quest is over before it starts." Winnie's back was straight, but her hands trembled in her lap.

Nick wanted to pull her on his lap and hold her until her shaking stopped. He wanted to simply open a door and find her daughter, make Winnie whole again.

"Yes, she can still talk. Some days are better than others. She has forgotten some things and gets mixed up but I think she can help you." Ruby got to her feet. "Let me go see if she's awake."

With that, the tall woman left the room. Winnie's gaze found Nick's.

"What if she doesn't remember? What if she makes a mistake and we go the wrong way?" She was always so self-assured, bossy even. To see her vulnerable was astonishing and humbling.

"Then we start again." He was foolish to speak as though they could wander Texas indefinitely. The Circle Eight needed him. He would have to return home. The round-up wasn't too far off and that dandy Vaughn wasn't enough of a cattleman yet to pull his own weight, much less Nick's.

"You can't mean we will keep looking forever."

This was when he told her they only had a week. That he had to go home or risk his family's ranch and their future. A ranch that supported his entire family.

"We will search until we find her." Nick could not understand how those words popped out of his mouth. What was he thinking?

Winnie's smile was brighter and more beautiful than any sunset that ever graced the eastern sky. And that was why he said what he did.

"I think I love you, Nicholas Graham."

His gut bounced to his feet and then into his throat. Twice.

He was saved from answering when Ruby came back in the room. "She's awake and ready to talk."

Winnie was sad to hear Josie was ill. She and Ruby were good people, even if they worked and lived at a brothel. The girls who worked for them were always treated well and protected. They were an anomaly in a world where women were treated like chattel, sold to the highest bidder. In Winnie's case, her father had been the auctioneer.

She shook off the dark memories of the man who had both defined and altered her life. He was gone and she lived on. She had much to be thankful for, not the least of which was the man by her side and the friendship of a few select people, two of which were Josie and Ruby.

The twins were hard to tell apart at first. They were nearly identical in looks but that was where the similarity ended. Ruby was a sensual being, her gait and mannerisms, the way she spoke, it all exuded a sexual being.

Josie was sweet and light, someone who spent her life caring for others. She started as a healer for the brothel and then word of her skill with herbs and medicines, and eventually birthing babies, spread. She was well loved and respected. When Winnie had discovered her pregnancy, she had fled to Espejo as soon as she was able to seek Josie's help.

Now the healer was sick and, if her sister was correct, dying. Ruby knocked lightly and opened the door in the corner.

"Here she is." Ruby stepped inside and held the door for Winnie and Nicholas. He looked like a cat entering a room full of rockers, twitchy and ready to bolt. Yet he stayed by her side and she loved him all the more for it. A woman nodded at them and left the room, obviously the woman who sat by the dying woman's bedside, taking care of her needs.

Winnie's blurted confession of love had been embarrassing, even more so when he appeared shocked. Ruby had saved Winnie by returning to the room before the awkwardness got worse. Perhaps Winnie had spoken too soon of her feelings for Nicholas. He was skittish when things like love were involved. She could only hope she didn't ruin any future they had together. Silly, but her emotions were running high.

The smell hit Winnie first. The stench of dying and sickness, a mixture of sour bodily fluids, vomit and a used chamber pot. She breathed through her mouth and put on her best smile.

However, she couldn't contain the gasp that escaped when she caught sight of Josie.

The previously healthy and beautiful woman was merely a husk of who she had been. Her beautiful hair had faded to the color of dishwater, sprinkled liberally with gray. Her skin hung off her frame as though someone had deflated her, stealing the life out from beneath her. Her sunken eyes topped cheeks that were gaunt and hollow. She was no more than thirty-five years old, yet she could have been mistaken for someone twice her age.

"Josie." Winnie's smile faded. Sadness washed over her at the condition of her friend. She sat down on the chair beside the bed and took Josie's hand, which was as fragile as a bird's wing. "Why didn't you tell me?"

Josie managed to shrug her slender shoulders. "I didn't want anyone to see me like this." Her voice was a papery whisper, her breath hitching on each syllable.

"Oh, sweetheart, I would have been here to help you as you have for countless others." Winnie's eyes pricked with tears at the advanced condition of Josie's illness. The descriptor "wasting sickness" was not nearly strong enough.

"Winnie is here about her daughter." Ruby wasted no time in getting to the point. It was what made her successful in a world of sex and fantasy.

Josie tried to squeeze Winnie's hand. "You want to find her."

"Yes, I do. And this is my friend, Nicholas Graham. He's helping me."

Josie's gaze flickered to Nicholas and then back to Winnie. "I would have done my hair if I'd known a handsome man would visit me."

Winnie managed a laugh although her heart was breaking for the sisters. "He is partially blind so don't worry."

Nicholas made a noise behind her and she glanced back. He stared at the wall as though it held the secrets to life.

"Can you tell me where you took Grace after I gave her up?" Winnie held her breath while she waited for a response.

Josie coughed, a deathly rattle that shook her entire sparse frame. "What do you remember about the birth?"

"I remember it hurt." Winnie let loose a hysterical chuckle. "Other than that I tried to not think about the baby other than to close my heart to her."

"I expected that was the case. You have to protect yourself from more pain." Josie sighed. "You aren't the first or the last woman to give a babe away to give them a better chance in life."

Winnie took a deep breath before she spoke. "I gave away a piece of myself that day. I never had anyone that was mine,

80

until Grace. And I turned my back on her. I won't be whole again until I find her."

"I hope you do." Josie's eyes started to close.

"Wait, please. Tell me what you did with her. What family took her in?"

Josie's eyes popped back open and in them, Winnie saw something that resembled regret. "You don't remember anything about her."

"No, nothing except she was a crying, wrinkled, red baby, breathing and healthy." Winnie tried to pull up something other than the brief glimpse of the newborn, but there was nothing. She had closed her eyes and refused to look upon the baby that had broken her soul in two.

"Red. Yes, she was that." Josie reached over with both hands and Winnie braced herself. "Grace is half-Indian or half-Mexican, I wasn't sure which."

A thousand conflicting thoughts slammed into Winnie's mind. Her daughter was half-Indian or half-Mexican. A child people would look down upon, a half-breed who belonged in neither world. Abandoned and neglected. Her throat closed up and tears spilled from her eyes. What had she done?

Winnie knew who the child's father was. Until now she hadn't been sure since there had been three men she'd been intimate with in the time Grace was conceived. It appeared the hacienda owner, Velazquez, was the man who had planted the seed. Her father had been trying to swindle the man out of his property and used her to distract him. She turned away from Josie and pressed her arms against her stomach.

Being a whore had brought her nothing but heartache. And now she had brought a child into this world and abandoned her without a chance. She was sick over her selfishness and foolishness. Winnie would never forgive herself.

"I took her to Fuller's Home for Orphans in Houston. They took children without questions. I didn't think a family would want her." Josie sounded as upset as Winnie was. "She was a beautiful child with hair as black as a raven's wing and dark brown eyes the color of coffee. She rarely cried on the trip there and she slept well even on the first night."

Winnie took no comfort in the fact the babe was sweet tempered. She likely wouldn't be now. "I can't believe I just let her go."

"You didn't just let her go. You sobbed hard enough I thought you might hurt yourself, or pop a lung at least." This from Ruby. "You told me you had no soul left and you wanted to give her a chance to live in a normal home."

"I threw her away." Winnie didn't hear Nick move, but suddenly he was there. His strong arms surrounded her.

She cried silently against his shoulder while the sisters murmured quietly behind her. Winnie's heart broke for all the mistakes she'd made in her life. She should have kept Grace and done what she could no matter how difficult. Selfish, selfish, selfish.

She hadn't realized she'd spoken aloud until he whispered in her ear.

"No, you are far from it, Winnie. Believe me, I know selfish."

She could barely breathe for the tears and snot clogging her nose and throat. "What if it's too late?"

He tilted her head back and scowled so familiarly she had the mad urge to laugh. "Too late? Was it too late for you? You escaped from your father and built a life of your own. Hell, woman, you own a boardinghouse and support yourself. I can't lay claim to anything of my own except my thoughts and my cantankerous nature."

This time she did laugh. "I'm afraid I made a mess of things."

"Nah. We'll figure it out. Together."

Her heart clenched hard and the love she had for this man surged through her. He might have been difficult, grumpy and stubborn, but she loved him. Desperately, completely, always.

"Thank you." She leaned back and attempted to locate the handkerchief in her reticule without embarrassing herself any further. He saved her again with a clean but serviceable red kerchief from his pocket.

"I'm sorry if I upset you." Josie interrupted Winnie's self-pitying ramble.

"No, please don't think you upset me at all." Winnie smiled shakily at her friend. "I'm only sorry I asked so much of you."

Josie's smile was sad. "I am your friend and always will be."

Winnie had to dig deep to find courage and fortitude to do what she must, no matter how hard it would be. Finding out what happened to Grace could shatter her, but she would see it through. "Is there anything else you remember that might help?"

Appearing nine years after a child was brought into the orphanage anonymously would be difficult to say the least. If she had something to go on aside from the baby being half-Mexican, it might help.

Josie snapped her fingers, barley a whisper of a sound. "Yes, I do. The baby had a heart-shaped birthmark on her hip. I remember remarking to Ruby about it."

Ruby nodded. "That's right. I remember it too."

Winnie smiled. "Thank you both." She turned back toward her friends and Nick kept one large hand on her shoulder. "I am sorry to have interrupted your day. I'm even more sorry I haven't come to visit you in so long."

There was nothing to be said about not knowing Josie was so sick. Neither sister would welcome or want pity.

"There is no apology required, you know that." Ruby smiled. "You make sure you come back and see us soon."

"I promise." Winnie hugged Josie gently and stood to leave. Ruby kissed her sister's forehead and walked to the door with Nicholas and Winnie.

Winnie had known Ruby for fifteen years. Seeing the madam again had brought back a wave of memories, ones Winnie had deliberately tucked away long ago. Ruby had been the woman her father sent young Winnie to learn from, on how to please a man. Nicholas would be shocked to know how much Winnie knew but did not acknowledge out loud.

Their shared past seemed like a lifetime ago, at a time when she existed but didn't live. Ruby showed her compassion, friendship and, eventually, love. No man could understand the bond between them, only that it was strong and everlasting.

They walked back to Ruby's room and sat down to talk. The tall woman had lost some of her energy, that which made her sparkle in a room full of lumps of coal. Infinite sadness painted her features.

"I'm sorry, Ruby. This must be so very hard for you." Winnie felt her friend's pain.

"It's harder for Josie. She knows she's dying and has accepted it. I won't let her give up, though, and she's fighting me and trying to die at the same time." Ruby's hands fistcd. "I can't give her up that easily."

Winnie wisely decided not to comment on Josie's declining health. It was too obvious, and too raw.

"You'll go to the orphanage and look for Grace?"

"Yes, straight away." Winnie glanced at Nicholas, who nodded. "I don't know how much luck we'll have but I have to try."

"It takes balls to face an ugly past and try to make things right." Ruby shook her head. "I don't think I'd have that kind of courage."

Winnie knew her friend had more than enough courage to face her own past but didn't believe she ever would. After Ruby crossed a line, she never looked back. Winnie envied that about her friend. Regret had become a constant companion and for once, Winnie was going to do something about it.

"Is there anything I can do?" Ruby was a force to be reckoned with.

"No, you've done more than enough. I know where to start now and I have Nicholas to help me." Winnie took a deep breath. "I will be back to see Josie. If anything happens before then, please send word to the boardinghouse."

Ruby's expression tightened. "I won't lie and say nothing will happen. No matter how much I want to control her sickness, I can't. I'll send word." It was a hard admission for Ruby, of that there was no doubt.

The trip back down the stairs was somber instead of full of trepidation and fear. Winnie knew as well as Ruby did that the dying woman upstairs had little time. There might not be another visit before there was a funeral.

Two young men were downstairs sweeping the floor and polishing the wood bar. They were young and nameless, looking at Ruby as though the queen had stepped into their presence. She nodded at them and they continued their work, their gazes slipping to her every few seconds.

"Thank you, Ruby. I can't tell you how much this meant to me." She hugged her friend, the persistent tears she never shed still stinging her eyes.

"You are always welcome here, no matter what. You know that." Ruby kissed Winnie on both cheeks and hugged her tightly for a near bone-cracking moment. "It was a pleasure to meet the man who has finally made his way into Winnie's heart."

Nicholas blinked a bit like an owl before he responded. "Thank you for helping her. It means the world."

Winnie wondered, for a fleeting moment, if he would acknowledge her love at all. If he never said the words aloud, she knew he loved her. His actions spoke of his feelings even if his mouth did not.

CHAPTER SIX

Nick didn't like seeing Winnie in such a state. She was scared, weeping and trembling, not at all the strong woman he'd met in Houston who had twisted his tail into a knot. He damn well didn't want to see it again either.

A half-Mexican baby was unexpected but not a big concern to him. People were who they were, no matter who their father's father was or what color their skin was. Nick understood it could be hard for children who were caught between worlds. But perhaps the girl had found someone who accepted her as a child, no matter the origin of her birth.

Then again, he knew how hard the world was and the babe might have suffered a worse fate than finding an adoptive family. Much worse. He wasn't going to mention that to Winnie, though. She appeared to still be shaking from seeing her friends.

There was also the matter of how she was well acquainted with a brothel madam and the inner workings of a rather famous one. He was bursting to ask her but didn't think it was the right time. From what he knew of her father, it shouldn't surprise him she had spent time with a madam. However, he had a feeling there was more to it than that, but he would save his questions for later.

He helped her mount the mare and made quick work of untying the reins and getting them on their way. Winnie remained silent and she was strangely subdued.

"You want to go to the orphanage now?" Nick didn't want to assume anything.

"Not quite yet. I think we need to ride back to Houston and have dinner. We need to have a plan before we go." Winnie appeared to be plotting.

"Are you thinking up a story, Miss Watson?" He had been a witness to the story Vaughn and Elizabeth had concocted to trap her father, Troxler. Winnie could have written fiction with all the ideas she had.

"Yes, I am." She glanced at him. "We can't fail, Nicholas."

"Then let's make sure we have our story solid before we go. Are you ready to step into this no matter what happens?" He was no fool. There was little chance of succeeding if they weren't prepared. As it was, their chances were slim to find Grace, but without a battle plan, they sank lower.

"No matter what, I am ready." Winnie had changed. Visiting the Ruby Slipper and the sisters had done something to her. He wasn't sure exactly what, but he could hear it in her voice, see it in her face and the way she held herself. Her shoulders were slightly slumped and a crease had appeared between her brows.

"Do we need more help?" He wasn't sure what they faced.

"I don't know." She sounded unsure of herself. Another thing that he didn't like. Not a damn bit.

"What do you know of the orphanage?"

She shrugged. "It's on the other side of the city, privately run and funded. Troxler never ran in philanthropic circles so I don't know too much."

They had to have a plan before they got to the orphanage. Nick would have to shake her out of her un-Winnie-like behavior. Trouble was, he didn't know how.

The next hour passed in silence, one full of endless thoughts and unspoken words. Nick was a simple rancher. He could track a lost beeve, a deer or elk, rabbits even, but lost children in a city? He was at a loss and that bothered the hell out of him. He'd started her on this quest and now he wasn't going to be of much use.

The dark hole that he existed in had held him captive for so long. Now when he looked up, he saw Winnie at the edge staring down at him as he hung on for dear life. He wanted to climb up and out. This was his chance to not only escape from his prison but to fill it in with dirt. To stamp on its ground and say goodbye forever.

Trouble was, he didn't know how again.

Frustrated and annoyed, he grew more fractious with each step the horse took. By the time they reached the outskirts of Houston, he had himself in a terrible knot. An epic knot that would take a mighty sword to cleave in two.

He couldn't stop himself. The darkness within him grew no matter what he did. His breathing grew labored and sweat rolled down his back.

"Nicholas?" She turned to look at him with her delicate blonde brows drawn down. "Are you feeling poorly?"

His chuckle was more of a rusty sob. "Every day of my life."

She rode close enough to touch him and put her hand on his. "Me too."

Just like that, his grip on the edge of the hole tightened. Winnie had pulled him back from the shadows that reached their tendrils around him. His eyes stung and he had to blink a few times to see straight.

Her fingers caressed his and it was as though she reached in and plucked his heart. It shook off a few more cobwebs and thumped steadily. For Winnie.

"Let's stop for dinner." She gestured to Houston. "There is a nice restaurant at the hotel up ahead."

Nick followed her lead to the building she indicated. The restaurant was nestled in the bottom floor of the Breakman's Hotel. Not the highest quality place, but definitely had an air of well-tended ownership. They were seated by a middle-aged, balding man with a lisp.

After ordering the day's special, Nick waited for Winnie to speak. He felt as though he was treading water in an endless lake, still gripping her hand, and hoping like hell the shore was visible soon.

"As I said, I don't know much about Fuller's Home for Orphans. I've heard the name before, but it's been some time." She clasped her hands together. "I am ashamed to know Grace was so close to the boardinghouse."

He gripped harder and yanked himself forward out of the hole, shaking his head. "You've been in the boarding house for five years."

"Yes." She frowned.

"You gave Grace up nine years ago. By the time you bought the boardinghouse, she might not have been there." He focused on the timeline and on Winnie. Being together was much better than alone. Much, much better.

Her mouth formed a small O. "I hadn't thought of that."

He seized on an idea. "Do you think your father knew about where Josie took the baby?"

She snorted. "Of course he did. The man knew when I had a bowel movement. He would have definitely known where my child was placed."

This time it was Nick's turn to reach for her hands across the table. "Then maybe she didn't stay there long. Maybe your father made sure she was adopted straightaway."

Her face brightened. "That's entirely possible. He would have considered the notion I would look for her. If she was close by, then he suspected I would try to find her. I didn't but I did leave his house for good. Mr. Troxler did not like being out of control."

"Then she was probably not an orphan for long."

She let out a sad sigh. "Then it might be harder to find her."

"And she might be happy with a family who loves her." Nick had a family who loved him, but he wasn't happy. It wasn't a good time to bring up that point, though.

"If she is, then I will leave her alone. As long as I know she has a good life and is happy, then I can be at peace." Winnie seemed calmer than when they left the Ruby Slipper. "I need to know she is well, Nicholas."

"I know you do and when we find her, and you see how well she is, you can move on with other things in your life." He didn't want to confess his feelings yet. She had told him she might love him, but that wasn't good enough for him to blurt out similar feelings. Oh, no, that was a definite no until he was absolutely certain of her love and only then would he ask her a more direct question.

Nick was the last person who would have considered marriage. He thought his siblings were a little odd to fall in love and act as crazy as could be over their mates. He hadn't understood it and had shown nothing but confusion and disdain.

Then he met Winnie.

She was a storm he hadn't expected, blowing him over with her power, strength and her thirst for life. He had been helpless against the onslaught of emotions that raced through him when he'd met her. When she was shot by her own father, in the act of killing him, Nick thought he might have died along with her.

Nursing her back to health had given him a purpose and it was amazing how that had transformed him. Going back to the Circle Eight had cut him off from her, as though he were a flower snipped from its stem. As with any bloom without its roots, he began to wither and die. Now that he had Winnie back in his life, albeit reluctantly at first, he felt the roots wrapping around him, pulling him to her. It would be a painful, if not fatal, experience if he were separated from her again.

"Nicholas, are you all right?" She must've seen something in his expression that caused her alarm.

"Just thinking about cut flowers," he blurted, a half-truth.

"I rarely cut the flowers because they die so quickly. If I leave them alone, they bloom and flourish over and over." She squeezed his hands. "If I haven't said this already, thank you for being here with me. I don't know of another person I would like to have by my side."

"Not even Vaughn, or Ruby?" He couldn't help himself. Jealousy over the people she counted as friends was inescapable.

"No, although I love them dearly, they aren't you. I need to—"

She was interrupted by the return of the waiter with their food. After the plates were set down and napkins unfurled, the conversation turned to banal topics. The weather, the couple in the corner couldn't take their eyes off each other long enough to chew and the old man who kept glancing at the door.

Everyday things, boring and unimportant.

His mind was wrapped up in the realization he wanted to marry her. Marry. Marriage. Husband. Wife.

The very idea made his legs shake and his heart run like a thoroughbred. She, picking away at her food, had no idea of the turmoil slamming around inside him. He didn't know if he'd have the courage to ask her, especially if the thought alone had him quaking.

"Do you agree?" She was looking at him with expectation on her face.

"Ah, sure." What he agreed to, he couldn't begin to imagine.

She dabbed her mouth with the napkin. "Good. I think a married couple has more of a chance of finding the information we need."

He nearly inhaled a green bean.

She pounded on his back as he fought to pull air into his lungs instead of green vegetable. His eyes watered and his throat burned from the effort to breathe normally.

"Married?" He managed to croak.

"Well, of course. How else do you suggest we go to the orphanage? You did agree."

Nick's face burned as his thoughts careened around. Had she proposed to him and he missed it? Or did she have another plan in mind.

He could not ask her. He simply could not. Whatever happened, he had to pretend he knew exactly what she was speaking of. If she wanted to allow people to believe they were married, he could do that. If she wanted to marry him, he would find a preacher.

Suddenly his thoughts around marrying her solidified, became very real. Possible. Excitement roared through him and he was finally able to take that deep breath.

"Yeah, of course I agreed." He used the napkin to swipe the sweat off his face. Holy God, next thing, he might piss himself if things got any stranger.

"Then we should pay for our meal and ride to the orphanage now." Her eyes sparkled for the first time since she spoke to

Josie. How could he possibly refuse her?

"Let's do it." He reached into his pocket but she put his hand on his arm.

"Please let me pay. This entire trip is for me. I cannot allow you to pay for a thing."

He frowned at her. "In my world, ladies don't pay for their own meals no matter whose idea it was." He carefully took her hand off his arm. "I will pay."

She opened her mouth to argue and he deepened his frown to a scowl. "If we're gonna be a married couple, then you need to let me be the man."

She closed her mouth and nodded. Relieved, Nick left enough money on the table for their meals and got to his feet. When he pulled out her chair and offered his hand, her eyebrows went up.

As they walked out, the old man who'd been watching the door looked up at them as they passed. He smiled sadly. "Hang onto that one, boy. She's one to keep."

"I plan to," popped out of Nick's mouth before his brain caught up with his tongue.

Winnie gifted the old man with a smile. "Thank you."

Perhaps the old man had been waiting for the woman he loved and lost. The lesson was not lost on Nick. He couldn't lose her now. It took his entire life to find her.

They stepped out into the warm sunshine. He again helped her mount the mare, her seat more comfortable than she had been this morning. They were on their way in moments, off to the orphanage to find a little lost girl.

The busy streets seemed to clear for them, giving them a path forward. He rode by her side, his outlook almost hopeful. Nick didn't allow hope to enter his life often If he didn't hope for anything, he wasn't disappointed. Yet when it pertained to Winnie, he didn't seem to be able to help himself.

Perhaps finding Grace would be simple and straightforward. Perhaps his grim predictions would not come to fruition. Perhaps they would be married before the summer was out.

Perhaps not.

They stopped at a ramshackle building with boards across its windows and a white paper nailed to the door. The words Fuller's Home for Orphans had been nearly scratched out, reading "F—ll—'s H—e f-r Or—s".

Winnie made a sound of distress. Nick's gaze snapped to her. Every drop of color had drained from her face.

"No."

"It's closed, Winnie."

"No. It can't be."

"I'm going to guess there are no children in his building. There might be rats the size of small children but no humans." He didn't know what possessed him to say such a thing. Perhaps it was the crushing weight of disappointment and the idea he had dared to hope for something. Nothing, of course, was ever going to come from hoping. He should have remembered that and not allowed his emotions to get tangled up.

"Don't be such a jackass," she snapped. "What's wrong with you?"

"A lot, if you ask my brothers."

"This isn't a time to joke, Nicholas." Her voice was tight with anger and hurt.

"I know. I don't mean to."

"It certainly sounded as though you meant it." She closed her eyes and her chin dropped to her chest.

Nick's heart twisted. He sidled close to her and dug deep for the courage he needed. No matter what, he needed to be at her side because he didn't want to not be there. Ever.

"I'm sorry, Winnie. My mouth doesn't check with my brain before it takes over."

She shook her head. "Someone must know about the orphanage. We can knock on doors and ask. This can't be the end."

"That's what we should do. People tend to live in one neighborhood. There has to be people who were here ten years ago. We'll knock until we find them." He didn't know where his optimism came from but it felt liberating to hear it out loud.

Some color had come back to her cheeks. "Thank you."

"I don't want you to give up. This whole thing ain't gonna be easy. I reckon a closed orphanage is just another bump in the road."

"Josie's illness was the first." She looked sadly at the ramshackle building. "And the worst."

He could imagine losing someone who was as close as a sister. His youngest brother, Benjy, was kidnapped when he was five. The Grahams had spent the next five years mourning their brother. Their brother Caleb had been the one to bring Benjy home. Nothing had been the same since. Nick had his own secret over Benjy's disappearance, one that festered in his gut since that fateful day.

He managed to swallow the lump in his throat that had formed. Benjy was safe now, perhaps never to be the same person he might have been, but alive. Nick couldn't allow himself to play the "what if" game when it came to his younger brother. Just couldn't.

"Where should we start?" Winnie pulled him back to here and now.

He looked around and noted a few relatively new buildings with fresh boards and signs proclaiming their retail missions. One building was two stories high but didn't have a sign. There were at least half a dozen houses on the street along with a milliner's shop and all were weathered wood structures.

"Let's go to the milliner's shop."

"A likely place to start. They may have been in that location for some time."

"That's what I thought too."

They rode over to the shop, nodding politely to those folks walking along the street who gave them curious stares. Houston was a big place but perhaps it wasn't so big. People tended to stay with who and what they knew. Strangers were just that—strangers.

Winnie, however, had such an open face and beautiful smile, she received few stares but much more welcoming gestures than Nick did. When they arrived at the milliner's shop, named "Hats Paradise", he helped her dismount. He was very conscious of being watched and did his best to keep a bland smile on his face. Winnie murmured her thanks and took his arm.

Their boots thunked against the oft-swept wooden sidewalk. He opened the door to the shop and a rush of ladies' perfume and mothballs swept across them. Nick resisted the urge to wrinkle his nose and chose to breathe through his mouth instead. Ladies' shops gave him the itches and he damn sure wouldn't be here if not for Winnie.

Someone had built shelves into the walls and they were currently full of dozens and dozens of hats. The store was full of hats of every shape, size and color. Some had features, sprigs of flowers, even some with what appeared to be fruit, which had to be fake, and miniature birds. There were straw hats, felt hats, beaver hats, lace hats and countless other types he couldn't identify. Someone really liked to make hats.

"Good afternoon?" Winnie called out when no one appeared to greet them.

"Be right out!" a muffled voice replied from behind a curtain. A sturdy sewing machine sat in one corner with an overstuffed basket of thread, buttons, ribbon and an assortment of geegaws.

A tiny woman with a dress as gray as a winter sky shuffled out from behind the curtain. She was likely no more than thirty years old but she dressed as though she were twice that. Her dishwater blonde hair was up in an excruciatingly neat bun while a pair of half-glasses perched on the end of her nose.

She looked them up and down before speaking. "Can I help you folks?"

Winnie pulled out her friendly smile. "Good afternoon, ma'am. My name is Winifred and this is my husband, Nicholas Graham."

"Graham, eh? I've heard tales of the Grahams, shot Mr. Troxler they did. Caused lots of trouble in town. That your kin?" The milliner narrowed her gaze at Nick.

"Ma'am, I surely did not shoot any Mr. Troxler. I live on a ranch two days' ride from here." He put on what he thought was his best smile, or he hoped it was. He had no idea their family had a reputation in Houston now. It was disconcerting

95

to say the least.

"Hmph. You do have the look of a rancher." She eyed his legs as if she could spot horse hairs on his trousers or something. He resisted the urge to hide behind Winnie. "I'm Harriet Gregson. I hope you're here to buy a hat."

Hell's bells.

No, they weren't, but he had a feeling the crotchety Miss Gregson was not about to give up any information if they didn't make a purchase.

"Of course. A woman I met earlier recommended your shop. Since we were nearby I thought we had to come in." Winnie sounded earnest. He was damn convinced.

Miss Gregson beamed. "I do have the highest quality hats this side of Houston."

"That is what I was told. I need a new bonnet for Sunday visiting." Winnie drifted over to the straw brimmed hats. "These would be lovely for a summer day."

Miss Gregson clapped her hands together. "You are so fair, the straw would not be the right hat for you. No, indeed, I have experience in these kinds of selections. I would recommend a green hat and I have just the thing."

The hat maker puttered around showing her wares, exclaiming every ten seconds about a hat and gushed when Winnie complimented one.

It was enough to make Nick lose the dinner he recently paid for with what little money he had.

Winnie, clever woman, had selected a hideous green hat with not only a feather, but one with two tiny birds in a nest perched on the side. The brim was wide, which it had to be to support the weight of the ridiculous concoction.

"This will be perfect, Miss Gregson." Winnie gazed at herself in the mirror on the wall. "You were right to recommend the green color."

"I told you so. With your fair hair, it's just the thing." Miss Gregson looked proud enough to pop. She went behind the small desk in the corner. "Now let me write up a receipt for you." She stopped, pencil in hand, and looked at Nick with a smattering of distrust. "You can pay for the hat, can't you?"

Nick was about to tell her she would have to pay them to take the hat when Winnie stepped in again.

"Of course we can. I am holding the funds since my husband has a hole in his trouser pocket."

Nick had no such hole and resented Winnie offering to pay again. It was bad enough she offered at dinner. He was not poor, but he did have to choose carefully how to spend what coin he had. She didn't have an entire family ranch depending on profits to survive season to season. Her money was for her alone. He had a hard time imagining that problem.

"The hat is seven American dollars. I don't take Texas redbacks. I will take gold or silver in trade, though." Miss Gregson, still poised with her pencil over the receipt book, watched Nick's face. He told himself not to react outwardly.

Inwardly he shouted at the top of his lungs.

Seven dollars? That could feed an entire family for a month!

"A reasonable price for such a fine piece of craftsmanship." Winnie handed the woman seven American dollars. He wanted to ask her how she had come by that money but it wasn't his business.

Nick wanted to tear the hat into tiny pieces, then burn it and scatter the ashes over Miss Gregson's stoop. Then he remembered why they had come into the milliner's shop.

"I wondered if you could help me with something." Winnie closed her reticule, her friendly smile still in place. "I wondered, do you remember Fuller's Home just across the street?"

"Remember it? Of course I do. There were some scoundrels who would escape from its confines and cause mischief." The milliner shook her head. "Mr. Fuller had his hands full with those young'uns."

Winnie leaned against the woman's desk and leaned down conspiratorially. "I donated money for several years. I too am a business owner here in Houston."

"Of course you are. I could tell that from the moment I saw you. She's a strong, smart lady, that one is, I told myself." Miss Gregson turned a sour look in his direction. "I don't expect your husband understands women in business."

"He is quite understanding, actually. His dinner wasn't to his liking and I'm afraid it's put him in ill humor." Winnie shook her head. "We were hoping to donate to Fuller's Home again and were disappointed to see it had closed."

Miss Gregson nodded. "Oh yes, it's been nearly two years since it shut its doors. After Mr. Wegman died, he was the housemaster, Bertha couldn't run the home alone. She was good with the young'uns but had no head for business."

"That's so sad. I remember Bertha when we toured the facility. She had a strict hand." Winnie was outright lying now and she did it without batting an eyelash. Nick, with seven siblings and had experienced prevarication of every shape and form, was impressed yet again with her.

"That she did. Luckily the rich folks up yonder needed a nurse for their own young'uns and hired her."

"That is lucky." Winnie adjusted her hat as she stood. "Which rich folks? I'd like to express my gratitude to them."

"Oh, that would be nice. They are a nice family." Miss Gregson walked to the door and stepped outside.

Nick and Winnie followed. She flashed him a triumphant grin and his lips twitched in response. Damn but that woman was beautiful.

The milliner pointed with one bony finger. "The big house on the hill with the green shutters and red door. I believe their name is Fritz."

They took their leave of the claustrophobic shop and mounted their horses once more. Winnie set off toward the Fritz house with a single-minded determination. Her green hat trembled with each clop of the horse's hooves.

He promised himself he would burn the hat after they found Grace. For now, he would endure looking at it.

"That hat makes my eyes hurt," he blurted.

She laughed, that musical sound that tugged at his gut. "I think it's unique, just like its maker."

"Unique is one word to use. I can think of a few more."

She tsked at him. "Be nice, Mr. Graham. She was a kind lady who gave us the information we needed.

"After you lied to her."

She shrugged. "Small white lies that won't cause her any harm. Besides, she sold a hat—"

"For a ridiculous sum of money."

"She sold a hat, which will help her survive another month in business. She was right about women business owners, you know. It's a man's world and difficult to survive." Winnie's expression had turned serious. "I don't have money to throw away but I thought it important, especially if her information leads me to Grace."

He couldn't argue with that, nor could he fault her logic. Nick constantly fought against what people assumed about him because of his brothers or his sisters. Not many knew who Nicholas Graham was. They called him "one of the Grahams" or "Matt's younger brother" or something similar. He had no identity outside of his family or the Circle Eight.

Until Winnie.

She made him feel like he was important, an individual in a sea of humanity. She made him feel loved.

He stared at her back as they rode up the hill. What would he do if he wasn't able to be with her any longer? A sobering thought. Ridiculous maybe considering a week earlier he did his best to avoid her.

Now he couldn't imagine not being with her.

Nick was in trouble. A lot of trouble.

Winnie's stomach quivered with apprehension as they made their way up the hill to the Fritz's large house. She had no idea if the woman, Bertha, was there or if she would be willing to speak with them about the children.

Bertha might not remember one little girl from nine years ago. She might not have even been there at that time.

There were so many things that could go wrong with this conversation. Winnie couldn't guess how many. Her dinner threatened to make a reappearance and she swallowed numerous times to keep that food where she put it. The good luck they'd found in the milliner's shop was just that—luck. She had manipulated Miss Gregson, but in the end the kind but unusual woman had a good amount of money for her trouble.

99

Winnie didn't have unlimited funds. Spending seven dollars on a hat she might not wear again may be called foolish. However, she would spend every cent she had if it meant finding Grace. Now that she was on the path to locate her, there was nothing—and no one—that would stop her.

Nicholas had been by her side the entire time. His reaction with Miss Gregson had been enough to make their farce real. Pretending to be married had its appeal. If she were honest with herself, being married had an even bigger appeal. It was too soon to allow herself to think about that.

"What are you going to tell them?" Nicholas had ridden up beside her, taking advantage of the lack of traffic on the quiet street.

"I hadn't decided yet. Perhaps the truth."

"You didn't tell Miss Gregson the truth." He eyed the hat. "About anything."

She touched the brim of the garish green hat. "She was very proud of her work. I was glad to help support her."

"Especially when it gets you the information you want."

At that, her cheeks heated. "I will do what I must to find Grace. No one was hurt by my prevarication."

"Agreed. I still hate the hat, though."

She didn't respond to his ridiculous statement. He didn't have to like the hat.

They made their way a bit further up the street, coming closer to the large house at the top. The green shutters and red door gave it a bit of whimsy in an otherwise plain edifice. No front porch, no Greek columns, no balcony. There were some rather nice bushes and trees out front, with a plethora of flowers with eye-popping colors. It was a beautiful residence and it was obvious the owner cared a great deal about their home.

When they arrived, the iron hitching post gleamed in the sunlight. Their groundskeeper or gardener kept the front of the house immaculate. She could hardly swallow the lump in her throat or quell the nervous shaking in her hands. Nicholas stood beside the mare and put his hand on her thigh. He looked up at her with sympathy in his eyes.

"I can ask questions and you can stay here if you like." He was gallant even if he hid it from the rest of the world.

"No, thank you. We need to do this together." She handed him the reins and waited while he secured the mare before returning to help her down.

The moment her feet hit the ground, her legs decided not to support her. Nicholas held her, his warm strength giving her the time she needed to recover from her momentary weakness. His heart beat beneath her hands, strong and steady. He didn't speak, but simply stood there, waiting.

"I'm recovered." She smiled at him shakily.

"Good, because I didn't fancy carrying you inside. Those rich folks might not care for it."

She laughed, grateful for his twisted sense of humor. "I suppose not." Winnie stepped back from his comforting circle and cleared her throat. "Are you ready, Mr. Graham?"

One dark brow went up. "Are you ready, ah, *Mrs. Graham?*"

A thrill zinged through her at the name. She was indeed ready and pleased to take his arm. They walked side by side up to the house, his arm an anchor in the storm of uncertainty.

The green door sported a shiny brass knocker. He glanced at her and waited. She nodded and he clanged the knocker three times.

They waited mere moments before the door opened. A woman dressed in a crisp black uniform with a blindingly white apron looked between the two of them.

"May I help you?" Her voice held a twang of Texas but she had definitely been trained to speak as a servant in a rich household would. The memory of the same type of language in her father's house rushed over her. She pushed aside the dark years and focused on tomorrow. On finding her daughter.

"Good afternoon, ma'am. We were hoping to speak with Bertha." Winnie smiled.

The woman frowned. "She is working. It's highly irregular for her to have visitors."

"If you would please allow us a few moments of her time, I assure you we will not keep her a moment longer than necessary." Winnie hated the pleading tone in her voice. "It's very important."

"Wait here." The woman closed the door, disappearing from view.

"Do you think she'll come back?" Nicholas scowled at the door. "Not the friendliest reception."

"Yes, she will come back."

"How do you know?"

"Because if she doesn't then we are at the end of this trail and that *can't happen*," she snapped. He was the unwilling victim of her tension.

"Oh." His brows eased.

She closed her eyes and pressed her fist to her forehead. "I apologize, Nicholas. I shouldn't vent my anger on you."

He made a derisive noise. "Why not? I do it all the time."

Again, she chuckled, her tension easing with his sense of humor. "Because I'm a nice person."

"I'm nice."

She laughed out loud. "You are incorrigible."

"That much I know."

The door opened suddenly and Winnie's smile faded. A woman in a blue dress stood on the threshold. She was at least fifty with silver hair in a loose bun. A smear of ink graced her cheek.

"Marta said you were here to see me. Do I know you folks?"

Winnie resisted the urge to blow out a breath of relief. "Bertha, my name is Winnie Wa—Graham and this is my husband, Nicholas. I apologize for showing up unannounced and interrupting your day."

"What do you want, Mrs. Graham?" Bertha watched them both with wariness.

"I am looking for a child that was brought to Fuller's Home. Miss Gregson told us you used to work there."

Bertha's brows went up. "Yes, ma'am, I did. No one has asked me about that place since it closed."

"Yes, well, I am looking for a child from nine years ago. I know it's been some time but I hope you can help me track her down." Winnie tried to keep the eagerness out of her voice.

This was someone who might have seen Grace. Held her, fed her, comforted her.

"Nine years ago? That was quite a while ago. I don't know how much help I will be."

"My wife is only asking you to try to remember, ma'am. That's all." Nicholas spoke softly. "Please."

"I suppose I can try." Bertha gestured to the house. "The children are napping for another half an hour. Let's walk in the gardens and we can talk."

Winnie's eyes burned. "Thank you. Thank you so very much."

Bertha patted her hands. "You aren't the first woman to come looking for a child who was left at Fuller's."

They walked around the side of the house, the perfect manicured grounds led to a stunning garden filled with all manner of amazing plant, flower and tree species. Winnie couldn't help but admire the skill of the person responsible.

"This is magnificent," she breathed.

"Oh, yes, it surely is. Mrs. Fritz does a lot of work herself. She's a fancy rose person, but she had a gardener who spends seven days a week picking, plucking and pruning." Bertha led them to a stone bench in a circle around a fountain. The water burbled merrily in the concrete basin, a soothing sound to accompany the twitter of birds and chatter of squirrels. If they lived here, Winnie would spend a good deal of time here. It was tranquil and very lovely.

They settled down on the stone bench before anyone spoke. Winnie took a deep breath. "Miss Bertha, I wanted to say thank you again for agreeing to speak with us." Her voice shook with trepidation, a bit of fear, and excitement.

The older woman flapped her hand, which was also smudged with ink. She must be doing more than nursing her charges if she was teaching them to write. "I wouldn't get my hopes up, Mrs. Graham. There were many children who came through Fuller's Home."

"I expected that was the case. Many children were orphaned during the war with Mexico and others abandoned." Her throat closed up so tight, she couldn't even take a breath.

Nicholas once again saved her. "We are looking for a girl who was brought to the home ten years ago. May of thirty-five?" He looked to her for confirmation and she managed to nod.

"Oh that was quite some time ago. We were just starting out." Bertha looked up at the clear blue sky. "Things were different."

"Yes, they were. It was before the war. Before Texas became its own." Nicholas held Winnie's gaze. "There were plenty of men doing anything they could to hurt others."

"That's the God's honest truth." Bertha appeared more relaxed and Winnie was thankful Nicholas was there to help her.

"The child was brought to Fuller's by Josie Fleming. She delivered the child." Nicholas paused and waited for Winnie to speak.

"She was half-Mexican. A little girl." Winnie was surprised by how ragged her voice was. The emotions that had run over her in the last twenty-four hours had drained her.

"Hm, we had Mexican children, of course. Many of them girls. Is there anything else that might set her apart from the others?" Bertha asked.

"The birthmark," Nicholas added. "Heart-shaped, on her thigh."

Bertha's eyes widened. "Oh my."

"You know who she is." Winnie didn't know whether to laugh or cry.

"Yes I do. Before I say anything else, can you tell me why you are looking for her?" Bertha had every right to know why Winnie and Nicholas were there.

That didn't make it any easier to tell the truth.

"She's my daughter, Grace. I-I gave her up because I was sixteen and unmarried." Winnie's voice gained strength. "I was afraid to look for her for fear when I found her, she would hate me. Nicholas helped me see what I couldn't."

He inclined his head in a small gesture of approval.

"You named her Grace? Too bad no one told us. When the babies come into the home, we gave them a name, made them a part of our big family. Or as much as we could." Bertha sighed. "There were too many children and not enough hands to help. After Mr. Wegman passed, everything fell apart. We did what we could with the ones that were left."

A few moments passed before Winnie was struck numb with a terrible, awful thought. "She was still there."

Bertha's expression turned to one of sympathy. "Yes, she was."

The world went gray around the edges of Winnie's vision. Nicholas was there, pressing her head down between her knees and rubbing her back. Misery and self-recrimination clogged her throat.

Grace had been waiting for her mother to come back for years. All her life. Then like a left over piece of meat, she was tossed out with the trash.

"What did you call her?" Nicholas asked.

"The girl? We named her Martha." At Bertha's words, Nicholas hissed out a breath. "But I called her Sunshine. She was a sweet child, always helpful and whip smart. I enjoyed having her there, that much is true." Bertha smiled with an obviously happy memory.

"Why wasn't she adopted?" Nicholas knew how to get to the heart of things. Winnie sat with her heart in shreds as they spoke over her head.

"Oh, it was her leg. It was crooked and she lagged behind the other children with crawling and walking. People didn't want a crippled baby or child. Most folks adopted for an extra pair of hands on their farm or ranch."

It was much, much worse than she had expected. Winnie sat up and took Bertha's hand into her own clammy ones. "Thank you for taking care of her. She knew love because of you."

Bertha didn't pull her hands away. "She was easy to love."

"What happened to her after Fuller's closed?" Nicholas wasn't giving up.

"I tried to place her with someone who needed help. Although she was only eight, she knew her numbers better than I did." Bertha squeezed Winnie's hands as if bracing her. "There was a feed store run by an older couple who had no children of their own. They took Martha to work for them."

Winnie's face flooded with heat. "She was given as a child worker. A young girl who couldn't walk like others was taken to work in a *feed store*?"

"There wasn't much else I could do, Mrs. Graham. No one wanted her."

Winnie leapt to her feet and walked away, the grass spongy beneath her feet. Her mind raced with thoughts of what her daughter had endured. Might still be enduring.

Crippled. Unwanted. Abandoned.

A warm hand on her shoulder stopped her wandering. "Bertha has to go back to work." Nicholas took her arm. "She gave me the name of the feed store."

Winnie could only nod, exhausted by the emotional storm of the day. She listened as he thanked the older woman again, then walked blindly beside him out of the beautiful yard. The sun still shone, the birds still sang, but everything had lost its color.

The lovely mare she had enjoyed held no promise now. She sat atop the saddle and took the reins when proffered. Nick looked up at her, his hand on her knee.

"Things we did, we can't undo. There's no soap and water to wash away mistakes. We accept them and move forward. We can't go back and we can't stand still." He was quite a philosopher for a rancher.

She smiled at him with nothing more than the muscles in her face. "I know."

"That is the first lie I've ever seen you tell." One corner of his mouth turned down. "Let's go home and you can get some sleep."

She didn't speak, but he took her silence as acquiescence. He mounted his own horse and they rode away. Winnie breathed, her heart beat and her body functioned, but she could hardly see beyond her own pain.

Her heart was in a thousand pieces.

CHAPTER SEVEN

Nicholas was worried. He wasn't one to worry about things. He complained and groused, muddled about and carried on. Damn sure didn't waste his time worrying.

Yet he worried now. About Winnie.

This whole situation with her daughter had turned her into a ghost of who she was when he'd first met her. Fierce, bossy and passionate, Winnie Watson had turned him on his ear until he didn't know which way was up.

Now because he had pushed her into finding the daughter she gave up, she had become a person he didn't recognize. Shaking, pale and lifeless. As they rode through Houston to her boardinghouse, he kept prompting her to verify they were headed in the right direction. He didn't know this complicated mass of streets. Yet she appeared to be almost slumbering on her horse.

There was a point in the yard of that big house, the largest he'd ever seen and certainly the fanciest, that he thought she would have the vapors. Hell, she did have the vapors, and nearly puked. What they heard was rough news and it hit her with a force of a mule kick.

And he worried. About Winnie.

They reached the boardinghouse in less than an hour but it seemed ten times that long. A ride pervaded by awkward silence and a nothingness that bothered him immensely.

He helped her dismount and then took the horses to the barn. They deserved some care after a long day of riding all over creation. He took his time currying them, checking their

107

hooves and providing them with feed and water. The quiet of the barn helped him think about what had happened that day.

A lot. More than he expected and it would take time to get it all straight in his mind. Winnie blamed herself for all that had happened to the girl, but it simply wasn't true. At sixteen, Winnie was still a child herself, and had a monster for a father who controlled her for another five years after her daughter's birth. Nothing was Winnie's fault. Not a damn thing.

Now the trick was going to be to make her believe it because if he wasn't mistaken, her heart was hurting and she needed kindness and love. Two things he wasn't very good at.

It seemed his relationship with Winnie was more complicated with each day that passed. He had been by her side, whether or not he helped was still an unanswered question. Damn sure she wouldn't have made it back home after speaking with Bertha if he hadn't been there. She'd been shaking and pale as milk. Finding out her child had lived in an orphanage for years because she was crippled had been difficult to hear.

Tomorrow they would go to the feed store and possibly find the child. The one piece of information that had hit Nick was the name given to Grace when she'd been left at Fuller's Home—Martha. What were the odds she would be named after his sister-in-law's grandmother, adopted by the Grahams who had passed away several months earlier. In Nick's arms, no less. He'd been the one to see the life disappear from her eyes. The experience had affected him more than he let on. Granted, she'd been quite old, in her seventies, and staying the night in the elements had been too much for her failing heart.

Now the child Grace was Martha. As if the older woman, outspoken and stubborn, had come back to show him the path he should take. If Winnie was able to find and adopt the girl, then Nick might have no reason not to marry her. An instant family and another Martha in the Graham household.

With that thought rattling around in his brain, he patted the roan mare's neck and put the curry brush up. "I guess it's time to go into the house. I think I've stayed away long enough."

The sunset painted the yard in brilliant orange and pink. He squinted and tugged his hat down farther on his forehead. He might have to go scrounge up food for supper. After their breakfast that morning, there didn't appear to be much left in the pantry.

He knocked on the backdoor before he entered the house. No one answered and the house was bathed in shadows. He turned the wick up on the lamp on the table.

"Winnie?" His voice echoed across the empty room.

With a frown, he walked through the kitchen, poking his head into the parlor and sitting rooms, also empty. The stairs loomed ahead and he took them quickly, because damn it all, he was worried. Again.

No lights burned upstairs. He turned toward Winnie's room in the corner. She'd chosen that to live in because of the two large windows. The room sat at the corner of the house. The other three rooms were meant for borders, but they lay empty now, waiting for their next resident.

Her door was closed, which was a good indicator she was in there. He rapped on the wood with his knuckle.

"Winnie?"

A muffled sound came from within.

"I'm coming in."

Another muffled sound. He opened the door, surprised it wasn't locked. If she truly desired privacy, she would have used the key. To his surprise, she wasn't in bed. She sat on the window seat, her knees drawn up toward her chest with her arms wrapped around her calves.

"Winnie?"

She sighed and turned her head toward him. Her eyes were buckets of sadness, brimming with ancient pain.

"I was never meant to be a mother."

He sat down beside her. "If that were true, you wouldn't have conceived her."

She snorted. "Any animal can breed."

"I don't like you when you do this."

Her eyes widened. "Pardon me?"

"You heard me. I reckon you're due to feel bad about what happened to the girl, but this—" he waved his hand at the empty room and her posture, "—this woebegone face and the moping needs to be over. I don't like it and it needs to stop."

Her mouth tightened. Good. It was a better reaction than the sad-faced girl.

"You have no right to judge how I behave."

"And you have no right to behave that way. The girl was well-cared for at the orphanage. Was it a perfect life? No, but she's alive." His anger for her grew. "Sitting around in self-pitying foolishness will not change anything."

"What do you know of her life?"

"I know her parents weren't murdered by a greedy bastard who wanted her family's land." He blurted. "I know her youngest brother wasn't kidnapped and held for five years by a bastard who did untold horrors."

Her arms opened and she reached for his arm. "Murdered?"

"Shot and our barn burned. I was fifteen years old. My father and brothers had survived the war, but in the end, greed and evil took my parents and brother from us. I was the one who convinced Mama to make Benjy stay home that day. He'd been driving me crazy, pestering me until I wanted to throttle him. Because of my selfishness, my brother lost five years of his life." His throat burned with fire. The Grahams had endured so much in the last eight years, more than any family should. "There are worse fates than living in an orphanage and not knowing your mother."

His anger faded as quickly as it had come. There were days he wanted to rail at the heavens for the unjustness. Then there were days his own guilt for what happened to Benjy threatened to overwhelm him. Until now, only his mother knew what he'd done and she couldn't speak the truth.

She sucked in an audible breath and blew it out again. "You're absolutely correct. I was lost in regrets and self-recrimination. There are definitely worse occurrences. I'm sorry about your parents and your brother. It was Benjy, right?"

He nodded tightly. "He was gone for five years until Caleb stumbled across him and had to steal him back from the man who had bought him."

She swung her legs around and snuggled up beside him.

"Poor child. He did appear to be very quiet and watchful."

Nick shrugged. "I try to talk to him but I don't want to ask him what happened. Sometimes it's better not knowing."

She squeezed his arm. "I can attest to that. Sometimes it is better. Now that I know her story I need to finish this. I need to find her and determine if she's happy and safe."

"And will you leave her be? Not tell her who you are if she is?" Nick didn't know if he could do such a thing.

"Yes, it will rip my heart from my chest to walk away but I can and I will." She got to her feet. "First, though, I think we need supper. Let me ask Consuela if she can come over and cook."

"Who's Conseula?" He was pleased to see the spark back in her eyes. The self-pitying, long-faced woman was not Winnie Watson. She was someone disguised as her who didn't deserve to take over such an incredible person such as Winnie.

"The cook for the boardinghouse. She lives two doors down and can make the most delicious tortilla soup in no time."

Nick stood and cupped her face in his hands. "That is more like it. I knew you were in there somewhere." He kissed her hard and stepped back.

She shook her head. "You are an insufferable ass."

"I know, but that's part of my charm."

She chuffed a laugh. "Let's eat supper and then prepare for tomorrow."

He had a better idea of what to do after they ate, but now wasn't the right time to mention it. After they had full bellies and Consuela returned to her own house, he would speak of it. His body craved her, this spunky woman with skin as soft as flower petals.

This woman who already held his heart in her tiny little hands.

Winnie closed the door behind Consuela's goodnight and leaned her forehead against the wood. The impromptu supper had been delicious, as usual, and the cook's gaze had kept straying to Nicholas. Her winks and nudges made Winnie regret asking the older woman to come over. It was embarrassing to know her desire for him was so obvious.

He sat behind her on the stairs, his elbows resting on his knees. As was his way, he'd been quiet during dinner, eating several helpings of the tortilla soup and corn bread. When the cook had brought out cinnamon sprinkled rolls for dessert, his eyes had brightened. The man obviously had a sweet tooth, given the fact he ate most of them.

Now they were alone again. The air crackled with all that was between them. What exactly that was, Winnie could not explain. She knew she loved him and at times, hated him for his abruptness and cruel words. Then she would remember it was who he was. His abrupt words weren't cruel but honest. They brought her back from the darkness that threatened her.

She turned and looked at him. He cocked his head and watched her, his face in the shadows. His hat had been abandoned for the meal, exposing his wavy brown hair. She knew first hand how soft it was and how the curls slid through her fingers.

"Feeling better?" his voice was pitched low, husky.

"Yes." She stepped toward him, her body thrumming insistently at the sight of the man she desired, despite all the odds.

Winnie put her knee on the second step and made her way to where he sat on the fifth step. He watched her, those blue-green eyes unreadable. When she reached him, he lifted his arms allowing her to slide between his knees.

The heat from his body surrounded her. She leaned forward and kissed him. His lips were warm and compliant as she nibbled her way from one side to the other. His breath gusted out as she lapped at the seam of his lips.

"You starting something?" he murmured.

"I was hoping to."

His lips twitched in what might have been a smile. "On the stairs? What if someone comes by?"

"The door is locked and I have no guests." She kissed her way across his jaw, the scrape of whiskers on his jaw rough against her lips.

"You run a boardinghouse. Anyone could come by." He

groaned when she reached his ear and nibbled on the lobe.

"Do you want me to stop?" She hovered half an inch from his neck, waiting for him, aching for him.

"Hell no."

Winnie laughed against his skin and resumed her explorations. His skin was warm and salty, his scent uniquely Nicholas. She reached for the buttons on his shirt, kissing the exposed skin. Down, down, down, she went.

When she reached his belly, his muscles were rock hard. When she touched his trousers, he jerked. His cock was already hard, straining against the flap of the material. She had never enjoyed seducing a man, but with Nicholas, she not only enjoyed it, she was excited by it. Her pussy throbbed with each touch of her lips on his skin.

She cupped him and he groaned. "You don't have to."

"Oh but I want to."

"I've never...that is...I haven't...oh hell." He was flustered and inexperienced in ways she hadn't been for a very long time.

"Then let me show you." She waited until he exhaled the breath he'd been holding.

"Yes."

A thrill raced through her as she released his staff. It sprang into her hands, hot and hard, velvet steel. She ran her hands down its length, reveling in the shudders that passed through him. He pulsed within her grasp. She lowered her head and took him into her mouth.

He moaned and grasped the banisters in both hands. "Holy fuck."

She sucked at the head of his cock, paying special attention to the underside. When she took his length into her mouth, he almost cracked the wood he hung onto. She laved him, suckling the tip before pulling him deep into recesses of her throat.

Winnie found a rhythm and he matched it, pushing up as she pushed down. She cupped his balls, fondling the already tight sacs. He cursed again and his thighs closed in around her ears. She nipped at him until he relaxed his legs.

"Jesus, Winnie, I can't...hell, you need to stop or I'm done for."

She licked her way up his length until she let him loose with a pop. He looked down at her, his eyes almost black from widened pupils.

As he watched her, she lifted her dress, her pussy wet with need. Thank goodness her undergarments allowed her to simply spread her legs and impale herself on his cock. She stopped and simply held him deep inside. Winnie had never understood what complete meant until now.

Joined with him in the most intimate way, she *was* complete. It was as perfect a moment as it could be.

Now it was her turn to grasp the banisters while he took hold of her hips, guiding her as she rode him. The sound of a ticking clock downstairs was the only other noise beside their harsh breathing and the slick slide between their bodies.

He pressed his face against her breasts, nibbling at her through the cotton of her dress. She clenched at the moment he bit her taut nipple.

"Jesus, do that again." He attacked the other nipple and her muscles contracted harder.

She fumbled for the buttons and released the front of her dress. The next thing she heard was the rending of her chemise, now lying in tatters. Her exposed breasts pouted with eagerness. He growled in triumph and sucked one deep into his mouth.

Her pleasure skyrocketed with his tongue and teeth performing their magic. Her speed decreased, selfishness over his attention to her breasts making her forget she was in charge of their joining. Instead she used her interior muscles to bring them both forward.

He groaned and switched breasts. The night air hit her wet, turgid nipple and she cried out when his mouth closed in on the other.

"I'm close, Nicky. So close." Her small movements were harder, faster until a wave of pure ecstasy washed over her, pulling her this way and that until she neglected to breathe for the intensity of it all.

He let her nipple loose and pushed her hips up and down. Ripples moved through her and she picked up the speed at which he slid into her pussy. He pulled her down hard until her thighs smacked into his. Her own orgasm prolonged with each pass.

His fingers dug into her hips and he uttered her name on a harsh whisper. She tightened to the point of near pain as he spent himself deep inside her. Stars danced behind her eyes and all coherent thought fled.

She laid her head on his shoulder and tried to catch her breath. Her entire body shook with the power of what they had just experienced. Was love the reason the pleasure had been so great? She could only hope her feelings were returned. Now was an ideal time to confess her deepest secret regarding Nicholas, but her mouth refused to form the words.

"Holy shit."

She smiled and her head lolled to the right. "Yes."

"Nicky? Did you really call me Nicky?" He sounded amused, a different emotion for the usually grumpy man.

"Did I?" She knew very well what she'd said. "Does it bother you?"

He was quiet for a few moments. "No. I haven't heard anyone call me that in years."

What remained unspoken was who had called him that.

"She sounds as though she was a wonderful mother."

"She was. The very best. She knew I was the middle child and she always made sure I had things the others didn't." His hands kneaded her back and she purred.

"Mmm, that feels good." She played with the buttons on his open shirt. "What did you have the others didn't?"

"She was fair to all of us. Everyone took turns doing chores, getting served first, and picking what book she read to us first." His kneading slowed. "But she made sure that I got a bit more dessert, or read a new book first. Sometimes she would take me alone to town and everyone else stayed home."

Winnie pictured the wonderful life he'd had with his parents. "I wish I had known her."

"Me too." His voice had dropped to a whisper.

She hugged him before she sat up and met his gaze. "Would you care to find out how comfortable my feather mattress is, Nicky?"

His smile, when it came, took her breath away. If only he did that more often than frowning. Nicholas Graham was devastatingly handsome.

"I can't think of a single thing I want more."

Winnie could, but for now, this was enough. Perhaps one day he would want to be in her bed permanently. Their bed. Together.

The sun rose early the next day, its rays pricking at Nick's eyes until he opened them. For a moment, he forgot where he was, only that he was warm, comfortable and a deliciously feminine form had snuggled up beside him.

Winnie.

She had been magnificent last night, showing him things he hadn't known women and men could do in a bed, much less on the stairs. He was spent in more ways than one. It was just past dawn, and normally he would be up and doing chores. Today he didn't want to move. Lying with her was the closest he'd come to peace in a very long time.

He'd spoken of his mother to her. It had been years since he'd allowed himself to even think about his mother, Meredith. Her brutal death and the sight of her lifeless body had haunted his dreams, awake or asleep. Last night he'd remembered her as she'd been all his life, not at the end of hers.

Although he'd been fourteen when she died, he hadn't been ready to lose her. It had been too abrupt, too shocking, too devastating. It had changed him from a happy teenager to a bitter old man in moments. Now he was older, more bitter and more unhappy. Only Winnie had pulled him from his morose existence to find a smidge of light.

If he lost her now, there would be no hope for Nick at all. He would not recover from it. His heart was truly tangled up with hers and there was no way to change it, not that he wanted to. Waking up beside her gave him a feeling he had forgotten— contentment. He wanted to hang onto that feeling for as long as he could.

She shifted and made a sleepy sound. He turned so he could pull her closer and she responded by tucking her head beneath his chin. The steady thump of her heart against his side was comforting.

"You're awake." Her voice was tinged with sleep.

"Not on purpose."

She chuckled, her breath warm against his skin. "I suppose we should get up."

"Or we could stay here a bit longer." He was never one to lie in bed. Ever. She had changed him in more ways than one.

His stomach yowled as if on cue.

"There's no food."

"Damn." He could survive a bit longer before he had to eat.

"And I need to bathe before we leave. I'm a bit sore."

Guilt gnawed at him. "I'm sorry, honey. I didn't mean to hurt you."

She sat up as though he had pinched her. Her glorious blonde hair had puffed out into a halo around her head and she sported a few sleep wrinkles on her cheek. She was also gloriously naked, her pink nipples staring him, quite literally, in the face.

"Hurt me? That was as far from hurting as you can possibly be. It was wonderful, amazing, the most pleasurable experience of my life." Annoyance had made her face flush a becoming pink color. She was magnificent when aroused no matter how it occurred.

"Then I apologize for saying hurt. I expect what we did made you sore."

"It did but I wouldn't trade it for all the money in the world." She huffed and got out of bed, allowing him to watch her magnificent, curvy body shrug into a wrapper. She flipped her hair and then leveled another glare at him. "Did you call me honey?"

Nick stared at her, helpless to answer. He had called her honey but he didn't plan it. The word had popped out of his mouth without a thought.

She came around the side of the bed, her hands on her hips,

her frown a miniature of his own. "Did you?"

"I, uh, I reckon I did."

He waited for the second storm to hit but instead her expression softened. To his surprise, she reached down and kissed him hard. Her scent, of woman, of beauty, washed over him.

"Do it again, Nicky."

"Honey." His voice had dropped to a whisper. She kissed him again, this time as softly as a butterfly wing.

He wanted to yank her on the bed and fuck her until neither one of them could move. He wanted to disappear inside the heat of her body. He wanted to marry her.

Holy shit indeed.

Winnie hurried to heat the water and took a standing bath in the hip tub rather than fill the big one. She wanted to get to the feed store that morning. There wasn't a second to waste. She had to see Grace. Or rather, Martha. The name Grace was one she had given the little girl because Winnie had given her away and with it, God's grace. Twisted but true.

Nick had gone to saddle the horses. He'd been so sweet in her bed this morning and she loved him all the more for it. And he'd called her honey. Twice.

She hugged that knowledge to her chest, an unexpected gift. Nicholas appeared to have softened in the time she knew him. She considered that he probably hadn't felt softness since he'd lost his mother. There was more to his story there, but she hadn't wanted to push. He'd shared something with her she recognized he didn't tell anyone else.

Another unexpected gift.

Perhaps his feelings for her were a mirror of what she felt for him. Hope warred with uncertainty and the need to protect herself. Winnie was tough because she'd had to be. The last few days were an aberration in her behavior and attitude. Nicholas's harsh words had been the mental slap she'd needed to snap out of the ridiculous pit of despair she'd been mired in.

She donned one of her best, a blue satin dress that had cost her a good deal, but she'd been told it matched her eyes. With a mind for where she would be going, Winnie pinned her hair up and added a matching blue hat. She pinched her cheeks for color and pronounced herself ready to go.

As she made her way downstairs, her stomach started fluttering. Today she would meet her daughter. Today the rest of her life would be decided.

It was a daunting thought.

She was determined to be strong. No more weeping foolishness. She'd been through so much in her life and survived. Now was the time to draw on that strength and do everything she could to make a place for herself in Martha's life.

Taking a deep breath, she went out the back door. Nicholas had the horses saddled and ready. He stood in the sunshine, as bright and appealing as any sight. Her heart thumped and her confidence jumped. She could, she *would*, do this.

He turned to look at her and the appreciation in his gaze warmed her. "You look pretty as a picture."

It was the first compliment he'd paid to her and she knew it was genuine. Many men would wax poetic about her hair or her eyes or her skin, but most were empty words. This man's words were worth more fortune than she could ever hope for.

She sketched a rather impressive curtsey, or something that resembled one. "Thank you, kind sir."

He shook his head and walked the mare over to her. "Let's get going so we can eat. My gut is rubbing against my backbone.

Winnie hid her grin. He picked her up and set her on the horse, an impossible feat for anyone but the strongest of men. Ranching was hard work and it showed in his physically perfect form, the sinewy muscles that rippled beneath his shirt. She had tasted them and ran her fingers along their lines. His hands lingered on her waist a few moments too long and she had to resist the urge to lean down and kiss him.

After the tasks of the day were done, they could find pleasure in each other's arms again. For now she had to force herself to forget how enamored she was of him.

"Are we married today?" His question momentarily stunned

119

her.

"Pardon?" Had he just asked her to marry him?

"Are we Mr. and Mrs. Graham today when we get to the feed store? I figured we might as well finish out this farce how we started it." He swung up in the saddle with his usual grace, not recognizing his words had sliced through Winnie's heart.

Farce?

"I suppose we should." Her smile was brittle and if she made it any wider, she might have shattered her face.

"Then let's get to eating so we can make it to the feed store before dinner. I expect it's busiest early in the day." He glanced at her and pursed his mouth. "Breakfast?"

"Of course. We must fill your belly before we act out our farce." She nudged the mare into motion, her previous elation wiped out by his callous disregard for her feelings. What was she to expect? He told her about his nature, his callous disregard for the softer things in life, but last night, he'd called her honey. She was confused and angry, two things she didn't need to work through today.

"Are you mad at me?" He spoke from behind her as they rode down the street toward her favorite breakfast restaurant.

"No, why would I be mad?" She bit her tongue to keep from lashing out at him. "I am simply nervous about meeting my daughter."

He made a noise in his throat but didn't speak again. It was for the best because if he had uttered another word, she might have had to shoot him. That would be a bad start to the day.

Nick knew something wasn't right but he didn't know what. The night before had been the most amazing experience of his life. Hell, his knees were still wobbly from all they'd done to and with each other. She had come out of the house and his foolish heart had almost taken over.

He'd nearly told her he loved her.

In the end, he hid behind his contentious self and hurried her along. Maybe she was anxious about meeting her daughter but he suspected it was something else. Something he had done and he had no idea what it was. He doubted she would tell him either. Women were perverse like that.

They ate breakfast in silence. Well, he ate and she picked at her food. He decided against asking if she was going to eat her biscuit and finished his own food. They left the restaurant in the awkward silence they'd arrived in.

She didn't speak until they were both mounted. "Tell me the name of the feed store."

Gone was the sweet, beautiful woman who had knelt between his knees twelve hours earlier. He wanted her to return because this Winnie was the businesslike harridan he'd met so many months ago when searching for his sister Elizabeth. The sweet, soft woman he'd woken up next to had vanished.

"Conklin's. I know right where it is. It's on the way out of town heading toward the Circle Eight. Near that Devereaux's furniture place." He had been surprised when Bertha had told him the name. He'd passed by it three times already coming and going from the city. Then again, nothing in his life had made sense since he'd fallen in love with Winnie. Why would this be any different?

They headed north toward the feed store, her back straight as a poker. Her beautiful blue dress had made her eyes glow in the same shade. Her hair about sparkled in the bright sunlight. He'd been honest when he told her she was pretty as a picture. Now she was cold as though she really was a fancy painting and not the hot, sensual woman he loved.

The idea she might not want to be with him for good was incomprehensible. He refused to contemplate it or it might damn well happen. On the other hand, he couldn't pine over her like a lovesick fool either. He shoved it all to the back of his mind. There was no use dwelling on something he couldn't control. Her daughter was the important mission now and that was what he kept returning to.

Martha. Little Martha, the lost daughter. Nick promised her he would help her get her daughter back and there was no way he would fail her. He'd sooner cut his own heart out.

No, they could not fail.

The ride to Conklin's took less than an hour but it might as well have been a week. The silence was crushing in its awkwardness. If they convinced the storeowners they were a happily married couple, he'd eat his hat.

"I reckon we should actually talk to each other if we're supposed to be married."

She snorted. "Most married couples don't spend the time to speak to each other."

At this, his ire rose. "Yes they do."

She didn't turn around. "Not in my experience."

"Then you don't know my family," he nearly growled. "My brothers are happily married, as are two of my sisters. Happy people who not only talk to each other but laugh too." She was silent and they were steps away from Conklin's. "Winnie." He pulled his horse to a stop. "Please."

"Please what?" She finally turned to look at him, her blue gaze sharp enough to cut him. "I can be a loving wife in our farce. How about you?"

Farce.

He'd used that word earlier. Now he saw what he'd neglected to. His choice of words had hurt her. Nick had no control when it came to his mouth. No doubt it wouldn't be the last time he unintentionally caused her harm.

Nick rode up beside her and tried to take her hand. She held fast to the reins, refusing to release. He simply put his hand on top of her gloved ones.

"I ain't good with words and sometimes stupid shit comes out of my mouth but I damn sure didn't mean to hurt you." He swallowed the lump in his throat. "I'm sorry."

"It doesn't matter if you meant to say certain things, you obviously felt them or you wouldn't have said them." Her logic baffled him.

"We won't convince these folks of anything if you can't look at me without growling." He had to make her see what would happen if she didn't snap out of her haze of anger.

Realization crept over her face along with a lovely shade of pink on her cheekbones. "I don't want to miss my opportunity with her."

"I know you don't." He sighed. "I'm sorry, Winnie."

She glanced at the storefront and then back at him. "When

this is over, we need to speak of what we have. I don't like this unspoken something between us. It's too hard on my heart."

Nick knew what she meant although he couldn't put it into words. They had something but it wasn't defined, which made it prickly and hard to hang onto. It damn sure made her prickly too.

"Fine with me. Let's go and get your daughter."

Her face softened a bit. "Thank you for everything."

He shrugged. "I would do anything for you."

She opened her mouth as if to respond but then nodded instead. After taking a deep breath and exhaling, she kneed the mare into motion. They were at the front of the store in minutes.

The front of Conklin's Feed Store was a gray color with two windows on either side of the door. The building itself was only two steps from the ground. A sturdy hitching post, oft used by the look of it, waited outside.

Nick dismounted quickly, peeking through the windows as though he would be able to see the girl. He secured both horses before reaching up to assist her down. She was also looking through the window, her face taut with tension.

"Winnie, c'mon down." He had to call her twice before she reacted.

She offered him a shaky smile before she leaned down. He grasped her waist and pulled her to the ground gently. He waited until she raised her face to look at him.

"I'm frightened."

He chucked her under the chin. "You? Fearless warrior? I reckon that's not true."

"I am far from fearless." She pulled a handkerchief from her sleeve and dabbed at her cheeks. "Right now I fear I may turn into a puddle of pitiful from this heat and my own cowardice."

"Then we'd best get inside before you do." He took her arm and marched up into the store before she could protest.

The inside of the store had an earthy smell with stacks of buckets, shovels, bags of all types of feed from chickens to horses. There were tins of horse liniment, curry brushes and hoof picks all stacked together on barrels. The light was muted

123

in the store. There was only one lantern list toward the back on a long wooden counter.

Winnie looked around as though someone was jerking her head from left to right, behind her and then forward. There was no one to see. The store appeared to be deserted.

"Is anyone here?" Nick called out.

A man popped up from behind the counter, startling Winnie. She jerked and stumbled against him.

"Easy," Nick whispered to her. "Nothing to be afraid of."

If he were honest with himself, there might be something to fear, but it wasn't danger. No, it was not finding Martha or worse yet, finding she had passed. There were bad things in the world and both of them knew that firsthand.

The man was in his forties, possibly fifties. His hair had receded to the point there was none left on the top of his head. Unfortunately he decided to grease up what hair he had left and comb it over the balding pate. His eyes were narrow, flanking a hawk-like nose and small lips that were currently pursed as he surveyed them. He had a medium build with muscled arms as though he did a great deal of work with them, but his chest and shoulders were not oversized. He was an odd looking man.

"You folks lost?"

Nick didn't like the man already. They were well-dressed customers in his store and he treated them as though he didn't want them there. What kind of foolish storeowner would behave like that? A rotten one.

"No, we ain't lost. We're here—"

She cut him off. "Good morning, sir. Are you Mr. Conklin?" Winnie had recovered her normal aplomb.

"Who's asking?" The man's impossibly narrow gaze narrowed even more.

"My name is Winifred Graham and this is my husband, Nicholas Graham." She smiled, her smile shining in the dim light.

Her pulse thrummed against his hand, fast and erratic. While she appeared the calm, cool proper lady, she was anything but on the inside. She was amazing.

"You looking for feed?" Conklin's gaze slide up and down

her body, pausing on her breasts before doing it again.

Nick heard a growling noise and realized it emanated from his own throat. Winnie squeezed his arm in warning.

"Not today but I will send my groom, Mr. Bartholomew, by when he returns from his trip." She stepped toward the counter.

Mr. Conklin hadn't relaxed his stance. If anything he watched her as a snake might watch a mouse meandering too close to its lair.

"You here to order then?"

"We would like to speak to you about something." Winnie put on a bright smile.

Conklin glanced at Nick and his mouth twisted. "If you ain't buying or ordering, then you need to get on your way."

"Mr. Conklin, we only need a few minutes of your—"

"No, I'm a businessman, not a fella to stand around chatting like a woman all day."

"Horse liniment." Nick snatched up a can and held it up. "I'll take one."

"That'll buy you a minute of my time. Then you get gone." Conklin waited while Nick paid for the tin, an inflated sum, which he tossed on the counter.

"We are looking for a little girl named Martha who used to live at Fuller's Home."

Conklin's expression tightened. "I don't know no girl."

"We know she was adopted by you and your wife when the home closed. We have a witness who confirmed the information." Winnie's voice remained steady and strong. To think she had no confidence in her strength. She was stronger than any person he'd ever met and that said a lot.

"That so? I don't know a girl or no witness." The man's hand fisted on the counter and Nick knew he was lying.

"Martha's parents have returned to claim her. There was a mistake and she shouldn't have been given to a new family." Winnie told the truth, if only a slightly tilted version of it.

"Fuller's Home closed two years ago. They took their time in claiming a crippled girl."

Triumph zinged through Nick. "We didn't say she was crippled."

125

Conklin's eyes widened. "Sure you did."

"No, we didn't." Winnie set her reticule on the counter. "We want to return Martha to her family. I realize this might be difficult to contemplate letting her leave, but I'm afraid we must insist."

"Insist, eh?" Conklin looked at Nick. "What are you gonna do if I kick you out and call the sheriff?"

"Send a message to my brother and brother-in-law, both Texas Rangers." Nick had never been so glad he had Texas Rangers in his family. Even if they weren't actively working, a Ranger was one until he died.

Conklin swallowed audibly. "You can't come in here and threaten me, talking crazy about a girl. I can shoot you where you stand and claim self-defense."

Winnie's smile had turned brittle. "I sincerely doubt you can reach your gun before I shoot you with the pistol in my reticule." Sure enough her hand gripped the hard object beneath the blue material. Well, hell, she was more than amazing.

"You wouldn't dare."

"Oh yes, I would. You will bring Martha out here and let us speak with her."

Conklin stuck his chin in the air. "I told you I don't know no g—"

As if he conjured her, the girl came through the front door, skidding in as children were wont to do. Her dark hair was in haphazard braids, flying behind her as she moved. She wore a plain gray dress and a tattered apron. Her right leg was indeed cocked inward as though her hip was misshapen. It didn't stop her from moving at a brisk pace, though. She barely spared a glance at Winnie and Nick as she made her way to the counter, a burlap sack clutched in her hand.

Winnie, however, sucked in a breath and trembled against him. He held her upright, noting the tears that sprang to her eyes.

"Be strong, honey," he spoke for her ears alone.

"Girl, what the hell are you doing? Get back to the house." Conklin's face had flushed a ruddy shade.

"Mrs. Conklin said to get this to you right away." The girl sucked in a great gulp of air after every two words as though she had run to the store.

"I don't care what the hell she said. Get out!" The girl jumped at his words and dropped the bag on the counter. Her shoulders remained back and straight as she made her way back out. This time she did look at Winnie and Nick, but simple curiosity was in her gaze.

She slipped through the door, leaving the store quiet as a cat. Winnie's mouth tightened as she looked at the store owner.

"Perhaps you can tell me again how you don't know Martha and there is no girl here?" She glanced at the sack now lying on the counter.

"I ain't gotta tell you nothing. You get out of here now." He reached for the sack but Nick snatched it instead. "Give that back."

"Not until you tell us about the girl." Nick held his anger back with more strength than he thought possible. He did it for Winnie.

The other man bared his teeth. "I don't have to tell you nothing. Her parents threw her away. I bought her. Fair and square."

Winnie gasped at the same moment Conklin's words sank into Nick's brain.

"Did you just say you *bought* her?" Nick's voice had dropped to a snarl. He and his family never believed in slavery and didn't hold with the practice of it. Child slavers were the worst and, considering what Benjy had endured, it was a surefire way to induce violence.

"You don't like it, that's too damn bad. I got a bill of sale." Conklin yanked the sack from Nick's hand. "Now get the hell out of here before I call the sheriff."

One thing Nick learned being in a family of eight siblings, he knew when to retreat and when to stand his ground. This was a time to retreat.

He tried to turn Winnie but she resisted. "It's time to go," he spoke quietly

"I'm not leaving her here." Winnie hissed, her color high

and her eyes suspiciously shiny.

"We have to. For now. We aren't giving up." He was able to move her toward the door.

"Don't make me do this." She started to pull back.

"For now, trust me." He opened the door. "Please, honey."

She closed her eyes and a single tear rolled down her cheek. "I want to shoot him."

"Me too." He managed to get her outside before she spoke again.

"I hope you have a plan for what we do now." Her fingers dug into his arm.

"We start by talking with Bertha again and finding out what son of a bitch was selling orphans." His jaw hurt from gritting his teeth and his fists hurt from clenching them. Keeping his anger inside was like swallowing a bullet.

"Do you think she lied to us?" Winnie's gaze searched the street for the girl, but the small figure was nowhere in sight.

"Maybe. Or someone else decided to make some money on the misfortune of children." He would find out who and make sure they ended up in jail. Caleb and Brody would help him. As soon as he could, he would get word to them and get them on the trail of the bastard.

When they stood by the horses, she gripped his shirt with sharp fists. "She was sold, Nick. Sold!"

"I heard, but we will make it right."

"I told myself if she was happy I would leave her be and let her live her life. She's not happy." Fury flirted at the corners of her words, along with pain.

"No, I don't think anyone who gets bought is happy." Nick put her up on the horse before she could break free and go shoot the son of a bitch Conklin.

"Leaving here now is tearing me up." She placed her hand on her stomach. "I might be sick."

"You can do it, Winnie." He took the reins of both horses and led them away. Nick felt the man's gaze following them. If they were lucky, Conklin would not punish the child for their visit. Their initial visit did not go well and their opportunity to meet the girl had passed.

Someone had sold the girl, which meant there was likely more than just one child involved. Maybe Fuller's Home closed because they ran out of merchandise.

"We should also find out if Josie knew who owned Fuller's." Winnie had started to be herself again.

Nick hadn't considered that but it was a good idea. They had to backtrack and find out what wasn't said. Perhaps they hadn't asked the right questions when they'd talked to Josie or Bertha.

"Do you have someone you can trust to send word to my family and Josie? The post is going to take too long."

She nodded tightly. "Write what you need to and I'll get someone."

Nick puzzled through everything they'd been told about Fuller's Home and Grace, who was now called Martha. There were some holes in what they knew. Finding information had been too easy. At the time, it hadn't occurred to him but now he recognized it had been obvious. Winnie had been eager to find her daughter after Nick suggested it.

No one could have possibly known of their plans until they spoke to Josie. From then on their journey had been too easy. It started with the woman who made the hats.

"Not that I want to go back there but we need to go back to the crazy hat lady."

Winnie's grows went up. "Do you think she's part of this?"

"Maybe. She talked to you about Fuller's pretty easy-like. I thought it was because she was cracked in the head, but maybe it was more." Nick didn't want to believe the strange woman was smart enough to outsmart them, but it wasn't impossible.

"She was nice."

"She was crazy."

Winnie frowned. "I would hate to think she was untruthful."

"I think everyone we talked to was untruthful. Bunch of liars."

She turned to look at him. "Not Josie."

"I don't know her but if you say she don't lie, then I believe you." He didn't think a dying woman would spread lies regardless. If Winnie trusted her, then Nick would.

"Thank you." She blew out a breath, rustling the stray hairs that had escaped her coiffure. "I still might be sick."

"Don't do it on this side. I only got but one pair of trousers with me."

It took a moment but she barked a laugh. "Sometimes I don't like you, Nicholas."

"We need to focus on finding the truth and being sick and womanly ain't the way. Being smart is. Brody and Caleb taught me that."

She inclined her head at him. "I bow to your experience here. I don't have two Texas Rangers in my family to call on. I, um, don't actually have a family. Not even Grace."

"You've got me." The words tumbled out of his mouth. He wanted to grab them out of the air and stuff them back in his mouth.

"I do?" Her mouth formed that perfect O again.

"Yeah, you do. I don't know if it's enough but you've got me."

She smiled, a genuine, heartfelt smile. "Thank you, Nicky."

He didn't want to complain about the nickname. It was his mother's pet name for him and it had been a very long time since anyone had used it. Somehow it fit when he said it. God forbid his brothers hear her use it though. He'd never hear the end of it.

"Now let's go see the crazy hat lady. This time I get to talk to her until she tells us the truth this time."

"Don't hurt her. We don't want to be as bad as the bastards who owned Fuller's."

"I don't plan on hurting her but I damn sure plan on scaring her." He couldn't wait to get back there, which was ironic, so he could make her tell the truth. Sometimes his size was an advantage he used wisely. There was nothing he wouldn't do for Winnie.

That was the truth.

Rebecca could hardly sit in the saddle. Weariness dragged at her from the top of her head to her feet, including her heart. After sitting for three full days with Pops, he had passed on.

She comforted the smallest Gibsons as best she could. They were all devastated by his loss, of course. He was old and sick, and his time had come.

Nothing she did had cured him of his disease, but she had made him comfortable. Tobias had growled and snapped at her no matter what she did. She decided to ignore him after the first two days. After the kiss.

He hadn't spoken to her since Pops died. They had buried him quickly and with little ceremony. Rebecca packed her things and prepared to leave. He saddled the horses and held the door for her, as if silently telling her, "Get out. You're no longer welcome."

They had ridden relentlessly forward, toward home. Toward the Circle Eight. She'd never felt so weary in her life. Even her hair seemed to be heavy on her head. Tobias ignored her, although he was escorting her, albeit with obvious reluctance.

The sun had set at least two hours ago. They were riding in near pitch darkness, which was dangerous. She didn't care. All she could think about was her bed and her pillow. Her behind was numb along with her thighs. She had ceased to feel pain, only a bone deep weariness.

She didn't remember falling asleep but the sensation of sliding off the horse woke her up with a jolt. A strong arm grabbed her and stopped her descent.

"Jesus, girl, can't you stay on the damn saddle?" He pushed her back up into a sitting position. She blinked and tried to get her bearings. "Do I need to tie you to it?"

Rebecca felt the unfortunate sting of tears. She refused to cry in front of Tobias. If he was going to be her husband one day, she had to show him how strong she was. This trip did not prove her theory about him being a hero, but to his credit, his grandfather had just died. She knew his pain well and it wasn't to be taken lightly.

"No, I'm tired is all." She yawned. "Thank you for escorting me home." She would use her manners. Even if her mother or Eva weren't there, she would do them proud.

His response was a grunt. They plodded onward and she kept pinching herself to keep alert. A short while later, a few pinpricks of light shone in the distance. Her excitement grew when she recognized the shape of the land. They were on the Circle Eight.

"You're welcome to spend the night at the ranch rather than ride back in the dark." Her brother Matt might not like it, but Rebecca could make him see reason. Maybe.

"No."

The man was impossible to talk to. Rebecca was going to have a lot of work if she was going to turn this man into a hero and a husband. For now she would focus on getting home, surviving her brother Matt's anger, and saying goodbye to the taciturn Tobias.

Nicholas and Winnie stood outside the hat shop for ten minutes banging on the door. It was no use. The building was deserted. Perhaps from the moment they'd left. Harriett Gregson had fled.

Winnie told herself not to jump to conclusions, but it was so very hard. This woman knew the owners of Fuller's Home, and someone there had sold at least one child, if not more. Innocents who were caught in adults' greed.

It had taken every ounce of strength she possessed not to snatch her daughter from Conklin's store with force. Nicholas had been right, of course. She had to be smart. Now they just had to make sure he didn't sell the girl before Winnie could get her daughter back. She would ask one of the boys she knew in the neighborhood to watch the store. Winnie was prepared to spend every cent she had.

For now they had to speak to Miss Gregson or Bertha. Obviously the milliner was gone so they would go back to the big house to speak to the former employee of the home. However, everything the nice older woman had told her was suspect. Bertha had worked there. She had to know what happened to some of the children.

They made their way back to the palatial house on the hill, Winnie kept herself moving through sheer force of will. She really wanted to gallop back to Conklin's store and take her daughter back through force. Her blood pulsed with the need to seek vengeance. Killing her father had been a side effect of her rage. Getting Martha in her arms, her real family, was an elemental imperative.

This time when they knocked on the fancy door, it took more than a few minutes for someone to answer. The maid they had seen earlier looked at them as if she'd never seen them.

"Can I help you?"

Winnie forced a smile to her lips. "I apologize for bothering you again today, ma'am. We need a few more minutes of Miss Bertha's time."

The maid's mouth tightened. "Miss Bertha is no longer employed here."

With that, she tried to close the door but Nicholas's foot shot out to stop its progress. "Could you tell us where she went? Please." His smile was more of a teeth-baring.

"I am sure I don't know." The maid looked at Nicholas's foot. "I can call the master or the sheriff if you don't remove yourself."

"I can call the Texas Rangers if you don't tell us where she went." Nicholas's words hit their mark.

The officious maid paled. "She was dismissed for not minding the children. I think she went to see a man she knows. A Mr. Fuller. That's all I know." She pushed at the door again. "If you don't leave, I'm gonna get fired too." Her gaze pleaded with them to understand.

"Thank you." Winnie took his arm and led him away from the door. They had to find Mr. Fuller and Bertha, and send word to the Grahams. There was much to do.

"Do you know who Fuller is?" Nicholas's arm was stiff as an oak tree beneath her hand.

"As it happens, I do. Mr. Troxler was active in society circles in Houston. I think I might have met Mr. Fuller when I was a child." Memories of the man flirted at the edge of her mind. Fortunately Mr. Fuller hadn't been one of the men her father had offered her to. If she remembered him correctly, he'd been a widower who had lost his wife and never had children of his own. He'd taken it upon himself to help the orphans, which had only intensified during the war with Mexico.

"Do you know where he lives?"

"No, but that will be easy to discover." She had to focus on what she could do and not what she couldn't. If she started to think too hard, she might do something stupid. Like snatch her daughter and run like hell.

"Good, then let's start with him. Maybe Fuller was in it to make money after all."

Winnie frowned at his suggestion. The man she remembered was kind and grandfatherly, not at all an evildoer like the feed storeowner.

"Or he is a kind man who Bertha feels she can go to for help." Winnie didn't want to believe everyone involved with the orphanage was a bad person.

"I ain't believing a thing anyone says anymore. Let's go to your home and get our messages out." He helped her onto the horse. "We need help to sort this out Winnie. This is bigger than we thought."

She could tell by the set of his jaw that asking for help was not something he looked forward to. She didn't blame him. She had a lot of pride herself and knew the pinch of admitting she needed assistance.

"Then we will send out the battle cry and get help." She was not without resources. There weren't many she counted as friends, but she had many acquaintances, some from the lower end of the social scale.

The trip back to the boardinghouse was significantly different than their trip out that morning. Both of them were lost in their thoughts; the somberness of their predicament weighed heavily.

As soon as they reached home, Winnie set out pen and paper and the two of them wrote missives. Winnie went to Consuela's house and paid her sons to deliver the notes. The trip to the Circle Eight was the longest and she happily paid more for that mission.

It was nearing suppertime again. Winnie turned down the offer of food from her cook and instead went home, weary of heart and mind. When she opened the door, she was surprised to see Nicholas sitting on the stairs again. Memory of their sensual encounter on the very spot the night before.

Tonight, however, he looked at her with a mixture of sadness and sympathy. She was so very weary. He stepped down and picked her up. Being held by Nicholas Graham was an experience she cherished. The very first time she'd found herself falling in love with him was in that very same position.

He started up the stairs and she thought to protest, but instead, she laid her head on his shoulder and closed her eyes. Tomorrow she would think about all she had experience that day. For now, she had to rest her body and mind.

Their battle had just begun.

CHAPTER EIGHT

Nicholas had taken care of his younger siblings as they grew up. He was no stranger to undressing a woman either. However, what Winnie needed was comfort. The shock of what they'd discovered, combined with her guilt, had devastated her. Her eyes held a haunted look, one he knew well.

He undressed her as he would have a child, with care and efficiency. Now was not the time to be aroused by her incredible, lush figure. Her blue eyes followed his every move until he had her safely in a lacy nightdress and tucked into bed.

She looked up at him. "Join me."

"I don't think that's a good idea."

"Please, Nicky. I need you to hold me. That's all." She lifted the corner of the blanket. "I can't be by myself tonight."

Another experience he also understood well. Nick shed his clothes and climbed in beside her. She snuggled up against him and to his surprise, he didn't feel uncomfortable. Instead he felt as though he was home. Perhaps it wasn't so much where he was as whom he was with.

The only sounds in the room were the gentle exhales of the woman currently attached to him and the thump of her heart against his rib cage. He closed his eyes and, within moments, sleep tugged at him. Without a shred of reluctance he let it claim him.

He was home.

The knocking on the door woke him. Nick opened his eyes

and was on his feet in a flash. He yanked on his trousers and shirt. As he checked his pistol, Winnie woke.

"What is it?"

"Someone's making a racket at the front door. Stay here and let me check. With all the shit that went on yesterday, I don't trust a damn soul except you and my family." He buttoned his shirt as he went down the stairs. Should have put his boots on but at least he was decent and armed.

He yanked open the front door to find a boy outside, no older than ten. His olive-toned skin blanched and his eyes widened at the sight of Nick, pistol in hand.

"What do you want?"

"I, uh, where is Miss Winnie?"

"Busy. I'm here, though." Nick gestured for the boy to get on with it. "Speak."

"I have a message for her." The urchin held up a crumpled paper.

"Fine. I'll take it."

The boy hesitated, clearly torn by his loyalty to Winnie. Even the little ones were in love with her.

Nick squatted down until he was eye level with the scamp. "I promise you I am keeping her safe. You can trust me. I won't let any harm come to Miss Winnie."

The boy had the audacity to scowl as though he were assessing Nick's worthiness to protect the beloved woman. "All right." He released the paper as though it were a historic document.

Nick got to his feet and patted the boy's head. "Now get off with you." He hustled the child out the door and closed it.

Winnie called to him from upstairs. "Who was it?"

He scowled. "Your smallest protector."

Nick turned to return to bed but before he went two steps, someone pounded on the door again.

"Dammit to hell." He opened it again only to find an older version of the original little boy. This one eyed him with borderline menace. "What do you want?"

"Miss Winnie!" he shouted into the house.

"Enrico, is that you?" Winnie responded, followed by a

series of thumps from upstairs. "I'll be right down."

Nick resisted the urge to roll his eyes. The boy clenched his fists as though preparing to fight for Winnie's honor.

"I haven't done away with her." Nick leaned against the doorframe. "I am an invited guest."

"A boarder? You look mighty suspicious to me." The young man narrowed his gaze.

"Not a boarder. A guest." Nick widened his stance, although the bare feet detracted from his ability to be tough with the young'un.

"Hmph. I'll believe that when Miss Winnie tells me."

"You related to the little scamp who was just here?" Nick held up the paper. "He gave me the paper that was meant for your Miss Winnie. He trusted me."

"He's stupid." The older boy had a lot of gumption.

Winnie clambered down the stairs, her hair still down around her shoulders. Her face shone as though she'd just washed it. She wore a yellow dress the color of a buttercup. The sight of her, still disheveled from spending the night in his arms, made his body clench with need. He wanted to see that every morning, every day every night.

"Enrico, good morning!" She turned her sunshine to the obnoxious boy on her porch.

The little ragamuffin had the gall to smile back at her. "Miss Winnie!"

"Did you get the information I asked you for?" She inspired everyone to do their best.

"Yes, ma'am." Enrico held out a paper to her.

She didn't open the paper. "Thank you. And did your cousin leave for the ranch yesterday?"

Nick stood up straighter. This topic involved him and his family.

"Yes, ma'am. Borrowed one Mr. Sylvester's fastest horses." Enrico looked quite proud of himself. He might have beat on his chest in triumph when Winnie patted his shoulder.

"Thank you so much." She handed him something and he continued adoring her with his gaze. "Please tell your mother I'll come to your house later if I need any more help."

After more stomach-turning foolish glances at Winnie, Enrico left them. Nick resisted the urge to kick the boy's behind as he walked down the porch steps.

Winnie opened the paper. "This is good news. It's the information on Fuller we need. And Conklin." Her smiling face had turned serious in only moments.

"Good, let's have some coffee and read what you got." He held up the other paper. "We've got double the news."

She took the paper and headed for the kitchen. He closed the door and followed. Today they would speak to Fuller and perhaps find a way to retrieve Martha from Conklin. He found Winnie in the kitchen with the papers laid out on the table, leaning over them.

Without asking, he set a fire in the stove, pumped water into the coffee pot and tossed in some ground beans. By the time the brew was on the stove heating, Winnie had sat at the table, still staring at the papers the boys had brought.

"What do the papers say?"

Winnie glanced up at him. "Fuller is dying. He has a wasting disease like Josie."

"That can't be a coincidence." Nick didn't believe there was such a thing as fate.

"You can't think my friends were part of this." Winnie looked stricken at the thought. "I refuse to believe that."

"I don't believe a lick of what anyone says except you or my family. Everyone else isn't to be trusted." He had let Winnie take the lead in finding information about her daughter. Now it was time for Nick to take control back.

"Josie isn't the type of person to sell children."

"Her sister sells women's bodies every day. I don't think it's a big leap to think they might want to make money off the babies that result from their first sales." Nick didn't want to shock her but he had suspected the sisters were involved.

"No, I won't believe it. Not Josie and Ruby. They saved my life. You don't know them like I do." Her face flushed with anger. "Many people get a wasting sickness. That doesn't mean they all know each other."

The coffee started bubbling behind him. "Then we go see

139

Fuller and see if he knows anything about Josie or Bertha."

"Fine. When you discover you're wrong about my friends, I expect an apology." She pointed at the paper. "Bertha seems to have disappeared, but there is information about Conklin. He has taken in six children over the last fifteen years. Aside from Martha, the rest of them are dead."

That hit him like a punch. His brother Benjy had escaped before a fate like these children. Different man, different situation, same innocent children involved. "Six? Damn, he's worse than we thought."

"Promise me we won't leave her there." Winnie's chin trembled. "No matter what."

His annoyance with her defense of her friends disappeared in an instant. He knelt beside her, ignoring the bubbling coffee and his growling belly.

"I promise. I've got a gun and a bad attitude. There ain't nothing I can't do if I set my mind to it."

She touched his face. "Thank you." Winnie leaned forward and kissed him softly. Her blue eyes held a myriad of emotions. He could hardly take it in and his own self-doubt bit him on the ass.

Nick jumped to his feet. "Let's get some coffee in our bellies and then get moving. We can see Fuller straight away."

He ignored the sigh from behind him and took down the cups from the shelf above the sink. He told himself he wasn't scared. Not a whit.

Mr. Fuller lived in a large house, not as palatial as the Fritz mansion on the hill, but larger than most folks' homes. He had enjoyed a moderate success, which allowed him to donate money to what he deemed worthy. His favorite was orphans and the Fuller's Home for Children had stayed open for many years, until Mr. Fuller grew ill and had to cut off his funding to pay for medical care.

Winnie hoped he remembered her. It would make their conversation much easier. Her stomach twisted as she and Nicholas walked up the steps of the house. The house was lovely but paint chipped on the shutters, the stairs were covered with dirt and stains, the bushes were overgrown and the entire building had an air of neglect.

The knocker on the door was missing, in its place a plain steel ring. Mr. Fuller had definitely fallen on hard times. She wanted to feel sorry for him, but held back until she knew of the part he played in selling children.

Nicholas squeezed her arm. "Are you ready for this?"

"Yes, more than I can tell you."

He nodded with his familiar grim expression and knocked on the door. And waited. And waited.

"Should we knock again?" Winnie tasted the tang of disappointment. "What if he's not here?"

A shuffling came preceded a creaking noise and the large wooden door swung open a few inches. Shadows danced across the person on the other side.

"What do you want?"

Winnie couldn't tell if the speaker was male or female, twenty or two hundred. She opted to put on her best smile and hope for the best.

"Good morning. My name is Winifred Watson Graham and this is my husband, Nicholas." She ignored the grunt from the man beside her. "We have come to call on Mr. Fuller."

A few painful moments passed. "Graham, eh? I heard about the Grahams. Rough lot of ranchers."

The stranger sounded female. Winnie stepped closer to Nicholas. "My husband isn't rough. He is here to escort me as I call on Mr. Fuller. He used to know my father, Mr. Troxler. I understand he's been ill."

"Yep, he's dying so he ain't wanting no visitor."

"Then now is the time to pay my respects before he can no longer hear them." Winnie kept the desperation from her voice but it danced at the edges of her mind.

"I reckon that's true." The door opened a little wider. "We hadn't had visitors for some time. I ain't got time for more than taking care of the old man."

Winnie took a deep breath before she stepped into the gloomy interior. The smell of decay, human and otherwise, mixed with the acrid scents of piss and vomit. She could finally see the woman and struggled to keep her smile in place. The stranger was of indeterminate age still, ancient with wrinkles, stooped in a brown drab dress. She was small, barely reaching Winnie's shoulder.

"You'd best wait in the sitting room until I talk at him." The woman hadn't introduced herself or told them where the room was, yet she turned and disappeared into the gloom.

"Happy place." Nicholas spoke, breaking the silence.

"I don't need your cynicism. I need your strength." She walked to the right and found a locked door, then another. He walked behind her, a quiet but solid presence. She turned around and tried two other doors, and to her surprise, one opened.

"Hope there aren't any spiders in there."

His statement forced a bubble of hysterical laughter up her throat. She slapped her hand across her mouth to stifle it. When she frowned at him for a chance, he shrugged.

The room had been a library but there were many empty spaces on the bookcases. Her instincts told her the books had been sold to pay bills. It was a sad house, a sad room and a sad fate. Perhaps he deserved it, but perhaps he didn't.

"This house stinks." Nicholas peered at the books that were left. "Rome's greatest conquerors? Sounds boring, no wonder he didn't sell it. Nobody would've bought it."

Winnie agreed with him but she wasn't about to tell him. He would continue with his nonsense and she needed to keep her wits about her, not fall into a pile of foolishness.

"It's rather gloomy and sad." Very unlike the house Josie lay dying. This house was dying like its master. Winnie shivered and folded her arms to ward off the chill.

"It's a death house." Nick had stopped at the remnants of a fire in the hearth, which was now a pile of ashes.

"I am not dead yet."

Winnie whirled around and saw a skeleton walking into the room. Michael Fuller had never been a big man, but he was of average height and build with a head of hair as thick as a dense forest. No more.

He had shrunken to the size of a twelve-year-old boy, thin

and gaunt, where his clothes hung off his body. His skin was the grayish and sagged where he had been formerly healthy. The man had the air of death about him and Winnie had to tell herself not to step back.

"Mr. Fuller. How lovely to see you." Winnie almost winced at the foolish choice of terms. "I hope you remember me."

"Troxler, right?" The man used two canes and shuffled, with obvious pain, to a wingback chair near the now cold fire.

"Mr. Troxler was my father, yes. I am Winnie Watson Graham and this is my husband Nicholas Graham." She managed to say the name Troxler without vomiting, which was a miracle.

"What can I help you with?" Mr. Fuller swept his arm to encompass the decay around him. "As you can see, I have stopped entertaining. I was going to have Miss Hettie escort you out, but I admit I was curious as to why you are here."

Winnie didn't know how honest to be with the man, but he had been truthful with her. She trusted her instincts and they told her he had nothing to lose.

"I am here because of Fuller's Home."

She let that sink in, watching his expression. A sadness settled over his features.

"One of the best ways to spend my money. It broke my heart when it closed." Mr. Fuller shook his head.

"Why did it close?" This from Nicholas. He stood to the side, his scowl in place.

"I ran out of funds and grew sick. There was no one left to keep the orphanage open after the housemaster passed on." Mr. Fuller looked at her. "This cannot be the only reason you are here."

"No, it's not." Winnie sat in the chair across from him. She clasped her hands together to hide the shaking. "Nine years ago, I had a child. At the time I could not be a mother to her. A friend of mine took her to Fuller's Home."

The man's brows rose. "You are looking for her."

"I looked for her and found her. She hadn't been adopted because of a crooked leg—"

"Martha."

143

Winnie swallowed the curse that nearly escaped. "Yes, Martha."

"She is your daughter?"

"I realize she doesn't look like me but you can be sure she was mine. The woman who delivered her identified her and the birthmark she bears." Winnie had to keep telling herself to breathe. This was too important to let her anger overcome her. "Since Martha was not adopted, and the home was closing, her fate was less than acceptable."

Mr. Fuller frowned. "I don't understand. She was adopted."

"No, she wasn't. Your former employee, Bertha, told us the same thing but when we went to the couple who had taken her in, we discovered Martha had not been adopted." Winnie gritted her teeth and paused. Nicholas's hand landed her shoulder and she leaned into his touch. He gave her the strength to do what she had to. "She was sold."

Mr. Fuller's eyes widened. "Pardon me?"

"You heard me. She was *sold*. Mr. Conklin bought her. He has a bill of sale. My daughter is now a *slave*, Mr. Fuller." Her voice shook with the barely controlled fury inside her. "Bertha has now disappeared and I cannot take my daughter home because a man owns her."

"I don't understand. How is that possible?"

"You tell me. It was your orphanage. Who else would know how it operated or how the children were treated?" Winnie leaned even further forward toward him. Nicholas's fingers tightened. "How many were sold? How much money did you make by selling these innocent children?" By now she shouted her words, her voice hoarse and aching with guilt and agony.

Her heart broke for the little girl she had refused, whose childhood was cut short by the greed of those charged with protecting her.

Mr. Fuller grew paler, if that was possible. "I did no such deed. Those children were not sold. I would not have allowed it."

"You're wrong or you're a liar." Winnie clenched her hands into fists. "You will help us fix this."

The silence in the room lay thick and heavy. Winnie

managed to pull in a breath although she shook like a leaf.

Mr. Fuller sank into the chair. "I do not doubt your word, Mrs. Graham. I do not think you would come to my house and speak falsehoods with your heart in hand."

"Then what are you going to do about it? I reckon we ain't doing a thing by sitting here and listening to the clocks tick." Nicholas wasn't one to keep his thoughts to himself.

"I do not believe there is anything I can do." Mr. Fuller sounded exhausted.

"The hell you can't," Nicholas growled. "You might not have known somebody sold those young'uns, but your goddamn name was on the building. You had better think of something. We will get our daughter back even if we have to steal her."

Winnie didn't know how to react to his words. He'd said "our daughter" and "steal her". At that moment, she had never loved him more.

"Who did you say bought Martha?" Mr. Fuller asked.

"Conklin at the feed store." Nicholas's tone was clear on what he thought of him.

The older man frowned. "I remember him. He had wanted to adopt children more than once but I never allowed it. Did you say Bertha gave you his name?"

"Yes, and now she's disappeared. Mr. Conklin knows who we are and we won't be able to enter his store again." Winnie hated the desperation in her voice.

"Bertha was a valued employee who loved those children. I cannot believe she would be involved in selling the young ones." Mr. Fuller inched his way forward in the chair, his cheeks had regained some color. "Where did you speak with her?"

"She was working at the Fritz house as a nurse for their children. In the hours between we spoke to her and returned to the house, she had been dismissed. We were told to speak with you."

"Me? I have not spoken to her in quite some time. At least a year." Mr. Fuller rubbed his chin.

"Why didn't you let Conklin adopt any young'uns?"

Nicholas stared at the older man, his expression carved from granite.

Mr. Fuller glanced away. "I saw the way he spoke to his wife, as if she were a dog. I cared about those children and didn't think Mr. Conklin had it in those children's best interest to adopt them. He wanted slav—" His gaze snapped back to Winnie's. "I apologize, Mrs. Graham."

She waved away his apology. Now wasn't the time for recriminations. It was time to get her daughter. "What about Bertha? Did she ever act suspicious about Mr. Conklin?"

"Not that I recall. As I said, she was devoted to the children. I never saw her raise her hand or her voice in anger." Mr. Fuller rubbed his stubbled chin with one gnarled hand.

The housekeeper Hettie came into the room with more speed than Winnie thought she possessed. Her eyes were wide and her face ashen. "Mr. Fuller, sir, there is a man wearing a silver star here to see you. Says his name is Layton."

Winnie looked at Nicholas and he bore the same expression of disbelief. Layton was the same man of the law who'd investigated her father's death. Who held Vaughn in his jail for months, preventing him from reaching Elizabeth's side. Was he following Nicholas and Winnie now?

"Show him in. I believe this situation calls for the police." Mr. Fuller attempted to get to his feet.

"Please don't trouble yourself, sir." Layton strode into the room, wearing his customary dark clothes and wide-brimmed hat. Hettie skedaddled back out the door. He doffed the hat and surprise crossed his face when he noticed the other two occupants of the room. "Miss Watson and Mr. Graham." His tone was one of suspicion.

"Layton." Nicholas sounded as happy as she felt to see the policeman.

"It's Mrs. Graham now," Winnie managed to say without tripping over her words.

"It's mighty strange to see you two here right after another murder. I don't trust either of you so I've had one of my deputies watching you. He let me know you were here. I ought to pull you in for questioning." Layton narrowed his gaze at

146

Winnie. "And don't think I forgot you conveniently fainted when that shyster escaped from my jail."

"I had nothing to do with Mr. Montgomery's escape. I am a good citizen of Houston and I resent your implication. Aside from that, I am the one who shot Mr. Troxler in self-defense. Vaughn had nothing to do with his death and you know it." Winnie spoke half-truths but she did so with fire in her gaze. His words finally sank in. "Wait, what murder?"

Layton's mouth thinned. "We found a woman's body on the north side of town and someone identified her as a former employee of Mr. Fuller's orphanage."

Winnie bit back a gasp. She knew who it was before the man spoke her name.

"Bertha Wilson was strangled and left in an alley behind a hat shop." Layton crossed his arms and widened his stance. "The Fritz's housekeeper said a couple had come to see her yesterday. You know who that couple was?"

Winnie wanted to hate the man, but found her common sense won out over her annoyance and dislike. "Yes, it was Nicholas and I. We were investigating the whereabouts of a child from Fuller's Home. Bertha was very kind to us." Her voice caught. "We came to Mr. Fuller when we'd discovered she had left the Fritz's employment."

"I find it mighty suspicious you two are involved in this death. It ain't been but a few months since your Pa died by your hand. Give me one good reason I shouldn't arrest you now." Layton stepped toward Winnie and Nicholas growled.

She got to her feet on shaky legs, holding up both hands. "Before the two of you do any harm to each other. I want to tell you all a story. One about a young woman who didn't think she had a choice."

Nicholas listened as Winnie told her story to Fuller and Layton. The men forgot Nick was even there, which was fine by him. It gave him a chance to study both of them. Someone was lying about the children being sold and he had a hard time believing it was this fragile old man. Certainly Fuller hadn't strangled Bertha.

Layton watched and listened but he didn't give away a single emotion in his stone cold expression. The man was a perfect man of the law, reminded him of Brody, his brother-in-law. Another who had devoted his life to upholding the law only to be felled by a woman and left the Texas Rangers behind.

Nick never understood it until he met Winnie and found himself caught in the same trap his brothers and brother-in-law had succumbed to. Now there wasn't anything he wouldn't do for her. The Circle Eight seemed a million miles away, the ranching work unimportant. All that mattered was making her happy and for that, they had to get Martha back where she should have been all along.

"I never sanctioned the selling of children." Mr. Fuller's chin shook with outrage. "Whoever is behind this also killed Bertha. Someone has made money off the sale of those innocents."

"Wouldn't be the first time. There's plenty of slaves in Texas, Mr. Fuller."

"Not in my house there aren't." The older man seemed to have found a well of energy to shout. "I opened that orphanage to help children who had lost their parents. I lost my only child and know the pain of separation between parent and child. If I helped at least one family come together, then my money was well spent. We helped hundreds find new homes and that is a mark on the world I am proud to own. Not child slaves."

Layton didn't look convinced. "No one would blame you."

"Goddamn it, I am not a slaver!" Fuller's passion convinced Nick the man was telling the truth. "Those children were entrusted to my care, not to my coffers."

"Then we have a mystery to solve, and a murder." Layton's words made Nick relax his stance, but only a little.

"I need a list of everyone who worked at Fuller's Home and their whereabouts if you know." Layton looked at Nick. "I expect you have information to tell me too."

"The milliner's shop. That's where we started looking for Winnie's daughter in Houston. The lady who makes hats made my gut instincts clench. She's part of this." Nick hadn't voiced it aloud, but it made sense.

"Miss Gregson." Winnie frowned.

"Yes, the woman who makes the ugliest hats on the face of the earth. Nobody who sells those hideous concoctions makes money at it. Plus, she charged you a small fortune and you didn't blink at the cost." Nick needed Winnie to see what he suspected all along. "She was testing us to see if we were really there for a hat or for something else. We fell right into that trap and she knew then we were sniffing around about something other than butt-ugly hats."

The moment she understood, Winnie paled. "She is part of this."

"Who is Miss Gregson?" Mr. Fuller frowned. "I don't remember a milliner's shop. Is it near the home?"

Now dread began to wind around his heart. Damn. He hadn't expected a woman to be involved but it made sense. Children naturally felt more comfortable around females. They would have trusted the women and done what they were told.

"Miss Gregson is the proprietress of the milliner's shop we visited. It's a few blocks from the building where the orphanage was housed. It's called Hats Incredible."

"I do not remember this establishment. It must be new." Mr. Fuller turned to Nicholas. "Describe her to me please."

Nick recounted the bird-like woman and watched the older man's face. "You know who we're talking about."

Mr. Fuller winced. "Yes, I believe it's a woman who used to work as a cook at the home. Her name is Rowena Halloren. She did her job but was never a pleasant person. I had to relieve her of her position when the home closed, of course."

Now Layton was interested. "You say this woman is now running a hat shop and changed her name. That ain't the first time somebody's done that in Texas."

"She is the one who led us to Bertha and conveniently told us things about the home as if she'd been a neighbor. Now we know she was lying. She set us up to run around after Martha so she could get rid of Bertha and disappear with whatever she's made from selling children." The words spilled from Nick in a rush. He should have followed his instincts to start

149

with and insisted Winnie do the same.

"You think she's left Houston?" Layton asked.

"No, she's got too much invested in that damn hat shop. I think she disappeared for a spell until we lose interest in finding her." Nick made a face. "Although her hats are ugly as hell."

"Are there records as to who adopted the children from the home?" Winnie had recovered some of her color. "I wonder if this Rowena had been selling children long before the home had to close."

That particular idea hit like a boulder in a lake. Mr. Fuller's mouth dropped open while Layton nodded his head. Nick had considered the slavery hadn't been a new business for Miss Halloren or whatever her name was.

"She has a partner." Nick was sure of this particular fact.

"Because she couldn't have killed Bertha by herself. Miss Gregson, or Halloren, is no bigger than a minute. Bertha is a healthy, robust woman. She couldn't have let that little woman strangle her without a fight." Winnie pulled two papers out of her pocket. "I think I know who the partner is." Her gaze met Nick's and in it he saw an apology. Whatever she'd discovered from her network of little spies had given her more information than she'd shared with him.

He told himself not to be hurt she hadn't told him. It wasn't relevant until now, until they had spoken to Fuller and found out Miss Gregson wasn't who she said she was.

"What information do you have, Miss Troxler?" Layton was apparently the type who needled people to get a reaction from them.

"That's Mrs. Graham, not Miss Troxler," Winnie said primly. "You should start thinking about finding this child slavery business and not poking at me any longer."

Layton had the grace to look at his feet for a moment. "What information do you have?"

"I had a few friends of mine find out some details about the home that were not well known in Houston." She sent an apologetic glance at Mr. Fuller. "While you had the best intentions, sir, I also know human nature. I suspected there was

150

more to this than one child."

"Please forgive me." Mr. Fuller leaned back against chair with an exhausted sigh. "I wanted to protect the children, not let wolves carry them away."

Nick believed him. He had expected the man to be a son of a bitch who didn't care a whit about the orphans, but he'd been wrong. The old man looked as though someone had punched him in the balls. Pain was clearly evident only his face.

"Tell us what you know." Layton didn't spare Fuller a glance.

"There have been children sold from Fuller's for more than five years before they closed, and for another year after. The buyers were unknown for most of them, while others were more public, like Conklin. Martha wasn't the first child he bought. The others are presumed dead since no one has seen them for years." The paper shook in Winnie's hands.

"What of Ruby and Josie? Were they involved?" Nick had to ask.

At the mention of the women at the Ruby Slipper, Fuller started. Nick watched the old man and saw no guilt.

"Josie Fleming?" Fuller stared at Winnie. "She is a friend."

"I suspect she was more than a friend." Nick didn't take his eyes off the other man. "Both of you have the same wasting sickness."

Fuller looked stricken. "She is sick?"

"Yes, she is." Winnie frowned at Nick. "According to her sister, she is dying."

Fuller put his hand across his eyes. "I did not know."

"She is being well cared for and is comfortable. I have to ask, Mr. Fuller, do you wonder if Josie was a part of what happened to the orphans?" Winnie was too nice. Nick would have asked in a bit more straightforward way.

"No. She is an angel on earth. The most beautiful woman I met after I my wife passed away." Fuller confirmed what Nick suspected. They had been lovers.

"How old are you, Mr. Fuller?"

"Fifty-two."

Nick was shocked. The older man looked twenty years older

than he was. The sickness had stolen much from him and Josie Fleming.

"I asked her to marry me once, but she said no." Fuller smiled sadly. "I need to see her."

"You can visit her if you like, but only after we help Mr. Layton find the people responsible for the atrocity of this child slavery." Winnie turned to look at Layton. "We need to start with the Fritz house."

"The Fritz house." Layton's brows went up, the first reaction Nick had seen from him. "The rich folks on the hill?"

"Yes. Mr. Fritz isn't who he appears to be."

"You have proof of this?" Layton was back to his dubious self.

"Not yet but I have information. Seven years ago, they lived in a much smaller house on the north side of town. Now, as every Texan struggles to feed themselves, they have a mansion with servants. How do you think they did that?" Winnie glanced at the papers in her hand. "Bertha worked there and Miss Halloren was right around the corner. They have been seen together for years along with Mr. and Mrs. Fritz."

"I can investigate the Fritzes within the confines of the law. If that's all you've got now, no judge in his right mind is going to accept that kind of evidence as proof of anything." Layton was right.

Nick thought about how his brother Caleb had stolen Benjy from the man who had purchased him. Child slavery was a very real problem and it happened right under people's noses. He would be proud to be part of stopping a ring of slavers, no matter how hard it was. What else could he claim to have done in his life? Until now, taking care of cows and mucking stalls was the sum of his contributions to the world.

He could make a difference. For the first time in a very long time, he was excited, eager and determined. It all started with the woman who owned his heart.

"Then we find the evidence we need." Nick earned a small smile from Winnie.

"I'm listening." Layton did actually appear to be listening.

"People who buy children aren't going to want to tell us

what we need to know. Even if selling and buying slaves happens every day, these children had no one to speak for them. They were left at the home to be adopted, not to line someone's pockets." Nick had a kernel of an idea. "If we can find the children who were sold, starting with Martha, we can build a case against those who betrayed their trust."

Layton studied him. "You're suggesting the children who were sold bear witness against adults?"

"Yes." Nick looked at Winnie and she nodded. "Children should have a say."

"Legally, they don't have a say until they're eighteen."

"Then we need to speak for them. We won't know what they need to say unless we talk to them." Winnie got to her feet. "I think it's an excellent idea. If Mr. Fuller can help us track down the children, we will find out who did the selling and stop them."

"I won't be able to arrest anyone based upon the word of a child." Layton, always not helpful, had to share his opinion.

Nick wanted to shout in frustration. "We can't do nothing."

"I didn't say we wouldn't do anything." Layton seemed to be the only calm person in the room. "I don't think children will be the right way to go."

"You need to find who was sold and find a real home for them." Winnie stepped over to Nick's side. He took her arm and tucked her close to him. She shook so hard, he was surprised her teeth weren't chattering.

"How many children were sold? Do you know?" The lawman was good at asking the hardest questions.

"We don't know until Mr. Fuller helps us." Nick caught the older man's gaze. "I know you're feeling poorly, sir, but we can't do this without your help."

Fuller's chin tilted up. "Until the breath leaves my body, I will do everything I can for the children."

"How about you, Layton?" Nick wasn't expecting much help from that quarter.

The lawman studied all three of them before he spoke. "I reckon y'all won't stop until you get what you want. No doubt you'll make my job harder when I have to arrest you for doing something stupid."

"I expect so." Nick wasn't about to let Winnie down and he would help her get Martha back, no matter what.

"Then I'll agree to be part of this if you all agree you won't break any laws. I don't like the thought of people selling orphans. It ain't right and I sure as hell don't want that happening in my town." The lawman stood up and put his hands on his hips. He didn't show much emotion but Nick sensed Layton was genuine in his intentions. Orphans didn't deserve to become slaves—they deserved a home.

"Let's get to work." Mr. Fuller looked more alive than he had the entire time they had been in his presence. His watery gray eyes sparkled and his skin had a pinkish tinge. "Hettie!"

This time when the housekeeper came in, she stared at her employer as though he'd sprouted wings. "Mr. Fuller?"

"The records I had you pack away in the attic. We need them now." Mr. Fuller looked to Nick and Winnie. "Perhaps you young folks can help her bring them down."

"Winnie can stay here. I'll help Miss Hettie." Nick didn't want Winnie traipsing around in the man's attic, no matter if he was helping or not. Winnie was Nick's responsibility and the upstairs of the house was unknown. Once a murderer committed the act, they could and might do it again.

"Perhaps I can make us some coffee?" Winnie waited for either Mr. Fuller or Hettie to tell her which direction the kitchen was in.

"Coffee's ready. I'll bring it in and then go up to get the records." The housekeeper eyed Nick as though he would ravish her upstairs.

"He's all bluster, Miss Hettie," Winnie assured her. "I sincerely appreciate your help with everything." The woman had the ability to make everyone, and anyone, feel good. Her beautiful blue eyes could hold a myriad of emotions. Now he saw gratitude, but he also saw the ghost of worry and anxiety. She wanted to march to Conklin's store and demand her daughter and not doing so was tearing her up.

Nick waited impatiently while Hettie retrieved the tray of coffee. He plucked it from her hands, silently wondering why people used fancy silver coffee pots, and then set it on the table by the fireplace. "Now we can go get what we need. Daylight's burning."

Hettie sniffed her disapproval but she headed up the stairs and Nick followed. The sooner they unraveled the mystery, the sooner Winnie's worries would be over. After that, well, he might have a family of his own, ready made, and not what he was expecting, but he knew family was not always about blood.

It was about love.

CHAPTER NINE

Winnie poured the coffee but her mind was upstairs with Nick. What would the records show? She had heard of Fuller's Home for years but hadn't been close enough to understand what the orphanage was all about. Other than the obvious task to watch over the orphans of course.

Mr. Fuller's burst of energy had started to wane. He watched Winnie with significant sadness in his gaze while Layton had his usual shuttered expression. The three of them sipped their coffee and sat in awkward silence while they waited for Nick and Hettie to return.

It seemed like hours but it was probably less than ten minutes before the pair came back with a crate full of papers. Winnie jumped to her feet and cleared the coffee service and put everything on the tray. Hettie took it from her and left the room, grumbling under her breath.

"Now, let's get to sorting." Mr. Fuller tried to lean forward but his weak body failed to function. He grunted and tried again. Winnie resisted the urge to look away from his struggle.

"Please, let me help." She took his arm and steadied him. His bones were birdlike, fragile beneath her touch. She pulled gently until he was able to sit at the edge of the chair.

"I remember when I could run for a mile without losing my breath." The older man was flushed from the effort expended to sit. "Now I can barely use the privy without assistance."

Winnie sympathized with the man. She had depended on others while she convalesced from the gunshot wound. It was an awful experience she didn't want to ever repeat.

"All we need here is your memory and your records. No need to feel uncomfortable." Winnie took a pillow from the settee and put it behind his back until Mr. Fuller was able to sit up without discomfort.

Layton watched them with a bored expression and Nicholas an annoyed one.

"Are we ready to get started here?" Her lover reached for the crate and pulled out the first ledger book.

For the next two hours, they combed through the records. The home's manager had been meticulous in his details. The four of them worked through more than ten years of orphans until they reached two years ago and the home had closed its books.

Winnie double-checked the information several times before she set the writing quill down. She blew on the still wet ink and examined the list.

"In the last three years of operation, there were twenty-seven children who disappeared from the records with no information as to who adopted them." Winnie would memorize their names, these faceless victims of greed. They deserved that much and more.

"Not enough to cause suspicion, but plenty to line someone's pockets." Layton had been surprisingly helpful as they reviewed the ledgers and papers.

"I can't believe it. I see the information, but I still cannot believe it happened under my nose." Mr. Fuller had paled with twin spots of color in his cheeks. No one could fake the level of distress he exhibited.

"Now that we know which children were sold, how do we find out who sold them and who bought them?" Nicholas had been quiet while they worked, watching and listening.

Layton shrugged. "I think most of them are gone and we won't find much. No one reported them missing—"

"Well I am reporting them missing!" Fuller shouted. "They were entrusted into my care and the people who worked for me *betrayed* that trust."

"We won't find them. Not without a lot of money." Layton

looked around the room. "And I suspect that money is in short supply for many of us."

Winnie couldn't argue with the lawman. Things in Texas were not as good as they were or could be. She'd heard rumors the Republic was going to be annexed by the United States and no longer an independent nation. She fought against the idea, but knew things could not proceed as they had been. Whoever had sold the children had done so out of greed, but probably also to survive.

"Then what do we do? I can't leave Martha to her fate at Conklin's hands." Winnie wanted to do more than just help one child.

"We get our daughter back." Nicholas crossed his arms.

"Legally, of course." Layton smiled but it held no warmth. "You Grahams have enough trouble sniffing at your heels without adding to it by kidnapping a child."

Again Layton made a good argument for staying within the bounds of the law. That didn't mean Winnie had to like it.

"How do you suggest we proceed? Legally, of course." Winnie heard the annoyance in her voice, but she didn't mask it.

Layton lifted one brow. "Do you have legal proof this is your daughter?"

"In a fashion, yes." She would need Ruby and Josie's help.

"Then get it in writing, solid proof, not just hearsay by a hooker and a madam." Layton held up his hand to forestall the words dancing behind her teeth. "Now if Mr. Fuller can corroborate her origin, that's something else."

"What about the children who were sold? Can't we simply bring charges against Miss Gregson and flush out her accomplice?" Winnie refused to believe they had no options.

"The only proof we have are records from an orphanage that closed two years ago. If you bring this in front of a judge, he'll laugh at your so-called evidence before he tosses you out of his court." Layton spoke without emotion. "Your option here is to appeal to what Conklin covets more than slaves."

Nicholas made a face. "What's that?"

"His own ass. You offer to adopt the girl and tell him he

won't go to jail. He might agree to it. I can't arrest him but you may be able to convince him I will. You two have quite a history of convincing people things are true." Layton got to his feet.

Winnie had to admit the lawman had a good idea. If she could threaten Conklin with jail, he might give her up. It was going to take a great deal of courage, but she was willing to try.

"Where are you going?" Mr. Fuller scowled.

"To do my job. I'll start investigating the Fritzes. If you find anything else that would prove these young'uns were sold illegally, you send word." With that the lawman left the house, leaving behind an awkward silence broken only by the tired ticking of a clock somewhere in the dusty house.

Winnie fought against the fatalistic attitude he'd left behind. "There has to be more we can do."

"You're damn right there is. I might not have the money I had but I still have social status and friends in society who can help." Mr. Fuller thrust up his chin. "My brother-in-law is an attorney. I will send for him and we will get Martha back. He can draw up adoption papers that cover the man not going to jail. It might convince him."

"I'm a rancher, Mr. Fuller. I don't know anything about lawyers or judges or courts. Tell me what I can do. My hands are restless." Nicholas flexed his hands as if to demonstrate his frustration at not doing something to help.

"Let me write a missive and you can deliver it to my brother-in-law." The older man looked at Winnie. "Perhaps you can help me by storing the records in the crate and adding more detail to the information we have."

Winnie was more than happy to help sort through the piles and put everything into some semblance of order. She kept her eye on the older man as he wrote a quick note. He could barely blow on the ink to dry it so she took the paper, made sure it was dry and handed it to Nick. He kissed her hard and looked into her eyes for a few moments before he nodded to Mr. Fuller and left the house.

She stared after him, wondering how her life had been turned upside down since she'd met him. No matter the outcome, she couldn't regret a moment of it.

"You love him." Fuller didn't ask a question, but stated a fact.

"Yes, I do." It was easy for her to admit. Too easy.

"It's good for a wife to love her husband and vice versa. I loved my wife very much." He looked off into a memory only he could see.

She gave him room to grieve and finished gathering up all the ledgers and papers. She organized them by year and month. She lingered over the ledger from May of 1835. Winnie couldn't stop herself from opening the book again. She ran her finger down the column until she reached "baby girl" from May 1, with Josie Fleming as the person who turned her over, now faded from the ink rubbing on the facing page.

She traced the note with her fingernail until emotions clogged her throat. Such a small entry for such a huge event in Winnie's life.

"Mr. Fuller, I would like to do something for the orphans."

He looked at her with a question in his eyes. "You already are."

"No, something more. I gave up my daughter and I've suffered every day since. The seven years she lived within your orphanage were happy ones for her." She paused and gathered her thoughts. The boardinghouse had been her crowning achievement. The accumulation of wealth and self-worth was tied to the house. She had bargained her way into buying it from the older woman who didn't want it after her sister had passed. Winnie had shed blood, sweat and tears to fix it up and make it into a thriving business.

It was all she had.

Until a fateful day a few month's earlier when she'd met a man named Nicholas Graham and her life had utterly changed. Now she knew what she'd shunned, what she'd ignored and left behind, meant more than what she held in her hands.

"I can offer you the deed to my boardinghouse to be the new Fuller's Home." She glanced up at his face, pleased to see he was surprised.

"I couldn't possibly accept."

"You can and you will. I'm sure you have good people who can help you run it. I'd like to call it Fuller's, of course." She smiled, knowing this was the right choice. "When I get Martha back, I will spend the rest of my life making up the time I've lost. I'm going to start by giving other orphans the home they need."

"Are you certain, my dear?" Mr. Fuller frowned.

Winnie didn't hesitate for even a second. She might lose her home but she would be gaining her family. She knew a moment of peace. It was the right thing and she had no regrets.

"Absolutely certain. I cannot imagine a better use for it." Another glance at the ledger and a thought slammed into her with the force of a punch. "There is no record of the Conklin's taking her."

"Correct."

"There are no records of any of the other twenty-six children who came but never left the home by legal adoptions." Winnie closed the ledger and looked at him. "There must be another ledger somewhere. No one continues to sell children without keeping track of the funds coming in."

Mr. Fuller raised his brows. "I suppose that's true. If this became a business, then they would record transactions."

"If we find that ledger, we find whomever has been selling these children. We have a weapon to use against Mr. Conklin and the rest of the people who bought those young souls." Winnie didn't know what she might find, but she knew where to start looking.

Hats Incredible.

Nick returned to Fuller's rundown house in less than thirty minutes. The brother-in-law's housekeeper took the note and Nick assumed there would be some sort of response, but he wasn't going to wait around for it. The whole situation made his neck itch and he wanted to be with Winnie. She grounded him.

He knocked on Fuller's door and, to his surprise, Winnie opened it. She stepped out with a flushed face and determination in her eye.

"I have so much to tell you. I have a theory and we need to get to the hat store to see if I can prove it." Winnie walked to her horse with more speed than necessary and waited, tapping her foot, for him to follow and help her mount the mare. "A ledger, Nicholas. There has to be a ledger of sales. I think Miss Gregson was the leader of this merry band of child sellers. She would have the ledger and I'm betting she left it behind at her store."

He helped her onto the horse and put his hand on her warm thigh, absurdly pleased by the feel of her leg beneath his fingers. "The ledger tells us what?"

"It tells us who she sold the children to and how much she was paid." Winnie smiled at him and his heart performed a somersault. "It's proof of her perfidy and a map to finding the rest of the lost children."

Nick had often wondered why his sister and brother-in-law had spent four years tracking down missing children. It was frustrating, hard work with little to nothing to show for it. Yet they persisted and only stopped when Olivia got pregnant. Staring into Winnie's beautiful blue eyes, Nick understood it. Every last impulse and moment was because of love, because a child deserved the love of its mother.

And Winnie deserved to love her daughter.

"Let's go look at those ugly hats again."

She grinned and he found himself grinning back.

"I decided to give Mr. Fuller the boardinghouse for a new orphanage," she blurted. "I can stay on and help if he needs me."

His brows went up. "I uh, that's an incredible idea. Are you sure? You won't have a home of your own."

"Home is family, not a place."

He smiled at her, love clogging his throat. "Home is family," he repeated. She was right, about everything. He was damn proud of her.

They rode back to the hat store at a brisker pace. Something told him they needed to get there before Miss Gregson came back. The proof of illegal child slavery could be sitting within the walls of the shop. Layton must have known they would go there. If all went well, they would find whatever proof Winnie needed and not get arrested.

His gut tightened the closer they got. He trusted his instincts and they were telling him to be careful. More than careful. By the time they arrived, his teeth hurt from clenching his jaw. Winnie must have been tense too because her gaze kept straying to the left and then the right.

Nick dismounted and looked up at her. "I want you to stay here."

Her mouth tightened. "No."

He had to make her understand her safety was more important than her pride. "Something isn't right and I think you know it. Let me make sure it's safe." She started to open her mouth and he squeezed her knee. "Please."

To his surprise, she nodded and didn't protest. He pulled the pistol from its holster as he walked toward the door. The small hairs on his neck stood on end. His hand tightened on the gun's grip. The door stood open an inch, barely enough to let light in, but enough to let him know his instincts weren't wrong.

Someone was inside.

He crept in on the balls of his feet, nearly noiseless in the silent shop. The bit of daylight he'd let in barely penetrated the shadows that hid what or who was there. His heart thumped steadily but he controlled his breathing, keeping all his senses on alert.

A shuffling in the back made him crouch to the right of the door. He strained to hear more but there was nothing. He started forward again. If Winnie wanted to search for the ledger, he had to find out whoever was hiding. Later they could figure out the details.

Another shuffling noise, this time to his left. He peered into the semi-darkness but saw nothing. The sounds from the street were muffled but he could imagine Winnie outside, impatiently waiting for him to find out who was in the shop. If he took more than a few minutes, he was sure she would follow him. He couldn't let that happen.

He stood up. "I'm tired of playing this game. Come on out and let's get this over with."

163

A loud noise to his right. He whirled, gun in hand. That's when his skull exploded. Hands closed around his neck and the world turned into pain.

Winnie itched to follow him but Nicholas had asked her to wait. He'd even said please. Yet she knew something wasn't right. She couldn't explain it, but it felt as though someone watched them.

A group of four men rode down the street toward her. She didn't want to look at them or consider if they were heading toward her. The air hung heavy around the hat shop, with anticipation and danger. Winnie trusted her gut and right then it was telling her the man she loved needed her.

Before she could make up her mind to ignore his request to stay put, she heard a thump from inside the shop. She slid from the horse with as much grace as she could muster and ran for the door. It took a few moments for her eyes to adjust to the darkened shop. She ran forward only to trip over something on the floor.

Winnie landed hard on her hands, sending pain shooting up her arms. Dirt and splinters ground into her palms. She heard a groan and realized what she tripped over was a body. A unique scent mixed with the tang of blood.

"Nicky?" She pushed herself to her knees, panic and fear clogging her throat. He needed her to be strong and she couldn't let him down.

She ignored the rustle of horses outside and ran her hands down Nicholas's body. She felt no breaks or wounds until she reached his head. Her hands encountered stickiness at the back of his skull that could only be blood.

Someone ran past her and she scrambled to find Nicholas's gun. Whoever it was ran for the back of the shop. To escape.

"Don't you disappear, you son of a bitch!" She couldn't leave Nicholas but she shouted at the bastard who had hurt him. More thumps and groans echoed from the direction the man had run. Frustration gripped her.

Footsteps outside the door notched up her fury. Her hand closed around the grip of the pistol and she swung to confront the next intruder in the seemingly innocuous hat shop.

"Stop!" She cocked the gun with one bloody hand. The shadows in the doorway stopped.

"Miss Watson?" The voice was familiar but she couldn't remember who it was.

"Stay where you are. I don't want to shoot you if I don't need to."

Someone snorted. "Sounds like another spitfire for a Graham."

"Miss Watson, it's Matt Graham."

Relief poured through her. "Someone hurt Nicky. They ran out the back. If you hurry you might find him."

Two of the shadows ran past her, boots slamming into the wood floor. She set the gun down and turned her attention back to Nicholas. One of the men knelt beside her.

"Winnie." Vaughn's hand landed on her shoulder. "We're here to help."

Fear and fury warred within her, and the sound of her friend's voice let it all loose. She swallowed the tears that threatened. She would not break down now.

"What are you doing in Houston? If Layton sees you—"

"Too late for that, Mrs. Graham." As if she'd conjured him, the policeman stepped into the shop. "I was hoping to see this man again."

"Mrs. Graham?" That was Matt's voice.

"Vaughn isn't guilty of any crime. You need to let him be and help us capture the child slavers!" She blew out a shaky breath. "But what we need right now is to find a doctor for my husband."

"Husband? What in the hell happened in the last week?" Matt scowled so hard his eyebrows touched.

"I will explain everything later." She got to her feet and looked to Matt, the oldest and watched as he glanced at Nicholas and then at her.

"Is there a doctor nearby?" He asked with a bite to his tone.

"There is a hospital a few miles from here. Someone needs to carry him." She cursed her own lack of strength. She couldn't even lift him from the floor.

"No one is going anywhere until I have answers." Layton blocked the door.

White-hot fury lanced through her. Winnie snatched up the gun from the floor and pressed it into Layton's chin. "If you do not allow him to leave and receive medical care, I will shoot you. If he dies, I will kill you."

Matt held up his hands. "I don't know you, Layton, but I agree with Winnie. I won't let my brother die because you don't have all your answers."

"Hey, there's something you have to see."

Winnie turned to see Brody, the brother-in-law with a gun in his hand. "Caleb has two men back here."

Layton stepped around her and she let the gun drop to her side. The weight of it heavy in her hands. She shook so hard, her teeth clacked together.

"Nick's hurt. You and Caleb can deal with the two men. Vaughn, help me carry him out to the horses. We're going to bring Nick ourselves."

Winnie almost wept at Matt's pronouncement. The men picked Nick up and brought him out to the horses. In the daylight, he was pale as cotton, blood dripping from the back of his head. Angry red marks encircled his neck.

She sucked in a breath. "He was strangled."

"Fuck." Matt glanced at her in apology. "Move. Faster."

They got to the horses in record time. Matt let Vaughn take Nicholas's weight. The oldest Graham swung up into the saddle and reached down to pull his brother onto his lap. The look on Matt's face was one of worry, fear and love. Tears stung her eyes at the sight. His family truly loved him so very much. If only he could see how loveable he was.

"Help her onto her horse and let's go." Matt was definitely used to giving orders.

Vaughn, an apology in his gaze, almost threw her into her saddle and handed her the reins. He mounted his own horse and the unlikely trio set out for the hospital.

It took less than ten minutes at the pace Matt set. People jumped out of the way given the pounding hooves streaking down the street. Winnie didn't care. She hung on and whispered to her horse, urging the mare to lead them to the doctor. Nick could be dying and she wouldn't let something like being polite to her neighbors get in the way of saving his life.

By the time they arrived, she was covered in perspiration but she ignored it. At that moment, she didn't care if she was covered in the worst offal. Nothing mattered but Nicholas.

She didn't wait for Vaughn, but slide down off the horse, landing with a thump. She ran into the hospital on shaky legs.

"We need a doctor quickly!"

The only person in the lobby was an older nurse. The woman was startled and dropped the tray she'd been carrying with a clang.

"Good heavens, ma'am! You don't need to shout."

"Yes I do. My husband was strangled and beaten. He needs a doctor. Please." Without permission, tears began to leak from her eyes. Emotional exhaustion threatened and Winnie hung on, determined to save Nicholas's life.

The nurse's expression hardened. "Then let's save his life. Bring him in to the first room on the right. I'll fetch the doctor."

Gratitude was pushed aside by urgency. Winnie ran back outside to see Vaughn accepting Nicholas's weight. Matt hopped down and took his brother back.

"This way." She held the door open for them. To her dismay, more tears fell down her cheeks. She couldn't take her gaze from Nicholas's still form. "First door on the right."

Matt entered the room followed by Winnie and Vaughn. The cot in the room had clean white sheets and Matt laid his brother down with a gentleness she hadn't expected.

"Get the doctor," he barked.

Winnie ran from the room, looking for the nurse. To her relief, the older woman was moving down the hallway with a young man behind her. No matter who he was, he had to save Nicholas's life. If he didn't, Winnie might not ever recover.

He had given her life back to her. With his gruff love and his insistence on finding her daughter. Winnie would have lived the rest of her life, unfulfilled and lonely if not for

Nicholas Graham.

She stayed by his side while the doctor assessed him. Matt stood on the other. Two people who loved him giving him their strength.

"Someone tried to kill this man." The doctor's pronouncement made Matt snort.

"I know that, doc. How about you save his life?"

The doctor, a sandy-haired man not much older than her, gave Matt a withering look. "That is what I am attempting to do, sir."

Matt nodded and folded his arms. "Then get to it."

Winnie watched the rise and fall of Nicholas's chest. The room was quiet except for the soft murmur of conversation in the corner between the doctor and Matt. The doctor had swathed Nicholas's head in bandages and his face was nearly as pale as the cloth. Nicholas lived but, according to the doctor, he'd seen people strangled who lived but never woke.

Winnie pressed her forehead into the side of the cot and fought for control. Emotion made her throat tight. How she wished she could turn back the clock and refuse the offer to ride home from the Circle Eight with Nicholas. If she had, he wouldn't be on a cot fighting for his life, half-strangled and beaten.

Then again, if she hadn't traveled with Nicholas, she would never have experienced the sweet joy of loving him. She wouldn't trade the time with him no matter what. An hour of wonderful was worth more than living for a hundred years in with a mediocre existence.

She picked up his hand and kissed one knuckle. "Don't make me follow you to heaven and drag you back by your hair. I wouldn't be happy with you."

He didn't stir at her words. Winnie pulled his hand to her cheek and closed her eyes at the feel of his callused skin against hers. When he twitched, her eyes flew open.

He watched her with his beautiful blue-green eyes. She yelped and kissed him as gently as she dared on his cheek.

"Nicky." The one word held so much emotion, she barely

got it out.

He cupped her cheek and croaked, wincing.

"Your throat probably hurts. Someone tried to strangle you."

His brows snapped together.

"Don't worry. I wasn't hurt. Your family arrived to help."

His gaze moved to Matt who stood at the end of the bed. Winnie saw a combination of relief and surprise cross his expression.

"Hey, Nick, heard you had a pinch of trouble." Matt nodded his head toward Winnie. "Miss Watson hasn't told us everything yet and I have some to share too. I reckon we ought to talk." Matt glanced at Nicholas's throat. "Maybe you should just listen."

"I've told him about Grace, or rather, about Martha." Winnie's heart stuttered to speak her daughter's name. "And all we discovered about the child slavery ring including how we plan to get Martha back."

Nicholas pointed at his bruises with a scowl.

"It was a fool named Willard. He used to do maintenance at Fuller's Home." Matt crossed his arms. "Now works as a gardener for the Fritz's."

"How do you know about him?" Winnie had barely left Nicholas's bedside for hours. It seemed she had missed a great deal.

Matt speared her with a look. "While you were here, Caleb and Brody interrogated Willard and the other man, Tucker."

She vaguely remembered mention of two men but she'd been too concerned with the injured man in her arms. Nicholas held up two fingers.

"Yep, Tucker was holding a gun to Willard, but he was no match for two ex-Texas Rangers." Matt's tone held grim satisfaction. "It appears you two had a shadow. Tucker followed you around Houston for the last two days."

Winnie's brows went up in surprise. "Two days? Who is he?"

"He was an orphan at Fuller's Home. Told us he was sold two years ago to a cotton farmer when he was sixteen. Little bugger ran away within a month but by the time he got back to Fuller's to help the other young'uns, it had already closed." Matt looked at Winnie. "He knows Martha well."

Winnie's heart galloped. "Then why was he following us?"

"It appears young Tucker has been trying to find the children who were sold and rescue them." Matt waited a moment. "Sound familiar?"

Although her cheeks heated, she refused to apologize for doing the right thing. "It's too bad the authorities didn't listen to him."

"Most don't pay attention to a scruffy young man with a chip on his shoulder."

"Where is he now?"

"He's at your friend Fuller's house. It seems the old man remembers him and invited Tucker to stay under his roof." Matt grunted. "I wouldn't trust him not to walk off with whatever he can carry."

"There is nothing to steal from Mr. Fuller. He's dying and he barely has enough to feed himself. If he offered to take in Tucker, it was done with genuine fondness." She would not allow Matt to speak ill of the old man.

"I ain't doubting Fuller, but I hope Tucker doesn't take advantage of him." Matt sat on the edge of the cot. "It's not the angry young man I want to talk about, it's the other one, Willard. He almost killed you, Nick."

Nicholas grimaced and Winnie squeezed his hand.

"The good news is, Willard had a book, a ledger, when we found him and Tucker behind that hat shop."

Winnie's hopes jumped. "The ledger! You were right. It was there." She beamed at Nicholas.

He nodded and managed to croak. "Woman?"

"Miss Gregson is nowhere to be found and Tucker hasn't seen her either. Caleb and Brody are chasing her down. She can't hide forever." Matt seemed very sure the woman would not escape. For that, Winnie was grateful.

"What about Layton? Is he part of this too?" Winnie didn't trust the lawman and she didn't want him to get his hands on Vaughn.

"He's working with my brother and brother-in-law but I don't think he's happy about it."

Vaughn poked his head in the room. "He's awake!" He stepped in with the other three men on his heels. "We wanted to talk to Winnie."

The Grahams were a serious lot and Layton fit right in with their fierce visage. Winnie didn't think she wanted to hear what they had to say.

"Maybe we should do this outside the hospital." She got to her feet but Nicholas grabbed her wrist.

"No." His gruff word cost him, judging by the pain in his gaze.

"Then we stay here." She sat back down. "Tell me what you have to say."

Vaughn was the one who spoke and she braced herself for bad news. "I spoke to Mr. Fuller's brother-in-law, the attorney."

It was going to be bad. He crouched down beside her.

"What did he say?" Her voice had dropped to a whisper.

"There is no legal precedent to take Martha from the Conklins. They have paperwork that was filed with the court properly. There are no record of her birth and no way to prove you are her mother." He swallowed as she absorbed the news. "And one more thing. Josie passed away the night after you visited her."

Winnie closed her eyes and refused to allow herself to cry. Martha was alive and so was Nicholas. Winnie would find a way to make up for what she'd done ten years ago.

"I'm sorry." Nicholas's gruff words made her heart melt.

She looked at him and managed a small smile. "You don't need to be sorry. I haven't given up, Nicky."

"I never thought to see Nick mushy over a woman." Caleb watched them. "But I think I see mush. And she called him Nicky."

"I think you're right. Ain't that a sight?" Brody was a cold looking man with his black hair and cool blue eyes, but she definitely saw a teasing glint in them.

Nicholas shook a fist at them.

171

"You deserve it." Matt shook his head. "What were you thinking disappearing like that? When I got your letter, I had about thought you dead. Not to mention what Rebecca just put us through."

"Bec?" Nicholas tried to sit up but Winnie easily stopped him. He was lucky to be alive and she knew it.

"She's home but she ain't leaving again until she's thirty. Maybe even forty." Whatever their sister had done, it had earned the eldest's ire for sure.

"We're glad you're alive." Caleb looked at Nicholas with a tenderness that surprised Winnie.

"It would make me angry if you died, you know." Matt was less affectionate but she heard the genuine concern and love in his words.

"I can tell you my wife would be mad if you died." Vaughn grinned at his brother-in-law.

Winnie stared at her friend. "Where is Elizabeth and why aren't you on your honeymoon?"

"She is home at the ranch. We made it to Galveston but as soon as she saw the ocean, the smell made her sick. I don't argue with my pregnant bride. We turned around and made our way back to the Circle Eight." Vaughn grinned. "She was happy to be home in our new cabin and bed."

"Hey now. Don't talk about our sister like that." This from Caleb.

"Hmph. You should talk. It was Aurora who taught her about sex."

Winnie laughed while Caleb sputtered. "She did no such thing."

"Your wife is an angel on earth. The things she knows. You must reap those rewards." Vaughn had been uncomfortable with his family but it seemed marriage agreed with him, allowing him to tease his new brothers-in-law.

At Vaughn's words, Winnie would swear the tough Caleb blushed. It earned a few guffaws from the others.

"These men are apparently not aware you are married, *Mrs. Graham*." Layton interrupted the foolishness. "I assumed you were telling the truth about your marriage."

172

It was a challenge the lawman threw down. Winnie considered how to respond but then to her surprise, Nicholas saved her.

He took her hand. "Wife." His fierce word fell across the room. No one doubted him, and for that blessed moment, Winnie felt like his wife in truth.

"We can leave that subject behind." Matt's words pushed the lawman to let it go, but in his gaze, she saw the truth. There would be a reckoning between them. Envy slashed through her at the way his family came to his rescue and protected their own no matter what the cost. She'd never had that. Vaughn and she had done what they could, when they could, and had true affection for each other as a brother and sister would, but it was not nearly the same.

She wanted a family, wanted the support, love and fierce protectiveness they all demonstrated, no matter how much they squabbled.

"What's the next step, Layton?" Brody spoke up from the corner, his face seemingly cut from granite.

"I interrogated Willard and he's no more than a simpleton. A big, brute of a simpleton. He might now how to prune a rose, but he is not the mastermind behind the child slavery ring." Layton's gaze found hers. "You were right about the ledger. It has damning information about all twenty-seven children."

"Twenty-seven?"

"Holy shit."

"Poor mites."

They all spoke at once and Layton cut them off with a sharp chop of his arm. "We will not find all of them nor do we have solid legal rights to take them back. Whoever was in charge of this was smart enough to make everything appear legal. The only evidence we have is this ledger."

"And Tucker," Winnie added. "He can testify what happened to him."

Layton looked doubtful. "Yes but he is a street ruffian. The judges in Texas don't take the word of a boy like him over an adult."

"He is an adult. Eighteen, right? He can certainly testify as to what they did to him. They accumulated wealth by selling children from an orphanage. How much lower can go you go?" Winnie was sick to think of it.

"Oh you'd be surprised." Caleb's expression was infinitely sad. "I've seen much worse."

"Much, much worse," Brody added. From what she knew, Brody and his wife Olivia had spent four years searching for their brother Benjy and rescued numerous children who had been kidnapped.

"We'll do what we can with the evidence, but as Mr. Montgomery told you, there is nothing we can do to break the legal right the Conklins have to Martha." Layton tapped his chest. "I won't break the law even if it ain't right that a child was traded for money. What I can do is investigate the Fritz family like I said I would. You do what you have to just don't tell me about it."

Winnie wanted to be angry with him but she couldn't. He was right. He was sworn to uphold the law, not break it. The lawmen in Texas were known for their fierceness but also their sense of honor. He was a pain in the ass and had put Vaughn through hell, but he was still right. She would battle Conklin on her own.

She looked at Nicholas and saw determination in his gaze. Whatever she wanted to do, she knew he would be at her side. It gave her confidence to do what had to be done.

"Then I fight Mr. Conklin for her."

The men all looked at her. Anticipation hung in the air. She knew what she was proposing was risky. Extremely risky. Winnie could lose everything, including Martha. However, if she did nothing, then she would be giving in. These people sold her daughter and she could not let that go.

"I will blackmail him into letting me adopt her."

Vaughn's eyes widened but the Graham family all nodded. Nicholas nodded at her.

"The man is a selfish bastard. He won't want to go to jail for a crippled girl. I can use the ledger and some friends." She had already decided and now that she had started down this path to accept her motherhood, she would stop at nothing.

"Dangerous." Nicholas's voice was a rusty whisper.

"I can and I will." She looked at the rest of the men, each of them obviously uncomfortable with her pronouncement. "Each of you would do the same. Don't dare judge me because I'm a woman."

"That isn't it." Vaughn took her hand. "You gave this child up nine years ago. Now you're willing to endanger yourself to get her back."

"Yes I am. She should have been in my care since she was born. I was a coward. No more." She got to her feet, sure of her path, undeterred by their doubt. "What would you do for your children?" She threw the question at Matt. He flinched.

"Fair enough. You are a woman grown. I ain't gonna judge you and what you want to do with your life. I do care that Nick is involved." Matt nodded at his younger brother. "He says you're his wife. Isn't this decision his to make?"

Winnie saw red. Fury raced through her and if she'd had a gun, she might have shot the eldest Graham.

"How dare you? A husband and wife are partners, not a feudal monarchy where the kind controls all decisions." She got to her feet, fists clenched. "That child is part of me, no matter if she has been lost for most of her life. She deserves a family. Would you deny her that? Do you even know how it feels to be at the mercy of someone else, unable to do anything but obey?" Her voice rose to a shout and the doctor poked his head in the door. "Get out!"

The man disappeared in an instant.

Matt widened his stance and crossed his arms. "I don't know what that feels like but I do know what family is." His brothers remained silent while Vaughn watched the play between Winnie and Matt. Layton leaned against the wall, clearly amused.

"Well I know what it feels like to live your life in fear. I lived the first sixteen years of my life with a monster. My father was evil incarnate. A greedy, selfish man who turned me into a whore when I was nine. If I can save that child even a moment of the horror I endured, then it's worth every cent I have." Her heart erupted with the pain of her past. Now that she'd opened Pandora's box, there was no closing it again. "I had a child at sixteen and gave her away because my father forced me to. I have paid for that since. Believe me, Mr. Graham, I didn't choose to be a pitiful old whore who killed her own father, but here I am. If you don't believe I'm good enough for your brother, that's your prerogative. He has a choice to love me just as I love him."

Nicholas struggled to a sitting position, batting away Vaughn and Caleb's helpful hands. He growled at them and looked at her. She saw the same raw determination in his gaze that rose inside her. She held out her hand and he grasped it with his own shaking one. He got to his feet and wavered for a moment before he steadied himself. She laced her fingers with his.

"You've made up your mind then. You're choosing her and her lost daughter." Matt kept his voice neutral but Winnie heard an edge to it.

Nicholas nodded tightly. She felt him shaking beside her and knew it cost him every ounce of strength he had to stay upright.

"Wife." When he repeated the word, tears sprang to her eyes.

"I can't judge your choice, brother. Hell I picked my wife over a bunch of turnips after Caleb mouthed off to her." Matt looked at Caleb, Brody and Vaughn in turn. "I needed to be sure."

Winnie started at his last words. "Pardon me?"

"Give us a few minutes, Layton." Matt turned to the lawman. Brody opened the door and ushered the sputtering policeman out. After it was family only, Matt spoke again. "I don't know you very well, ma'am, but I do know Nick well. He's struggled with a lot since our parents died. I think you know what I mean."

Winnie did. She'd sensed the same darkness in Nicholas that she struggled with in her life. "That makes no difference to me. I love him for who he is, the good and bad."

"Good. He needs someone with a mouth as sharp as his. I think you're doing the right thing no matter what Layton says.

176

That girl deserves a family." Matt surprised her more than she thought possible.

"But I thought you were against my plan. You were testing me?" Her original fury dissipated only to be replaced by annoyance. "You don't trust me."

"I trust my family. I trust Nicholas. You weren't part of the Circle Eight until now."

Winnie sucked in a breath and tried to calm her racing her. "Are you making me part of your family?"

"It seems Nick's already done that. I'm just agreeing with his choice."

Winnie let the tears fall, overcome by the sense of belonging and the strength the Graham family had surrounded her with. She glanced at her sleeves, stiff with Nick's blood and used her hands to wipe the tears from her cheeks.

"Thank you."

"You're welcome. Now help your husband back onto that cot before he falls." Matt reached for Nick at the same time Caleb and Vaughn did. Winnie let them take his weight, still reeling from Graham family acceptance.

"Now, you are going to stay here and let the doc take care of you." Matt shook his finger at Nicholas. He raised his gaze to Winnie's. She was struck by how much the brothers looked alike, the beautiful blue-green eyes unique to the family. Matt was a harder, older version of the man she loved, but now he was her family. "The rest of us are going to get Martha."

Winnie's heart leapt. "Truly?"

"I suggest you change your duds, but yep, we ain't leaving her with the bastard who bought her."

Winnie hadn't thought about where she would live, but it didn't matter, as long as she was with Nicholas and Martha.

She knelt down and kissed Nicholas gently. He was pale but calm. There was a peace in his gaze as he stared at her. Whatever they shared had affected both of them at the deepest level.

"I love you." She had never spoken the words in earnest until she'd met Nicholas, until she had finally found where she belonged.

He mouthed, "I love you," and she smiled so hard, her face hurt. To her amusement, he turned a scowl at his brother.

"I'll take care of both of them, I promise. We'll be back later, no matter what. With all of us." Matt took Nicholas's hand and squeezed it. "Ready?"

Winnie had never been more ready in her life.

CHAPTER TEN

Nick hated lying in the damn cot with the damn bandages and the damn doctor hovering over him. He wanted to be out there with Winnie and his family. If a bastard hadn't tried to kill him, Nick would be.

His mind drifted as he lay there. To her of course. She'd told him she loved him. Twice. The words had washed over him, soothing him as nothing had ever done. The years of fighting his own demons faded in the light of what they shared.

He'd meant it when he called her wife. They might not be legally wed, but to him, they were married in their hearts already. Life would not be worth living without her and he refused to consider that possibility.

Matt promised to keep her safe and help her retrieve Martha. He trusted his brothers, Brody and, to his surprise, Vaughn. They would do what was needed.

He must have fallen asleep because the next time he opened his eyes, Layton was back in the room. The lawman leaned against the open doorframe, his stance relaxed.

"I know you can't talk so I'll do much of the talking." Layton shifted his feet and glanced at his feet. "No matter what you think of me, I'm doing my job. I arrest people who commit crimes and try to keep Houston safe."

Nick blinked twice.

"I plan on getting to the bottom of the child slavers. Rotten bastards ought to hang from their balls. I can't step outside the law to punish 'em, though. I know you and yours will get that girl back." Layton looked up at Nick. "I was going to arrest your brother-in-law but I figured the rest of your family would bust him out, or your wife would."

Nick's lips quirked up. She was a woman with a spine of steel.

"Mr. Nick?" A little dark head appeared in the door. It was Enrico. "Miss Winnie sent me to tell you they were headed to Conklins."

Nick was not surprised to find she had sent one of her errand boys to assure him. He gestured to the boy to come in. With a suspicious glance at the lawman, the boy slunk in and stood in the corner.

"I'll be on my way. I'll send word when I know more about the folks responsible." Layton tipped his hat and left the room.

Nick didn't know what to make of the man. He'd insisted on arresting Vaughn for a crime he didn't commit, harassed Winnie, and yet he obviously had a heart. A puzzle Nick wasn't keen to solve.

"I don't like no police." Enrico frowned at the now empty doorway.

Nick made a motion with his hands as though he was writing. Enrico nodded. "You want to send a message?"

Nick nodded.

The boy pulled a piece of paper and a stub of charcoal from his pocket. Nick found himself smiling. Enrico was an enterprising young man.

Nick wrote only two words. *Love. Wife?*

Enrico smiled and folded the paper, tucking it into his pocket. "I'll be back, mister."

Nick had to watch the boy leave and lie there waiting. His crude marriage proposal would either be received well or laughed at. Then of course, there was the matter of his woman doing battle without him by her side. His head throbbed and his throat burned. It was going to be a hell of a long day.

Winnie smoothed her hand down her hair and looked at her reflection with a critical eye. She was washed, dressed and coiffed once again. The Graham men waited downstairs for her. All four of them were going to Conklin's store with her. It was like having a personal army of muscled gunmen. She couldn't say it didn't feel good but she wished she didn't need them.

A soft knock sounded on the door. She opened it to find a very worried looking Vaughn. Without hesitation, she fell into his arms and accepted the comfort. Her emotions were in tatters and it was wonderful to have her friend there to support her.

After a few moments of pure self-pity, she pulled back and took a deep breath. "Thank you."

"My pleasure." He smiled sadly. "Are you ready to give everything up again?"

She had left behind everything except the clothes on her back when she escaped from her father. For two years, she'd hidden from him, with Vaughn's help, and survived. The next three years, she worked hard and smart, doing anything and everything to earn enough money to live, then to thrive, and finally, to buy the boardinghouse. It was a personal triumph to come from eating scraps from a slop bucket outside a restaurant to being a business owner.

Now she was starting anew again. With Nicholas and Martha.

"Yes." Winnie didn't hesitate. This was when she proved to herself that she was the person she wanted to be. Someone the Grahams would be proud to call their own.

They headed downstairs where Matt, Caleb and Brody waited in the parlor. Seeing that room full of men made it appear so small. They were an intimidating lot.

"What's the plan?" Caleb looked to Matt.

To her surprise, Matt turned to her with his brows raised. He was deferring to her. "Winnie?"

She had been thinking about what to do since they'd left Nick at the hospital. Mr. Conklin knew her so the approach had to be done carefully. Wisely.

"Since Mr. Conklin and I are acquainted, I'm going into the feed store alone. If he sees this wall of muscle, he may refuse or, worse, bring out a gun and threaten to shoot us if we don't leave."

"I don't like that." Matt frowned.

"You can watch me through the window while I speak to him. Trust me. I have lived in Houston all my life. I've learned how to manipulate people, not that I wanted to. For once, the underhanded skills my father taught me will be used for good." She glanced at each of them. "I'm going to offer him a deal to give up Martha in exchange for not being prosecuted for buying her illegally."

Vaughn scowled, Brody twisted his mouth, Caleb shook his head and Matt crossed his arms.

"I'm ready to battle for her against anyone and nothing any of you say will change my mind. I'm going up against him alone." Her stomach twisted at the thought of the man refusing to give up the girl, but she had to fight for her daughter.

Now all of the men spoke at once, each growing progressively louder as they argued against what she had decided on. Winnie clapped her hands over her ears and walked out of the parlor and out of the house. She smiled at Enrico who walked toward the house, a puzzled expression on his face.

"Miss Winnie, do your ears hurt?"

"You have no idea."

It took a few seconds before the Graham men followed her out. They wore the same expressions but at least they weren't shouting.

"I have a note from Mr. Nick." Enrico held out a small paper.

Winnie didn't expect to hear from Nicholas so soon. It had been less than an hour since she'd left the hospital. She wasn't sure what she expected but it wasn't what the note contained.

Love. Wife?

He had told her he loved her and asked her to marry him with two words. Her heart smiled with the promise of what they would share, what they already had, and the love that overlaid it all. She folded the paper and tucked it into her stays. Nicholas would rest beside her heart as she faced the second hardest moment in her life.

Confronting her father and the ensuing gunfire encompassed the end of who she had been. A rebirth of sorts and now, she would be born again. This time as a mother. She looked up to find all of the males watching her.

"Is there a note to send back?" Enrico scratched is head.

"No note. Just please tell him yes." She smiled at the young man and pressed a coin into his hand. He saluted the men and winked at her before he ran down the street back to the hospital. "If you insist on coming with me, we need to go now before it gets any later. I want to be back at the hospital before supper with my daughter so she can meet her new father." She thought she saw a muscle twitch in Matt's face but he nodded and gestured for her to precede him.

After they all mounted the horses, they rode toward the feed store. Her pistol weighed down her pocket on the other side. Her anxiety grew with each step the horse made toward Conklin's. Her mind ran through all the worst possibilities from death to arrest or possibly the man had already sold Martha to someone else.

The last thought forced bile up her throat. She swallowed the acrid taste and promised herself no matter what, or who, had her daughter, she would find her. Nothing would stand in the way of Winnie and her family again. Ever.

Some folks stopped and stared as the group of them passed. As she expected, they were visibly intimidating on horseback, armed and fiercely frowning. She'd held people at bay for so long, not allowing most people to get close to her with few exceptions. Ruby, Josie and Vaughn were the only true friends she had made. Until Nicholas. And now Josie was gone.

Winnie understood loss but not at the scale of losing someone you loved. Her daughter had been an infant, someone she had refused to allow herself to love because she knew she'd be giving the baby away. What she hadn't understood then was she already loved her daughter. The loss was a constant ache she had long since accepted as part of life.

It wasn't a sudden loss but rather like a wound she'd kept putting salve on but would not heal. Now it was time to face that loss and finally close the wound that had festered in her heart for so long. Her hands shook but her heart and head were ready to do what she must.

Vaughn helped her dismount with true concern on his face. "Are you sure about this?"

"Never more sure about anything." She patted his arm. "Thank you for your friendship and your support. Elizabeth is a lucky woman."

He smiled and took her arm. Winnie allowed him to walk her up the steps, but then she turned and held up her hand. "This is where you stay." She glanced at the Grahams standing at the bottom of the steps. "All of you. If I need you, you will know it."

"Not if he knocks you out and drags your body to the back of the store." Brody was not quite a chipper sort of man.

"Or slits your throat." Caleb wasn't much better.

Matt raised his brows as if to confirm their predictions. She pinched her lips in exasperation. "Then wait on the porch where you can see me through the window but don't come inside unless I call you." She turned, not waiting to see if they listened to her.

"Do you have a gun?" Matt asked.

She patted her pocket. "Always."

"I do like her."

"She's got gumption."

"Not a lick of sense, though."

If the situation were not so dire with regard to Martha, she might have laughed at their antics. Their foolish behavior had chased some of the nervousness away.

She wiped her damp palms on her skirt and entered the store. As it had been previously, the store was empty and smelled faintly of sawdust and oats. She forced herself to walk forward. Her mouth had gone cotton dry and she needed to pee.

"Can I help you?" a small voice asked. As if in a dream, Winnie turned to her right and saw a figure emerge from the shadows. A girl with a crooked gait.

A child who had already laid claim to Winnie's heart.

"Martha?" Winnie's voice was a trembling whisper.

"Yes, ma'am." She stepped closer and allowed Winnie a

better look at her. She wore the same shapeless clothes and her hair was in a crude braid. There was a smear of something on her cheek but she had a lovely face. Although her skin was more olive toned, like the man who had fathered her, the girl was petite and the heart-shaped face was a copy of Winnie's.

The girl's dark eyes watched Winnie warily. "You were here before."

"Yes, honey, I was. I've come back for you." Winnie smiled although her hands itched to snatch the girl and run like hell.

"For me?" Martha looked surprised.

"Yes, I was speaking to Mr. Fuller about you."

The girl's expression softened. "Mr. Fuller is a nice man. He got sick and the home closed."

"I heard about that. I was very sorry to hear it closed. The home was a good place for children." Winnie searched for the right words. "I'm sorry, Martha, but I am very, very late in coming back for you."

"I don't—"

"Girl, what the hell are you doing?" Conklin stormed in, his face a mask of rage. He raised his hand and slapped Martha hard across the face before Winnie had a chance to realize what he was going to do. She shouted and threw herself between them. Martha had fallen to the floor with a small whimper. Up close, the man was worse than she expected. His lips were pulled back to expose his teeth as though he were a dog in a fight. His scent was malodorous, rotten.

"Get the fuck out of my way and out of my store, bitch." His foul breath gusted across her face.

"No. I came here to do business. Isn't that what you are? A businessman?" Her calm tone appeared to confuse him. She wanted him off balance.

"A'course I'm a businessman. You see the store, right? It says Conklin's Feed Store." He reached for her, but Winnie stepped back, toward the girl. Martha scurried back a few feet but didn't run.

"Then I have a proposition for you." Winnie's heart pounded so hard, her ribs nearly cracked.

"You were here with that son of a bitch already. I threw you

185

out then. I can throw you out now." He reached for her again and the door swung open, hitting the wall with a resounding crash.

"You touch either of them again, I'll rip your fucking arms off." This was Vaughn. The man she had called friend for years, and she'd never seen him violent. Behind him stood the Grahams and she was pleased to see Conklin's expression change from fury to fear. She was glad they were there to support her, even if she was too proud to ask for it. Home was family.

"What is this?"

"I told you. It's a proposition. Are you ready to listen?"

Out of the corner of her eye, she saw Caleb cross to the girl and kneel. Soft murmurs followed and she could have kissed Nicholas's brother for his gentle approach to her daughter. She remembered he was father to two little girls himself. He was probably an amazing parent.

"I'm listening." Conklin crossed his arms and glared at her.

"Two years ago you bought a child illegally. I'm offering to adopt the girl from you. If you don't sign her over, I will make sure you go to prison for your crime."

He jerked at her words, guilt crossing his features. "I ain't never done such a thing." The man was a filthy liar. He'd already told her he'd bought Martha. Now with an audience of armed men, he lied.

"We have a ledger that proves otherwise. Plus, I've been speaking to Mr. Fuller, who remembers refusing to allow you to adopt a child from the home." Winnie kept her voice even when all she wanted to do what shoot the man. "You also told me yesterday you had a bill of sale."

"I don't know what you're talking about. Everybody knows Fuller is out of his head dying."

"Not true. He is alive and very clear-headed. At this moment, he is meeting with his brother-in-law, the attorney, to track down all the children who were sold from the home along with the police." Winnie let that sink in, watching the other man's face. "You have a chance to avoid prosecution and, potentially, the loss of your business."

"By giving the girl to you."

"Yes, you walk away with your good name and you don't go to jail." She told herself not to touch her gun, although she wanted to shoot the man with a fever that burned her.

Conklin's gaze narrowed. "How do I know you won't send the law after me if'n I do give her to you?"

"That would be foolish. I could call the law now and the girl would no longer be yours to own. I am offering you a fair deal." Winnie had learned how to manipulate people early on. Now was the time to use all her skills. "I think the two Texas Rangers behind would be happy to take you into custody if you refuse."

She waited while he mulled over her words. Hope warred with fear like a hurricane in her chest.

"What do you want with a Mexican cripple anyway?" His gaze sharpened.

"I knew her mother. I want to return her to the woman who gave her up."

A tiny noise behind her made Winnie wince. The girl might not be keen on the plan to be reunited.

"Some dirty Mexican whore gave up a defective girl and you're gonna be a good Samaritan and bring her back?" Conklin snorted. "You're lying."

One of the men growled and the shop owner's gaze flicked to a spot behind her and then back.

"It doesn't matter where she goes from here, does it? She is unable to work as much as someone who was not crippled." Winnie was anxious to make the deal and leave this awful store for good.

"I ain't letting her go. It's gonna cost me plenty to pay somebody to do her work." Conklin had seen through Winnie's words and his avarice reared its ugly head.

"This is a one time offer. You refuse and the police will take you into custody." Her bluff was just that. Her face was impassive, smooth as porcelain, just like her father taught her.

"That's a load of shit." Conklin crossed his arms again. "No matter how many guns you got at your back, I ain't just giving up this girl. She's my, ah, daughter."

"She's nothing more than your slave." Winnie's voice shook with rage and she struggled to keep it under control.

Conklin shook his head. "You want this cripple and you're gonna pay for her. Five hundred or you get the fuck out of my store."

Boots shuffled near the door and Winnie held up her hand to stop the Grahams from jumping into the negotiations. She had to do this on her own.

"I will give you no money for her. She is not a thing to be bought and sold. She is a child." She pointed behind her. "The Texas Rangers or the girl. That's your choice."

"It ain't a choice. They need to get out of my store and so do you."

"No, we aren't leaving without Martha. Although I could ask them to shoot you." Fury had pushed aside any fear and Winnie pulsed with it. The note from Nicholas crinkled against her breast and she drew strength from the sentiment contained within. "What's your decision, Mr. Conklin?"

He stared at her, then at Martha. When his gaze returned to Winnie, she saw his decision in his eyes.

"I ain't going to jail for that little piece of shit. You can't prove nothing. Take her. She don't do nearly enough work anyway."

Winnie let out a breath slowly. "Vaughn, would you please go to Mr. Fuller's house and ask him to send his brother-in-law here as soon as possible?"

"On my way." Vaughn's footsteps echoed as he left the store.

"I'm going to take the girl outside for now." Caleb spoke in her ear. "She's heard enough."

Winnie nodded and the door closed once again. She stared at Conklin, hating him, at the same time, grateful for accepting the offer. She didn't have time to consider the fact he could change his mind before the papers were signed. It was done, and soon she could leave this awful store and never come back.

Later she would think about what they would do after they left the store. For now, knowing Martha was free of the man was enough.

Nick counted the cracks in the ceiling for the forty-seventh time when Enrico came back into the hospital room on stealthy feet. The boy peered at him until Nick beckoned him forward.

"Did you give her the note?" His voice had come back somewhat but it hurt to speak.

"Yup. Found her at the boardinghouse." The boy stood a few feet from the bed as though poised to run at any moment.

"I ain't gonna hurt you boy. Hell, I can't even sit up." He told himself not to scowl. "Did she give you a note in reply?"

"Nope."

Nick's heart stopped beating. It couldn't be true. She didn't reply because she didn't have anything to write with. That had to be it. Nick had asked her to marry him. She couldn't not respond to him. Not possible.

The blackness he'd lived in whispered at him. Since he'd been with Winnie, he hadn't had a single dark moment like what he had for as long as he could remember. Just being with her, loving her, had stopped the shrieking in his soul. He refused to believe she wouldn't be part of his life any longer.

"Are you sure?" He couldn't stop himself from asking.

Enrico shook his head. "No note, but she did ask me to tell you yes."

Yes.

A single word that held the world in its grasp.

Nick closed his eyes and savored the sound of it. No matter that it was through someone else's voice. It was Winnie's voice he heard. The slightly husky, melodious tones that caressed his ears.

Sweet Jesus. She said yes! He had himself a real fiancée. As soon as he was vertical he would find a preacher and marry her. He didn't care if anyone else was present. The sooner he married her, the sooner he could banish the shadows from his life for good.

"Then what?"

"Then she left with all those men. They rode off together and none of them looked happy." Enrico made a face. "They all had guns too."

"Don't worry. That's my family."

Enrico's brows went up. "I hate to get into a tussle with your brothers."

Nick chuckled, which made his head hurt, but it still felt good. "I got my ass handed to me more than once, but I can give as good as I get." A smile crept over his face.

"Do you gotta note you want to send back?" Enrico had walked back toward the door. He obviously wanted to skedaddle, no doubt to get back to she whom he worshipped.

"No." It was tearing him up to know she was there without him, facing that bastard who owned her daughter. Their daughter. Martha would be his. Each time he thought about the girl bearing the name of Granny Dolan, he allowed himself to believe the older woman was giving her stamp of approval.

"Miss Winnie usually gives me a coin." Enrico was an entrepreneur.

"Boy, I ain't got nothing but what you see. Tell you what, ask my brother Matt and he'll make sure you get a coin, okay?" Nick was impatient to know what was happening. "Now get."

Enrico skidded out the door and disappeared from view. Nick was left alone with his thoughts again. The next hour went by with excruciating slowness. He must have dozed a bit because the sun coming through the window had dropped low in the sky. Unbelievably, the daylight was fading. It must have been evening already.

No one had come to tell him what was happening. He missed his brothers, he missed Winnie with an ache. He could hardly stand the thought of waiting another moment for news. His throat ached and damned if he didn't have to take a piss.

A commotion in the hallway had his ears straining to hear more, but no one appeared in his room. His head screamed and his throat throbbed. He reached for the edge of the cot and pulled himself to a sitting position.

Winnie watched as Conklin signed his name on the adoption agreement. Mr. Fuller's brother-in-law, a sandy-haired man named Marcus Tuttle, had kindly written up a legal agreement in less than ten minutes within arrival time. Then he made a second copy.

"Your turn, ma'am." Mr. Tuttle handed her the quill.

She dipped into the inkpot and signed her name on both papers. For now, she wrote Winnie Watson. Soon, she would write Winnie Graham. Her family was nearly in her grasp.

Mr. Tuttle sanded the signatures and set them on the counter.

"Mr. Conklin, this paper gives Miss Watson immediate custody of the child Martha." Mr. Tuttle handed the copy of the adoption release to Conklin.

"Yeah, fine. As long as it says I ain't going to jail, that's all I care about."

"It was an interesting clause, but yes, the agreement has that information in it as I've read it to you." Mr. Tuttle glanced at Winnie and nodded ever so slightly.

Winnie reached for her copy of the adoption paper and folded it, tucking into her reticule. She looked at Conklin

"I will wait here with Mr. Tuttle while you retrieve Martha's belongings."

Conklin snorted. "Miss High and Mighty, still, eh? I ain't doing a damn thing. You wanted the girl. That's all you get. She ain't got nothing to gather."

That was fine with Winnie. A fresh start for both of them.

She turned to Mr. Tuttle. "Thank you for all your assistance today. How much do I owe you?"

The attorney waved his hand. "I won't take a fee for this. Consider it a favor for my brother-in-law. He deserves a bit of goodness in his life."

Winnie nodded and put her chin in the air. "Then I bid you good day, Mr. Tuttle." She wasn't about to speak to Conklin again. She wouldn't spit on him if he were on fire.

Caleb and Brody waited with Martha back at the boardinghouse. Vaughn waited for her by the door of the feed store. He offered her a small smile and his arm. This time when she left the boardinghouse, her heart had never been lighter. Life had kicked her enough times to deaden her sense of hope and goodness, but both had survived. And now, what she had was worth all the pain, all the heartache, all the tears.

She had a family.

Nick managed to make it to the boardinghouse before he almost fell off the horse. He'd ripped the bandages from his head and it felt like a damn hammer was drumming on his skull. He slid off the saddle and leaned against the saddle, blowing as though he'd run to Louisiana and back.

Caleb and Brody sat on the front porch with Martha between them. Nick's heart lodged somewhere in his throat.

She'd done it. Goddamn. Winnie had gotten the girl back. Now two ex-Texas Rangers guarded her as if she were a royal princess. She looked so small sandwiched between them, her gaze solemn. He knew he looked like shit but this was the first time he'd be speaking to her as her father.

He swayed a bit on his feet at the thought. A wife and a child of his own. Less than six months ago, the only thing he worried about was fall round-up and which calf would kick him. Now he had a huge responsibility. She was dark haired and olive skinned but damned if she didn't have Winnie's heart-shaped face and pert nose.

"Shouldn't you be at the hospital?" Caleb gestured to his appearance. "I mean, the bloodstained shirt and the pale, sweaty face is a clue you left too early."

"I couldn't lay there while Winnie went to battle with that son of a bitch." Nick's voice sounded like he'd been gargling rocks but at least he could talk. He took halting steps toward the porch. Caleb and Brody rose and walked into the small front yard.

Martha watched him, her expression blank. "Are you my new owner? I thought it was the blonde lady."

Her words were like a punch to the gut. How a child could even ask that question spoke to the evilness in the world where there should be good.

He made his way to the porch and sat on the step below her, leaning against the railing. "No, I'm not your new owner. No one is. Miss Winnie made sure no one could ever own you again."

"Oh." Martha scrunched up her face. "Is that the blonde

lady?"

"Yep, that's her."

"She's tough." A small smile crept across the girl's lips.

"That she is." He looked at Caleb. "Is she on her way?"

"She was signing papers with that attorney. Vaughn and Matt are with her." His older brother rubbed his chin with one hand. He lowered his voice. "That's one female who could rival Aurora for balls of steel."

"And Olivia," Brody added. "She'll fit right in, this almost-wife of yours."

Nick knew he wasn't fooling anyone by telling everyone they were married. They soon would be of course.

"We'll take care of your horse while you get to know her. She's powerful quiet." Caleb smiled at the girl. "We'll be in the barn, honey. Can you keep an eye on my little brother for me? He got hurt today." He and Brody left Nick alone with Martha.

She nodded and peered at Nick's face. "Your voice sounds bad and it looks like you got beat."

Nick told himself she was a little girl and didn't mean to insult his manhood. "I did, but the law got hold of him."

"The law gets you if you beat people?" Her eyes were wide.

"Yep. Especially if you try to strangle somebody." He pointed at his neck. "Miss Winnie and I were trying to get you away from that man. Some people didn't want us to."

"You got hurt trying to get me?" Her voice was barely a whisper.

"I did, but I'd do it again. Every day if I had to." He meant every word of it, much to his surprise. This child hadn't had someone to speak for her, protect her and love her. Now she had two, plus many more on the Circle Eight.

"Why?" This was the first emotion she'd shown. Confusion and suspicion.

"Because that's what you do for family."

She cocked her head. "Are you my family?"

His heart clenched at the hope in her voice. He wanted so much for this child to understand how much Winnie loved her and how much he wanted to. Nick had only seen the girl twice,

193

but he considered her as his own already.

"Miss Winnie and I would like to be. Would you like a mother and father?" The question hung in the air between them, full of promise and the future.

Martha looked at him and then down at herself. She wore the horrid sack dress and shoes with holes in the soles. Her crippled leg was tucked beneath the dress. She touched her ankle and Nick noted the dirt crusted under her fingernails. First thing they'd do is feed the child, then bathe her and clothe her in something more suitable to a young girl.

"I'm a cripple." Her voice was so small he barely heard her.

Nick knew his response to her confession would determine a great deal of the future with this child. "You know, only the most special people have a bum leg."

Her head snapped up. "What?"

"God picks the strongest people to give a bum leg to. Because only the strongest can survive and do what other people do with two good legs."

She scrunched her face again. "Is that true?"

"Absolutely. People who are crippled have to be strong. They're the ones that show the rest of us how to do it." He swallowed and his throat caught on fire. If he didn't stop talking, he might do something stupid like pass out. He closed his eyes for a moment.

"I'm strong."

Her little voice made him smile. "I know you are. So does Miss Winnie." For some reason, he decided it was a good idea to stand and find some water to cool his throat.

Then the grass smacked him in the face and everything went black.

Winnie rode flanked by Vaughn and Matt. Everyone was quiet on the ride back to the boardinghouse, but it was a good quiet. A peaceful quiet.

It was the first time in a very long time that she didn't feel on edge, as though she had needed to be ready to do battle. Surrounded by the Graham men, she felt safe. And with her daughter waiting at the boardinghouse, excitement raced through her.

Things were almost perfect.

As they approached the boardinghouse, she saw Caleb and Brody standing in front of the porch steps looking down. Her peaceful feeling flew away on the breeze. She kneed the mare into a faster gait.

"What's happened?" she yelled as she yanked on the reins to stop the horse

Caleb looked at her with his hands on his hips. "My foolish brother left the hospital and passed out in the yard."

Winnie slid out of the saddle and landed with a jarring thump. Her teeth clacked together but she ignored her own discomfort and ran to Nicholas's side. He was pale as milk and the bruises stood out like purple and red paint on his skin. To her surprise, Martha knelt beside him, worry clearly written on her face.

Winnie looked at the Graham men. "We need to get him inside." She held out her hand to Martha who shook her head and scampered back on her own. Winnie wasn't hurt by her daughter's refusal. Trust would come in time.

The four men nodded and picked up Nicholas's limp form.

"Where do you want him?" Matt asked.

Winnie thought through the possibilities. The parlor contained only the settee, which was too small, and the wingback chairs. The sitting room had only comfortable chairs. That meant Nicholas had to go upstairs, which would be nearly impossible given the width of the staircase and the width of the men's shoulders.

"Wait here." She moved faster than she thought possible into the boardinghouse and up the stairs. After grabbing the quilt from her bed, she made her way back downstairs and slammed out the door.

All four men holding Nicholas scowled at her.

"He ain't exactly light."

"I think we need to tell our little brother to stop eating so many of Eva's biscuits."

"And gravy."

"And the tamales. Jesus, he scarfs them down like nobody's

business."

Winnie had no time for their foolishness. She shook out the quilt onto the soft grass. "Please lay him here." After they set him down, she looked at him again and hoped he hadn't done permanent damage leaving the hospital too early. She turned to Vaughn. "Can you please get a basin of cold water, a rag and a cup?"

After Vaughn left to do as she bade, she lowered herself to the quilt and pulled Nicholas's head onto her lap as gently as she could. He was warm but not overly so. He had dark smudges beneath his eyes and his lashes were impossibly long for a man. She would have to tease him about that when he woke.

Martha sat at the corner of the quilt, her gaze on Nicholas. Winnie didn't look at her yet. She wanted the girl to feel comfortable on her own without being pushed. Winnie looked at Caleb. "Can you please go down the street to Dade's store? It's three blocks east of here. Ask for crates and sacks for packing. Also—" she glanced at the girl who hadn't moved an inch, "—if you would please get some clothes and a pair of good shoes for Martha."

She handed him her reticule. "There is plenty of money in there to pay for whatever you need to purchase."

He promptly handed the reticule back with a frown. "Grahams take care of their own."

With that, he sealed her opinion of him completely. He was a good man, no matter the tough exterior. They were all good men.

"We'll go get started packing in the barn," Matt said loudly.

"There isn't much to pack since I don't own any horses, but Bartholomew's things are in what was the tack room." She smiled at the memory. "He refused to sleep in the house and spent time fixing up his own space."

"Are there crates in the barn we can start with?" This was from Brody. "I don't fancy carrying a man's private things in my arms."

"There are a few crates in there in the loft." She glanced at both of them. "Thank you."

196

Matt nodded. "Caleb already said it but I'll say it again. Grahams take care of their own."

Winnie's throat tightened and she managed to convey her thanks with her eyes only because she couldn't speak. Being part of a family was overwhelming but it was also like a warm blanket on a cool night. Comfortable and safe.

Vaughn walked out of the house with the supplies she requested. He set them down and pointed at the house. "I'll start packing things in the guest rooms."

"Thank you, my friend."

He smiled and returned to the house. Winnie was alone with Nicholas and Martha. A soft breeze rustled the leaves on the trees and the late day sun warmed the air around them. Another silence descended, but Winnie welcomed it. The lack of noise gave her the opportunity to find that peaceful place in her heart again. She wrung out the rag in the water and wiped Nicholas's face.

"Thank you for taking care of him." Winnie finally looked at her daughter.

"He's a nice man."

"He's the best man I ever met." She cupped his cheek. "I love him more than life." *And I love you too, little one.*

His eyes opened and her heart stuttered. Those beautiful blue-green orbs regarded her with the love she never thought to receive.

"Hi."

The smile that spread across her face was one of relief and joy. "Hi, Nicky."

"My head hurts." His voice was like sandpaper.

She dipped the cup in the water and held it to his lips, letting some dribble into his mouth. He swallowed then winced. He sighed and closed his eyes.

"I want to tell you a story, Martha." Winnie knew it was time to be completely honest with her daughter. "Once there was a sixteen-year-old girl. She became pregnant by a man she barely knew. She was ashamed by her actions but not of the child. Her good friends took her in and helped her through the pregnancy. She delivered a beautiful baby girl and her friend

197

Josie took the baby to a man who would take care of the child. Mr. Fuller is a wonderful man who gave children a home until a family could find them and adopt them." Winnie heard Martha's small intake of breath but didn't stop. "For many years, the girl missed her baby and had a huge hole in her heart. Then she met a man and fell in love with him. Her heart healed but there was still an empty space in her life for the baby she'd given up."

Nick smiled at her and Winnie drew courage from it, his love and support. Her heart ached with the knowledge she had lost nine years of her daughter's life. Unforgivable. Almost.

"The girl found the strength to find her baby nine years later, only when she found her, someone held her captive. The girl and the man she loved did battle to free her, to give her a home and a family she deserved." Winnie finally looked up at Martha. "Now the girl hopes her daughter will forgive her."

Martha pointed at herself. "Me? I'm the baby?"

"Yes." Winnie's voice trembled right along with the rest of her. "Please forgive me."

Martha looked down at her leg. "I always thought my parents gave me up because my leg was crooked."

Tears gathered in Winnie's eyes. "I didn't know your leg was crooked. I couldn't look at you or I wouldn't have been able to give you away. I wasn't worthy to be your mother, Martha."

The girl frowned. "How do I know you're really my mother?"

"You have her face and nose." Nicholas reached out and tapped said nose. "And her stubbornness."

"You were born May first and you have a heart-shaped birthmark on your hip. I named you Grace because you were the part of me that deserved God's grace." Winnie let the tears run freely down her cheeks. "You took a piece of my heart with you when Josie brought you to Fuller's Home. I'm sincerely hoping I can convince you to give it back."

"Grace is a pretty name."

"You're a pretty girl." Nicholas touched Martha's foot. "Just like your mama."

Martha met Winnie's gaze. "You want to be my mama and be a family with Mr. Nick?"

"More than anything." Winnie took Nicholas's hand held the other out to her daughter. Time seemed to stop as the girl regarded the outstretched hand. Winnie's arm burned but she wouldn't drop it. Not if she had a breath in her body.

Martha crept closer and put her own shaking hand in Winnie's. A sob escaped from her throat and she pulled Martha in for a hug. The girl's scent surrounded her.

"Hey, how about me?" Nicholas's scratchy voice penetrated the haze of joy.

Winnie laughed and both of them leaned down to hug Nicholas. She finally had a family of her own, one she would hang onto with every fiber of her being no matter where they lived. They were her home.

"Can we do one thing before we leave Houston?" He squeezed her hand. "Will you marry me?"

Winnie thought she might shout with joy. "Yes, yes yes!"

With Enrico's help, the preacher arrived within half an hour. Martha shyly handed her mother wilted wildflowers she'd gathered in the yard. The ceremony took less than a few minutes while the groom lay on the quilt in the yard, the bride holding his hand and his brothers surrounding them. Martha watched with wide eyes.

Winnie had never heard sweeter words then "I now pronounce you man and wife."

The Graham men congratulated Nick with slaps on the back and her with pecks on the cheek. She thought she'd never stop smiling so great was the joy in her heart.

Martha looked at the flowers and looked up at Winnie with her solemn brown gaze. "Are we a family now?"

"Yes, sweetie, we are." She took both their hands. "I promise to love both of you forever."

"Good because I always wanted a mama and papa."

CHAPTER ELEVEN

"What do you mean you don't want any furniture?" Matt's voice echoed across the house. The night creatures sang outside as they determined what to pack and what to leave behind.

Winnie scowled at him. "Mrs. Cassidy left the furniture for me. If Mr. Fuller and Mr. Tuttle are going to set up a new orphanage they will need it."

"I suppose that makes sense. Damn foolish to give it all away, though." Caleb had an opinion too.

"I will take all the linens and my bedroom furniture, which belongs to me." She was adamant, no matter how much they argued with her. Nick knew she was stubborn but this was an extra helping of it.

"You talk to her. She's your bride, right?" Matt looked at Nick who was sprawled on the settee, a more uncomfortable a piece of furniture he hadn't run into.

"It's her decision, not mine." Nick never thought he would actually say that out loud, but there it was. How he had changed in the last few months. All because of Winnie.

"What about the kitchen? Are you leaving the dishes too?" Matt flopped down in one of the chairs by the fireplace.

"I can't cook," she confessed to all of them. "Nicholas already knows, but I can learn. We will take some of the dishes, pots and pans. There isn't any food to speak of."

"I found out." Brody rubbed his belly. "Never thought I'd miss my wife's coffee."

The men all chuckled, knowing Olivia and her fierce ways.

Incongruous that she was a mother of two and couldn't actually make good coffee.

"Fine, I won't argue any more. I just want to get all this gear together so we can leave when the sun comes up." Matt waved his hand in dismissal. "We need a wagon."

Nick smiled. "I know where we can get one."

Winnie chuckled and shook her head. His brothers looked at him questioningly. He just raised his brows and widened his smile.

"You're both crazy. Good thing you picked each other to marry." Caleb leaned against the door to the kitchen.

Small footsteps sounded from the stairs and Martha peered into the parlor. Her hair was in fresh braids, and she wore a pretty yellow dress and shiny, black shoes. Nick gestured for her to come in.

Winnie made a sound halfway between a squeal and a shout. She took Martha's hands. "You look positively lovely."

"Pretty as a picture," Vaughn offered.

"Wait until Eva sees her. She won't let that child out of her sight. Not to mention the twins." Matt managed a genuine smile for the girl. "I have two little girls named Margaret and Meredith who will love to meet you."

Martha was quiet but she managed a small smile. Nick knew it would take time for her to feel comfortable around the boisterous clan. It was good for her to meet the loudest straight off. All the young'uns were loud but she would have an easier time with the children.

She sidled over to Nick and perched on the edge of the settee. He told himself not to feel superior that she had chosen him over his brothers. Just as Winnie had done. Made him want to puff out his chest like a gamecock.

"Let me start sorting what to pack. You four, come with me." Winnie marched upstairs and his brothers and brothers-in-law followed, grumbling all the way.

He was alone with Martha, his new daughter. It was intimidating to say the least.

"We're going to live on a ranch called the Circle Eight." He kept his voice low, almost a whisper, and found it didn't hurt as much to talk. "I have seven brothers and sisters."

Martha turned to look at him, her eyes wide. "Your parents must have loved each other lots."

Nick smothered a chuckle. "They did but they died before you were born. My brother Matt raised us and most of us live at the ranch. Mr. Brody married my sister Olivia and they have a cotton farm not too far away. You, Miss Winnie and I will live on the Circle Eight. I'll teach you how to ride a horse and you can run and play with all your new cousins."

Her mouth twisted. "Horses kind of scare me."

"We've got all sizes, including ones small enough for girls. My nieces ride all the time." He was pleased when she moved closer, almost snuggling against his knees.

"I'll try my best to learn." Martha said solemnly.

"I know you will. There was a lady who lived with us we called Granny Dolan. She was Matt's wife Hannah's grandma and a smart, strong woman. She passed on a few months ago before I met Miss Winnie." The memory of Martha dying in his arms was still sharp. "I miss her a lot but you know what?"

"What?"

"Her first name was Martha."

The girl gasped. "You had a granny named Martha?"

"I did. And she would have loved you very much. I think she's smiling down at us right now." He had never thought himself one to believe in spirits, but believing in his adopted grandmother's love wasn't hard to accept.

Martha nodded sagely. "Will it take a long time to get to the ranch?"

"Two days or so. Maybe longer since we have to use a wagon. I have to ride in it." He made a face, but knew his brothers would not budge on this particular issue. Nick simply couldn't ride for two days on a horse. It wasn't possible given he had almost died that day.

"I can sit with you and keep you company."

Her offer made Nick's heart squeeze tight. "I'd like that."

This whole having a family thing might not be so hard. He had a feeling he would like it quite a lot. In fact, little Martha had already wormed her way into his heart.

Life would be good. Really good.

The morning arrived too early but Winnie dragged herself up out of the chair in the parlor. Her back hurt and her tongue was fuzzy with sleep, but she stretched and shook off the last vestiges of her restless slumber. After folding the blanket she used, she glanced at Nick, who was still asleep on the settee.

To her surprise Martha had insisted on sleeping in the other chair. She opened her eyes and looked at Winnie with a question in her gaze. Winnie put her finger to her lips and pointed outside. Martha stood and folded the blanket. Winnie held out her hand and to her relief, her daughter took it. Together they crept out of the room as to not disturb him.

Winnie found the Graham men had already been to Mr. Sylvester's livery and returned with a rather sturdy looking wagon pulled by two equally sturdy horses. Her brows went up to her hairline.

Matt was busy arranging crates in the wagon bed. "Morning."

"Good morning, I hope Mr. Sylvester gave you a good price. I will reimburse you, of course." To Winnie's surprise, Martha gave the horses a wide berth. Nick had to teach another female how to work with horses.

"He didn't want to take any money. Said it was a wedding gift or some such. Gave you the mare you'd been riding too. Caleb left forty dollars on his workbench when the old man wasn't looking." Matt clapped his hands together. "We need to get moving. Daylight is burning."

Winnie didn't point out that the sun had barely begun to rise. "Of course. I need to say goodbye to my friend down the street. We will be back in a few minutes. Nicholas is still sleeping."

"Lazy as always." Caleb winked at her as he stepped onto the wagon with another crate.

Winnie couldn't express her gratitude more to these men. Her heart overflowed with all she'd received when she accepted Nicholas into her heart. The Grahams were a wonderful family and she was so very lucky.

"Will you come with me to my friend Consuela's house?" she asked Martha.

"Okay."

It was very early but Winnie had to say her goodbyes to her past and embrace her future.

They loaded the wagon with all of Winnie's possessions and made a pallet for Nick to lie on. He made a face as he spied the crude bed even if it was lined with her best quilts. Martha sat on the wagon seat, his horse and the roan mare were tied to the back.

Winnie strode out of the house and slipped the keys into her pocket. She clapped her hands together and smiled. "Ready?"

"Not if I have to ride in that damn wagon."

"Don't worry. I promise not to jostle you too much." She climbed into the seat beside her daughter. They stared at him with identical expressions of anticipation. He couldn't help but appreciate how much they looked alike in that moment. He could endure the ride. What awaited at the end of the journey was more than worth it.

"Fine, but I ain't gonna like it." He hoisted himself into the wagon with Matt hovering behind him. "I'm fine. Let me be."

Matt harrumphed and didn't move. Typical pushy big brother. When Nick stumbled, Matt steadied him. Nick was embarrassed enough not to thank him. He didn't need to. Matt knew.

"We have one stop to make before we leave Houston." Winnie looked at him. "We need to say goodbye to Mr. Fuller and give him the keys to the house. All of us do."

Nick nodded. "Let's get going. Perhaps we can find some food and coffee along the way."

She chuckled. "Check the basket beside you. Consuela said to tell you goodbye."

To his delight, there was ham, biscuits and a jar of hot coffee. He took a swig of the hot brew and groaned. When the wagon moved, he almost choked on a mouthful.

"Who taught you how to drive this?"

"Bartholomew started the process, then you taught me how

to use the reins on the horse, and this morning, Caleb showed me how to drive the wagon." She smiled in triumph. "I need to know these things to be a rancher's wife."

There wasn't anything she couldn't do if she put her mind to it. He endured the jostling while he devoured the breakfast. He didn't realize how hungry he was until he swallowed the first bite. His throat hurt but not enough to stop him from eating. He hadn't eaten anything since yesterday morning.

She stopped the rig in front of Fuller's house. "You ready to see Mr. Fuller?"

Martha looked at the house. "Is this where he lives?"

"Yes, it is. I'm sure he will be happy to see you." Winnie managed to make her way down and held up her hands to help her daughter.

Nick grudgingly accepted Matt's help. After swaying for a moment, Nick found his feet and joined his girls at the door.

"It's damn early to be calling on folks," he whispered to Winnie.

"Your brothers insisted on leaving at dawn." She knocked again and a young man answered the door. He had hair as black as pitch, bright green eyes and a scar that ran across his left cheek. Surprise chased across his features.

"Martha?"

"Tucker!" The girl ran into the young man's arms with a muffled sound of pleasure.

"You two obviously know each other." Winnie smiled. "You must be Tucker. Thank you for helping us catch the man who tried to kill my husband."

The boy let Martha loose with a smile. He looked at Winnie and then at Nick. "You're, ah, welcome."

"We wanted to say goodbye to Mr. Fuller and give him the keys to the boardinghouse. We're leaving for the Circle Eight." Winnie didn't make a move to pull Martha back toward her and he knew how hard it was for her. She had to give the girl time to get used to having parents.

"He's just having his breakfast. I'll go let him know." Tucker glanced down at Martha. "You want to come with me?"

Martha opened her mouth and then looked at Winnie, a

question in her gaze.

"Of course you can. We'll wait here for you."

Martha's smile was genuine, as bright as the sun behind them. Winnie squeezed his arm and he knew she felt the same rush of happiness at the sight. The girl was beginning to heal.

Within a few moments, the two young people returned, their faces wreathed in more smiles.

"Mr. Fuller cried when he saw Martha." Tucker patted the girl's shoulder. "We're both powerful glad she's all right."

"Can we see him?" Winnie didn't want to overstep but she wanted to thank the man.

"He's not doing well." Tucker led the way into the house, up the stairs and toward a room with an open door. The house still smelled as though it was neglected but there was a lightness in the air. Perhaps the young man staying with Mr. Fuller was the right thing to do.

"The Grahams wanted to see you to say goodbye." Tucker walked into the room and they followed.

The older man appeared even smaller than he had a few days earlier, but there was pleasure in his gaze. He sat in a large four-poster bed with a tray in his lap.

"We won't keep you, Mr. Fuller." Winnie walked in and put the keys in the old man's hands. "I wanted to say thank you for everything. We got Martha back from Mr. Conklin. Legally and permanently. Thanks to your brother-in-law and you. The boardinghouse will be the new Fuller's Home."

"I'm so very glad to hear that and to see her." Mr. Fuller glanced at the girl with affection. "She will be happy with her new family. Mr. Tucker and my brother-in-law will help me track down some of the other children. Mr. Layton has also promised to help. The new home will help many children."

Nick was glad to hear the rest of the children would not be forgotten. For now he had to focus on building his own family but he wouldn't forget about the rest of them. "We will help as we can. You need only send word to the Circle Eight."

"Thank you. You two brought my life back. And Mr. Tucker here reminded me why I opened the home to begin with. This hooligan needs a firm hand to keep him in line." Mr.

Fuller spoke around the smile he couldn't quite conceal.

"I don't need no keeper." Tucker crossed his arm. "But I do appreciate a warm bed."

Nick held out his hand to the young man. "Thank you for saving my life."

The boy shook it firmly. "I knew you were looking for Martha and helping Mr. Fuller. I aim to do the same."

"Thank you for everything, Mr. Fuller." Winnie took Nick's hand. "Please do correspond when you can and I will do the same."

Martha hugged Tucker one last time and then returned to her mother's side. Together they left the house of the man who had changed their lives. The mood was more solemn than when they arrived. Nick was considering how long the older man would live to fight the fight but perhaps Tucker would carry on what he started.

The next two days were sheer hell. Nick had never been so bounced around in his life. He felt like a nut in a barrel that rolled down an endless mountain. Every muscle in his body ached right along with his head and his throat. Matt drove them toward the ranch as hard as he could.

The men took turns driving the wagon to give Winnie a rest. Martha, true to her word, sat in the bed of the wagon with Nick and told him the stories she knew. Most were fanciful ones about princesses and dragons, but she was a natural storyteller.

When they passed the huge tree that marked the property line of the Circle Eight, Nick was ready to weep. They were home. Finally, finally home.

The sound of a horse galloping for all its worth alerted them that someone had spotted them. Catherine came tearing up on her favorite stallion, her blonde hair streaming behind her. She yanked the horse to a stop beside the wagon, her gaze incredulous.

"What in the world?" The youngest Graham had a wild streak a mile wide and insisted on wearing britches and riding hell for leather everywhere she went.

"We brought Nick home." Matt waited for Cat to ask more.

"With Miss Watson and a little girl, and a wagon full of home goods?" The young woman eyed his prone form. "Who kicked your ass?"

"Watch it, brat. There's a lot more to this story," Caleb warned. "Get to the house and tell Eva we'll be there in ten minutes."

Cat scowled just like a Graham but she kneed her horse into motion and soon she was a blur of girl and equine streaking across the rolling hills.

"Who was that?" Martha asked.

"That's your Aunt Catherine and she's a pain in the a—behind." Matt pointed. "There is your new home."

They rode onward, Martha's eyes widening the closer they got to the house. People came from everywhere including the passel of young'uns running around the yard. Dogs barked and birds flew shrieking from the trees. It was near deafening.

"Who are all these people?" Martha whispered in his ear.

"This is your family, honey. Your cousins, aunts and uncles." He smiled as her mouth dropped open.

"It's like being at Fuller's again."

He supposed she was right. Loud, raucous children and adults trying to keep the peace. Fuller's was the only real home she'd known until now.

"Are we gonna live here?" She looked at Winnie.

"Yes, honey. This is our new home." Winnie pulled the wagon to a stop and crawled in beside them. Just for a moment, it was the three of them, cocooned in the crates.

"There are a lot of people out there." Martha's voice shook ever so slightly.

"It's family. They're loud because they're happy to see us." Nick took the girl's cold hand and rubbed it between his own. "Your cousins are all younger than you so you'll be in charge in no time."

"Oh." Martha looked at Winnie. "Will you hold my hand until I feel safe, Mama?"

Winnie sucked in a small breath. Nick knew the girl calling her Mama had surprised and delighted her. Her eyes were suspiciously moist. "Forever if you need me to."

"Okay. Then I'm ready." Martha took her hand and then his. "As long as I have Mama and Papa."

It was Nick's turn to be speechless. Life had been so dark, full of shadows and despair. Now he had everything he never knew he wanted. Love had changed him and given him gifts he could barely absorb. He kissed Winnie and then Martha.

"Always."

ABOUT THE AUTHOR

Beth Williamson, who also writes as Emma Lang, is an award-winning, bestselling author of both historical and contemporary romances. Her books range from sensual to scorching hot. She is a Career Achievement Award Nominee in Erotic Romance by Romantic Times Magazine, in both 2009 and 2010.

Beth has always been a dreamer, never able to escape her imagination. It led her to the craft of writing romance novels. She's passionate about purple, books, and her family. She has a weakness for shoes and purses, as well as bookstores. Her path in life has taken several right turns, but she's been with the man of her dreams for more than 20 years.

Beth works full-time and writes romance novels evening, weekends, early mornings and whenever there is a break in the madness. She is compassionate, funny, a bit reserved at times, tenacious and a little quirky. Her cowboys and western romances speak of a bygone era, bringing her readers to an age where men were honest, hard and packing heat. For a change of pace, she also dives into some smokin' hot contemporaries, bringing you heat, romance and snappy dialogue.

Life might be chaotic, as life usually is, but Beth always keeps a smile on her face, a song in her heart, and a cowboy on her mind. ;)

www.bethwilliamson.com

CPSIA information can be obtained at www.ICGtesting.com
Printed in the USA
LVOW08s2155240516

489818LV00004B/197/P